I0831269

METROGNOMES

THE SHAMAN'S APPRENTICE

Also by Glenn Slade Clark, Jr.

Cry, Wolf: Shadow of the Werewolf

The Chronicles of Nightfire, Texas:
The Vampire Murders
The Haunting of Alexas Mansion

The Great Debate

METROGNOMES

THE SHAMAN'S APPRENTICE

Glenn Slade Clark, Jr.

Illustrated by Molly Brimer

2016

Metrognomes: The Shaman's Apprentice

First Edition: October 2007
Second Edition: March 2016

Published by Clark Ink, LLC.

Cover art by Molly Brimer.

ISBN-10: 1-61815-070-7
ISBN-13: 978-1-61815-070-7

For the Youth Group
at White Rock United Methodist Church;
past, present, and on into the future.

Contents

Acknowledgements

It would be an unforgivable crime not to mention the people who contributed to this project in ways that have proven so invaluable: Jay King, who gave Kazkal No'tall his name; Helena King, who gave Jy'ty'tity hers; Valerie Clark, my sister and primary editor, who was never afraid to drown my pages in red ink, doodles, and amusing comments; and, of course, Molly Brimer, my illustrator and dear friend, without whom I would have never written this book in the first place.

All of the people mentioned above have helped immeasurably in making all the long hours spent on this project the most fun I've ever had writing a book.

METROGNOMES

THE SHAMAN'S APPRENTICE

1
The Shaman's Apprentice

The small home of the gnome shaman Malík was hidden underground, beneath the root of a great tree. The great tree itself was one among many in a wooded area, deep within a human city. The main chamber of Malík's tiny dwelling filled with the light emitted by the sorcerer's glowing staff. Malík spoke a few magical words, and a ray of light shot forth from the jewel at the top of his staff and into the potion that was brewing in the kettle.

Malík's apprentice, Ak'ten, watched without interest. The only thing about Malík's work that afternoon that had triggered the lad's interest at all, in fact, was how different the priorities of a gnome of fifteen were from the priorities of a gnome of three hundred seventy-five. All Ak'ten really wanted to do was go outside and see what sort of fun was eluding him in his master's dark and stuffy home.

"It's not so stuffy, lad."

Malík had heard his thoughts. Ak'ten hated that.

"You're surrounded by books; a world of knowledge. How could any gnome want to go outside before having read every tome in this vast library?" Malík chuckled to himself.

Ak'ten shrugged and looked out the window. The sun was shining brightly, the birds were singing, the flowers were blooming. Worst of all, young gnomes were playing. Young gnomes who *hadn't* been chosen at birth to be the shaman's apprentice. Of course, Ak'ten had to concede, he was lucky to have been adopted by Malík. He had been a stray, a gnome without a clan. Malík had rescued him from the fate that awaited such gnomes; the fate of servitude. The future Malík hoped to pass to Ak'ten through a shaman's education was very grand indeed. Still, Ak'ten yearned for something else. Something more exciting. Ak'ten wanted to be a warrior.

"How much longer will this take, Malík?"

The aged shaman studied his restless apprentice. *Was I so impatient at fifteen?* he wondered. After having been the shaman of Tribe Qadash for well over three hundred years, Malík had only seldom managed to think back as far as his youth. It seemed a fleeting dream at times, that he himself had ever been young, had ever lacked the long, thick beard that marked him as a shaman, had ever just wanted to go outside and bask in the sun. "Hopefully not too much longer, Ak'ten. Djreena No'tall is very sick. This potion will ease her suffering and help her to heal quickly. There's just one more ingredient to add, and then we can take it to her."

Ak'ten had mixed feelings at the mention of Djreena No'tall. On the one hand, she was the aunt of Ak'ten's hero, the mighty warrior Kazkal No'tall. In Ak'ten's daydreams, he was Kazkal's apprentice, going on adventures, learning to become a warrior, and defending the tribe from gremlins.

Alas, that would never be, as Ak'ten had been told so many times. Strays couldn't join the army. Strays couldn't do *anything* but serve the ones with clans. Unless they were lucky enough to possess an inborn affinity for the magical arts and be noticed by a shaman right away, as Ak'ten had been.

But then, even if Ak'ten had known his own clan and carried their name, he couldn't have been Kazkal's apprentice. The position was already filled by Kazkal's cousin An'sep No'tall. An'sep was only two years older than Ak'ten and had been training with Kazkal since the age of twelve. Ak'ten knew that he would make a better warrior than An'sep, if only Kazkal could see it.

This brought him back to the other feelings stirred up at the mention of Djreena No'tall. For, while Ak'ten was eager to help Kazkal's beloved aunt, he was far less than eager to help the very same gnome, when he remembered that she was An'sep's mother. Such thinking was wrong, and Ak'ten knew it, which is why he forced it aside. It was not right to let jealousy color one's perspectives. At the same time, however, he just didn't like An'sep. And he knew the feeling was mutual.

Thinking of Kazkal's family brought Ak'ten back to his daydreaming. Ak'ten wanted the life of a warrior so very much. He had even grown his hair out, which was not usually allowed for a shaman's apprentice. In fact, it was seen as quite a scandalous rebellion by Malík's peers. For some reason, though, Malík had allowed it. Ak'ten's jet black hair was now very long, hanging down past his shoulders. He smiled, wondering if it were longer yet than An'sep's.

It was the way of the gnome warriors to grow their hair out as long as they could. It was similar to the tradition of the shamans, once their apprenticeships had ended, in which they grew out their beards. The difference was that the warriors would spar, to practice their skills, and the object of their sparring matches was to clip their opponent's hair. Thusly, the longer a gnome warrior's hair, the higher his rank. Ak'ten had been in sparring matches with some of the apprentices, and he had never been beaten. He knew that it was shameful for the warrior hopefuls to be bested by the likes of him. He knew they all detested him for his skill. He also knew that one day at least one of the warriors would have to realize what potential he had. Surely the rule could be broken.

It was easy for Ak'ten to think this, because Ak'ten had always been quite good at breaking rules. He was by no means a bad gnome. He was simply uninhibited. And he knew he caused Malík much grief.

A grumble from Malík caught the lad's attention. "Oh … drat!" The old gnome put a jar down on the table, as he breathed a frustrated sigh. "It seems Djreena will have to wait a bit longer. We are out of fairy powder. The final ingredient."

He shook his bearded head. "How could I have let this happen? I just haven't been keeping up with inventory like I should. Perhaps I should assign that task to you." He looked at Ak'ten somewhat crossly. "Especially since it was you who drove me to distraction this past week with that slug wrestling escapade you led the Jinto boys on." Another sigh, as he put a hand to his forehead. "I thought their mother would never stop telling me what a horrible guardian I was."

Ak'ten, though always bound and determined to do what he'd set out to do, never liked it when Malík got into trouble over him. "I said I was sorry, Malík. It's not my fault. Not … really. The slugs were just right there in the mud and …"

"I know. You just *had* to jump in and give them a fight. And the Jinto brothers just *had* to jump in after you, all of you ruining your clothes beyond repair." Malík actually laughed at that. Andra Jinto was a troublesome gnome. She always insisted that things be just so. And when they weren't, she would point her finger and blame others—loudly. It was irritating, even to an ever patient shaman like Malík. He couldn't help but be amused at the sons fate had given her. He felt it showed the humor of the gods. "That *poor* woman."

Malík continued to laugh, and Ak'ten joined him, relieved to have avoided another lecture on what he considered a dead issue.

"So what are we to do about Djreena's potion?" Ak'ten asked.

Malík thought for a moment, then looked to his apprentice with a smile. "Well, it seems you'll have your wish today. I need you to go and collect the fairy powder. And hurry back.

Djreena needs us to be swift." Malík considered the bottle of troll whisky that had been the source of Djreena's stomach problem. "Hopefully this will teach her once and for all not to accept drunken gifts from her father-in-law. Where Meso came by a bottle of troll whiskey is beyond me, but not so surprising. The old codger picked up his fair share of connections and questionable allies during his days as a warrior." Malík shook a myriad of memories from his head with a small smile, and he looked at his apprentice. "Well, what are you waiting for? Go get that powder."

"But where . . .?"

"Just about anywhere, Ak'ten. You know that. We live near so many fairy trees, and the fairies with powder are impossible to miss, if there isn't any powder lying around out there."

Ak'ten nodded his head, went to his room, and came back with all the necessary equipment tied to his belt. This included a pouch full of charm dust, his flute (just in case), and, of course, an empty pouch for bringing back the fairy powder. "I'll be right back, Malík."

"Hm. See to it, Ak'ten, my lad. I have heard such promises come from your lips before." Malík's tone went hard. "Your haste is *very* important. You have never sampled troll whiskey before, but I will see that you do if Djreena has to suffer any longer than necessary. You would rather be flogged, I guarantee."

Ak'ten's eyes went wide. "Don't worry, Malík. I'll be back." Ak'ten smiled to reassure the old gnome, as he walked out through the small home's hidden door and into the all too distracting summer afternoon.

"Ak'ten! Over here," came an urgent whisper.

The shaman's apprentice looked to see Arco Jinto peeking around the giant tree that stood watch over the great underground tunnel system of Tribe Qadash. "Arco, what is it?"

The eight-year-old gnome looked to either side of him before he spoke again. "We're playing Seek with Keela. She's the seeker. Have you seen her?"

"No, but I only just stepped outside."

"Booble! Gigga moon *put*!" came the excited voice of Tana Jinto.

"Aha! Found you!" Keela shouted triumphantly. "Come on out!"

Ak'ten chuckled, as the other brothers followed Arco out of their hiding spot. Arco was the youngest of the three brothers. His cohorts in crime were ten-year-old Tramino, and twelve-year-old Thereo.

Keela was only a year older than Thereo, and she stood beside Tana Jinto, who imitated the older girl's posture, crossing her arms and looking at the boys crossly. "Rules were no hiding above ground. We could all get in trouble for this, you know! Especially since you left me with your baby sister, and I had to bring her with me."

"Well," said Thereo, "you didn't *have* to find us!"

"Right. But I did. I knew you would cheat! Boy's *always* cheat! And I wasn't going to be bested by cheaters!" She looked down at her toddler side-kick. "Boys!" she huffed.

The two-year-old huffed as well. "Beego!" She shook her head, then fell over, landing on her face. She sat up immediately and laughed about it.

Keela took notice of Ak'ten then. She studied him, realizing how glad she was at that moment that boys didn't usually wear shirts. "Hi, Ak'ten. Wanna join us?"

All of the Jinto boys rolled their eyes, knowing that Keela had the biggest crush on Ak'ten. The boys, of course, loved Ak'ten too. They looked up to him in much the same way that Ak'ten looked up to Kazkal No'tall.

"I can't today," Ak'ten said. "I have to gather some fairy powder for Malík."

Keela looked defeated. "Oh."

"Hey!" Arco shouted. "My father said Meso No'tall was in his tavern last night and going on about Kazkal again. Did you hear that Kazkal chopped off a mud troll's head with the No'tall Battleaxe!?" The boy was beaming with excitement.

"Oh, yeah," Ak'ten answered with the pride of an expert. "That's old news. I heard it from Kazkal himself."

The boys were impressed.

Keela was not. "That is so gross! Why do boys like stuff like that? And when they grow up, why do boys *do* stuff like that?" She looked down to Tana.

Tana answered, "Boggo, em stippled! Dis *stippled*!" And she very well meant it.

"Stippled, dippled," a strange voice rang before laughing.

All turned to see the tiny pink form of a fairy flying towards them. She paused just above them, jabbered something that none of them understood, then took her leave with a smile and a wink.

"There you go, Ak'ten! Take her powder!" Tramino suggested enthusiastically. "Then you can play with us."

Ak'ten laughed. "No, Tramino. Those kinds don't have powder. Only the really fat ones do. And I need one who's about ready to burst."

"Have you ever seen a fairy burst before?" Arco asked.

"Yeah, several times. Bursting fairies are bigger than *we* are!"

"Really?" Arco was amazed. It was difficult to imaging the tiny fairies he'd seen, creatures that could likely sit on his shoulder without causing him to strain, getting *so* fat that they were bigger than he was. So fat, in fact, that they burst!

Keela seemed bothered. "Does it … hurt them?"

"I don't think so." Ak'ten shrugged. "As far as I can tell, they think it's pretty funny when they burst. Because they go back to normal size and fly off right after. And then there's powder all over the ground right where they burst."

"That is so great!" Thereo said. "Can we come too?"

"Sorry, Thereo. I have to go fast, or else Malík is going to make me drink troll whiskey. Besides, your mother would kill us all, I'm sure. She still hasn't calmed down from last time, with the slugs."

"Oh, yeah!" the boys shouted in unison, and all laughed heartily.

"*That* was great fun!" Arco said. "Well worth our mother's wrath."

Just then, a squirrel crawled out of the brush, and a familiar voice asked "What have we here?"

"Uh-oh," Said Arco. "Here comes trouble." He and the other boys went to stand behind Ak'ten, looking as dangerous as they could.

"An'sep!" Ak'ten smiled craftily. "So good to see you. What brings you by? Is Kazkal out looking for a better apprentice?"

The older gnome slid off of the squirrel, followed by two other warriors' apprentices. "No. Kazkal is actually preparing for a mission. He has a quest. You, of course, don't know about it, because Kazkal doesn't find you as worthy of his trust as I am. He's going to be promoted, if he succeeds. And he *will* succeed. As for the three of us, we had riding practice. How 'bout you, stray? Out looking for your parents again?"

Ak'ten knew he would get in trouble if he fought An'sep again, but he really wanted to wipe the smirk from his rival's arrogant face. "No. I was looking for *your* mother. But I didn't know the way to the brothel, so I had to stop and ask directions."

An'sep raged. "How dare you! At least I *have* a mother! At least I'm not a stray who could never be a warrior no matter how hard he tries to *look* like one!" An'sep eyed Ak'ten's long hair angrily, remembering their last battle, in which Ak'ten had bested him. An'sep was sure the shaman's apprentice had cheated. Used magic. It was the only way.

"Go back to the warrior camp, *An'sep*!" Arco shouted. "You're just mad because Ak'ten would make a better warrior than you! And Kazkal *knows* it!"

An'sep drew his sword. "Fine, then! Let us put your boasting to the test!"

Ak'ten grinned in a predatory fashion. "How much hair do you want to lose, An'sep? If we keep on sparring like this, you'll have nothing left!"

An'sep almost stopped, as he remembered the snipping Ak'ten had given him the time before. It had been so shameful to be clipped by a cocky little stray who had no formal training. An'sep ran a hand over his long, wind-tussled, blonde hair. Hair that had once been even longer. Hair that had once reached to well below his waist, but now stopped at the small of his back. Anger overcame him then, and he moved towards Ak'ten.

"Wait! An'sep!" came the voice of one of the other apprentices. "He has no weapon! There's no honor in it!"

An'sep stopped. "This is true. Give him your sword then, Ras'kaal."

Ak'ten interrupted. "Ah! So that you can give me a trick sword, perhaps specially prepared for my defeat?"

"I am not the cheater here, magician! But to appease your suspicions, *I* will fight with Ras'kaal's sword, and you with mine." He then tossed his own sword to the ground in front of Ak'ten and took the sword of his friend.

"An'sep," came the voice of the third warrior's apprentice.

"What is it, Jared?"

The other young gnome removed his shirt and armored vest as he answered, "Be fair. He has no armor. Let him take mine, as I would like to repay him for a potion he brought to my sister when she had the Gray Fever."

"I am always fair, Jared. Though I doubt such slight armor will do him any good."

Jared tossed the protective coverings to Ak'ten and smiled, nodding encouragingly.

When Ak'ten had slipped into Jared's armor and lifted the sword from the ground, An'sep said to him, "Now that you see my good faith, give me your word that you won't use magic to best me!"

Angrily, Ak'ten grumbled, "I didn't use magic the last time! But you have my word! So come!" He raised the sword and prepared. His friends and An'sep's all backed away to give them room. The squirrel that had carried the warriors' apprentices scampered off as soon as the young gnomes' blades met, but no one made any attempts to stop it. All they knew was the battle that raged before them. A battle that could only end in humiliation for whoever was defeated.

Grim determination painted the faces of both young gnomes. They circled each other, each lunging when they thought they had a shot at pinning the other, but each missing the mark repeatedly. Though they both hungered for victory, they also held each other as highly in respect as they did in contempt. Each knew the other was skilled, though both were loath to admit it. The other gnomes were shouting things such as, "Teach the stray a lesson!" and "You can show him, Ak'ten! He's nothing but a stupid peezwizz!" The combatants

tried to tune them out, though what did get through made them all the more eager for success.

Suddenly, An'sep leapt into the air, somersaulted over Ak'ten's head, and landed behind him.

Ak'ten was quick enough to spin around and block An'sep's blade before having his hair snipped.

An'sep took advantage of Ak'ten's surprise, however, and power-kicked him in the abdomen, knocking him to the ground. An'sep actually growled as he fell on the younger gnome.

Ak'ten was ready though; for as An'sep descended, Ak'ten, ignoring the pain in his belly, met the other gnome with his feet and launched him over his head. An'sep hit the ground hard, and Ak'ten jumped up only to leap and land on An'sep. He tried to get to An'sep's hair, but An'sep knocked him off and came at him with his angry blade. Ak'ten was forced into a defensive position, blocking every furious blow. It seemed that An'sep had forgotten this was only a sparring match in which blood was not to be shed. All the more reason for Ak'ten to forget it as well.

The terrified onlookers grew silent. No one noticed the return of the squirrel, or its rider.

Ak'ten ducked down, letting An'sep's swing go unblocked, knocking the older youth off balance. He then kicked out from his squatting position, hitting An'sep in the chest. Determined not to fall again, An'sep did a back flip. As his long hair lingered in the air behind him, Ak'ten, quick to respond, slashed out with his sword, taking some more length from his opponent.

An'sep landed on his feet, but his grin faded, as he saw the smug look on Ak'ten's face and the locks of blonde hair on the ground. "No!" he raged, and he lunged at Ak'ten with his sword.

Ak'ten's eyes went wide. He realized that An'sep meant to take his blood. He raised his sword to defend himself, but both gnomes stopped cold at the commanding voice, which spoke sternly, "An'sep!"

Both young gnomes turned to see Kazkal No'tall sliding off of the squirrel. The mighty warrior walked over to them, and he looked angrily into his apprentice's eyes. "A warrior only truly loses his battles, when he cannot learn from his defeat and accept it gracefully. Warriors thank the gods for both victory and defeat; for it is in defeat that he learns his weaknesses, and it is in knowing his weakness that he gains new strength."

"Yes, Kazkal … I …" An'sep bowed his head in shame.

"You were told not to spar with civilians again, apprentice." Kazkal looked sternly to Ak'ten. "No matter how skilled they may be. It is against our rules." He looked back at An'sep. "You lose your battles, when you lose your temper. Now, get your sword and shake your victor's hand. Then you and your friends are getting back on that squirrel and riding back to camp. We will discuss your 'riding practice' with General Argon."

An'sep and the other apprentices all looked at each other with fear.

Kazkal mounted the squirrel and said, "Well, get on with it, lad! I have a quest awaiting me!"

An'sep swallowed. "Yes, Kazkal. Forgive me." He walked over to Ak'ten, who still looked smug. He extended his hand, and as the other gnome took it, he spoke quietly, menacingly, as he sneered, "You may have beaten me, Ak'ten, but you're still just a stray. It was a good fight, but you will *never* be a warrior. You will *never* come between me and Kazkal. And I will *never* stop dreaming of the day when we spar again, and I clip your hair to the scalp, knock you to the ground, and make you eat both dirt and blood."

Ak'ten nodded warily. "Good fight, An'sep."

An'sep snatched his sword from Ak'ten's hands, turned, and went to the squirrel.

Ak'ten removed the armor he'd been lent and handed it back to Jared without a word.

After the apprentices had all mounted the squirrel, Kazkal spoke directly to the shaman's apprentice. "Ak'ten. You've been warned. You are to stay away from An'sep." He paused, then decreed, "Malík will hear of this." He commanded the squirrel and rode away as fast as he had come.

Ak'ten stood, trembling slightly. How was it that all he ever need do was step outside, and he was in trouble again?

Arco was the first to break the silence. "Whoa! That was *great*!"

The other boys chimed in with laughter and shouts of approval.

Ak'ten forgot his fear of punishment then, as he was bombarded with affectionate nudges and pats on the back—the adoration of his friends.

Keela shook her head and huffed. But she forgot her anger, when Ak'ten looked her way and grinned like the little scoundrel that he was, melting her young girl's heart.

Not much later, Kazkal was alone in the forest. To humans, of course, this was no forest at all, but to gnomes such as Kazkal, who stood only nine centimeters tall, this was hardly less than a jungle. Kazkal trudged forward without weapons; for that had been one of the conditions of his quest. If he returned successful, he would be named a commander in the army of Tribe Qadash. Every other warrior believed in his ability to do this. The general seemed more than confident. And An'sep, even as Kazkal left him at the general's mercy, probably to receive cooking duty for a week, had more confidence in Kazkal than he had in the very gods. Kazkal hoped that An'sep would learn. An'sep was a good apprentice, but he was so proud, and he was terribly possessive.

Ak'ten was another matter. The boy seemed to crave Kazkal's attention as much as An'sep did. It was true that Kazkal had noticed the skill of the shaman's apprentice, but there was nothing to be said for it. Ak'ten's fate was sealed. He was a gnome without a clan. It was forbidden for him to become a warrior's apprentice. He needed to accept the hand the gods had dealt him. He was lucky to be anyone's apprentice at all. And he had the magic. That was for sure. Kazkal shook his head, and he muttered to himself, "Boys grow."

Just then, a sound in the grass caused his pointed ears to perk. It was a sound he'd been trained to recognize, and

Kazkal's heart began to beat rapidly. It was a slithering sound. Kazkal stopped in his tracks. The snake, however, had already noticed him and taken a hungry interest. Kazkal's eyes darted all around, looking for the beast. All went quiet, and Kazkal knew better than to trust it. Still, he couldn't wait around all day. Snakes were masters at the waiting game. If Kazkal moved, the snake would strike. Yet moving seemed the only way to get past this game and bring the monster out into the open.

Kazkal took a wary step, and the snake leaped out of the grass, striking the ground where the gnome had stood, just as Kazkal leapt out of the way. Kazkal landed on his back, but sat up quickly, searching for anything that he could use as a weapon. There was nothing. No stones. No sticks. Only grass and dirt. A gnome's fistful of dirt was nothing against such a viper as this.

The snake reared up, eyeing Kazkal ravenously.

Kazkal prepared for either the end or some last minute inspiration provided by the gods; for there was nowhere to run that the snake would not have him, so long was its terrible body.

The snake made ready to strike, but was distracted as another gnome sprang forth from the grass, tossing a powder into the air. The snake was in a daze, as it inhaled the substance.

The newcomer then removed a little wooden flute from his belt and began to play the most enchanting tune the snake had ever heard. So charming was this tune, in fact, that when the little flute player stopped his blowing and ordered the snake to leave and go far, far away, nothing seemed more appropriate to the creature. It slithered away in an absent-minded state of reptilian bliss, forgetting all but the magical tune and its own sudden need to be far off elsewhere.

"Ak'ten," Kazkal breathed out with relief. "Thank the gods! It seems they would not have me devoured before my quest had even begun. What did you do to the monster?"

Ak'ten shrugged proudly. "Charm dust. A shaman never enters the deep forest without it."

Kazkal stood then and brushed himself off. "Which brings to mind another question. Why are you in the deep forest at all?"

Ak'ten looked away from Kazkal's accusing stare. "Malík needs fairy powder. I came out here to find some."

Kazkal knew better. "Awfully convenient. You shouldn't have followed me, Ak'ten. This is a dangerous mission I'm on." He smiled. "But I am truly grateful for the rescue."

"I really am looking for fairy powder, Kazkal!"

The warrior eyed the lad suspiciously. "Even so, there are many fairy trees closer to home than this. But now I must insist that you stay near me, for I would never rest again were I to send you back through the forest and have you meet your death. There are many things more terrible yet than vipers in the area. But I can't have you interfering once we get to the tree I'm after. You'll have to wait for me at the bottom."

Ak'ten nodded, and they began to walk. "What is this mission exactly?"

"I am to climb that great tree off in the distance and take a feather from a most terrible bird without losing my life."

Ak'ten laughed. "Why so grim, Kazkal? That won't be anything for you! You're the mightiest warrior we have!" The youth beamed.

"Oh, Ak'ten. If only I saw myself as you and An'sep do."

Ak'ten went quiet at the mention of Kazkal's apprentice. When he at last spoke, he asked, "Why can't I be a warrior like you, Kazkal?"

Kazkal hated that the question had come to him so directly. "Um … because … you're a stray. You know the law. Strays can't join the army."

"I know," Ak'ten confessed. "That's what you and everyone always say, but *why*? I just want to know why."

"Well, because … um … it's … uh …" Kazkal rolled his eyes and released a great sigh. He then looked at Ak'ten earnestly. "I don't know, lad. I have no answer that would satisfy either one of us." He smiled and put a hand on Ak'ten's shoulder. "Look, you have *great* skill. I admit that you would make an excellent warrior, and I'm not the only one who sees it. However, the laws, as they stand, forbid it, and it's not within my power to change them. The gods made you come to us as a stray for a reason. You must be *meant* for the lot you've been given. Now, that doesn't mean you should stop honing your fighting skills. It just means that you should put what the gods want first. The gods clearly want you to follow in Malík's footsteps, or they wouldn't have brought your little stray hide to his attention." Kazkal grinned and mussed the boy's hair. "Now, let's get over to that tree."

Despite the rejection, Ak'ten was warmed by Kazkal's words. He had said that Ak'ten would make an excellent warrior, and Kazkal wasn't the only one who'd seen it. Ak'ten's mind was racing excitedly with possibilities of whom it could have been that Kazkal referred to. Maybe it was even the general! Ak'ten's stride picked up pace, as did his energetic daydreams.

When the pair at last arrived at the great tree, Kazkal repeated his order to Ak'ten. "Now, stay here. I'll be down shortly, if all goes well."

Ak'ten nodded.

Kazkal began his lonely climb. This was it. He would either succeed or fail. He had to admit that Ak'ten having gotten himself involved only made him more determined to succeed, for once he acquired the feather, he still had to see the lad safely back home to the tribe's shaman. More than just his own life depended on his success now.

Something pink came into view. It was not very bright, however, which is why at first Kazkal didn't recognize it as a fairy. He hadn't realized this was a fairy tree. He didn't know if that would help or hinder his efforts. He continued to ascend the vast wall of bark and twigs. The fairy came very near him then. Kazkal noticed that it looked sick. He hadn't known that fairies could get sick. It began to jabber, as fairies were wont to do. But even its jabbering nonsense seemed off for a fairy. Kazkal clearly picked out the word 'Fenrir' mixed in with the rest of the gibberish. He went cold. For why would an ailing fairy speak the name of the villain who'd killed his father when he was yet a child?

"What do you suppose she meant by all that?" Ak'ten asked.

Kazkal looked beneath him, to see that Ak'ten had been climbing after him all along. "Ak'ten! I told you to wait at the bottom of the tree!"

Ak'ten smiled and did his best to shrug without losing his grip.

"And I don't think it meant anything. Fairies are senseless. An utterly mindless people."

"That's not true. Malík won his position as an expert on fairies. He can interpret their gibberish very well."

"Bah," Kazkal said. "Anyone can read meaning into something that has none. It's finding meaning when it's truly there that most gnomes seem to have trouble with."

Just then the fairy swooped back down. Ak'ten had climbed up almost beside Kazkal by this time. The fairy looked at them with twisted, unfairy-like eyes. She croaked out some words, and an evil grin curled her lips. "Gnomes of a feather … gnome from a basket wet." She looked crookedly up at Kazkal. "Death found one … and he lived with it." She looked to Ak'ten. "Death, from the basket … he delivered it." She looked away from them then, to the human city beyond the trees. "Death … waits in shadows. Shadows wait in the temple of the unknown god. Death and shadow … envelope … please …" She looked at both gnomes. "Grow strong. Deliver it." A confused look came over her then. "Fairies hurt … fairies flee … fairies die so suddenly." She smiled crookedly.

Just then, the wind whisked past them, as the terrible bird itself swooped by, snapping the miserable fairy up in its beak and making a quick meal of her.

"Good gods!" Ak'ten shouted.

"It's the very beast we seek!" Kazkal looked determined.

"But where will we go? We are still on the trunk, and we're too high to just jump!"

Kazkal fumed quietly. Perhaps he should have sent the lad home after all. For what could he do to save him now? The bird, having swallowed the fairy already, circled back for more. "This is not good." Kazkal had nothing else to say, as he thought quickly and prayed to the gods. It was not easy to think positively after the eerie nonsensical words of the ill fairy. In fact, Kazkal thought that he had never heard anything so haunting in all his twenty-five years.

"Fine then, bird! Let's see if you make such a fast meal of Kazkal No'tall!" the warrior shouted, hoping that the bird's attention would be spent all for him, sparing Ak'ten.

Ak'ten had no idea what to do or say. He was trying to think up some spell that could save them, but none came to mind.

The bird came at them, and Kazkal managed to tear off some bark. He tossed it directly into one of the bird's eyes, as it tried to snatch him from the tree. The bird lost its focus then and flapped its wings wildly, changing direction. The repeated force of the wind from beneath the bird's wings proved too much for either gnome, and they lost their grip. They both howled as they fell, feeling that they were falling to their death, and the bird would be left to pick at their remains.

Just then, something warm and squishy took hold of them, and their fall was stopped. Ak'ten realized what the great, fat, pink thing was, and shouted with joy, "A fat fairy! She's ready to burst!"

Kazkal was concerned and bewildered. "Burst? Isn't that a bad thing? We still have enough of a fall to end us once we hit the ground."

"Oh, yeah. Well, maybe we should just hold on real tight. Grab a roll."

"Are you crazy, lad?"

"Well, what else are we gonna do?"

The fairy was smiling like an idiot. Much more fairy-like than the creature who'd been snapped up by the bird only moments before. She giggled as she squeezed the two gnomes, like a child with her dolls. She hugged them harder and harder.

Kazkal felt his eyes threatening to pop out if she didn't release them. He choked out a comment. "Maybe … we'd be better off … if she would just … burst."

Ak'ten was too constricted at the moment to reply.

Just then, a surprised look appeared on the fairy's face, and she began vibrating violently. The gnomes tried to shout out in fear, but they sounded ridiculous, as their voices quaked along with the fairy.

The bird had lost his disorientation and sped towards them once again, not finding any threat at all in the swollen fairy.

"Wh-e-e-e-e-e-e-en i-i-i-i-i-i-i-i-s she-e-e-e go-o-o-i-i-i-ng to stoo-o-o-o-o-p?" Kazkal shouted to Ak'ten.

"Ah-ah-ah-ah-ah-ah-ah-ah-ah," was all the lad could manage in response.

And then, the fairy burst. Ak'ten and Kazkal found themselves howling again, along with the terrifying squawk of the terrible bird, as they plummeted once more towards the earth so far below.

And when they stopped at last, it was not to hit the hard earth and splatter in all directions as they'd expected. Rather, it was to land softly in a mountain of something pink and somewhat tasty. Ak'ten emerged from the strange substance that had saved their lives, and he laughed. "Fairy powder!"

Kazkal forced his head through the surface of the pink powder. "Wonderful. And what of my quest?" He noticed Ak'ten's eyes looking over his head. Kazkal looked up, covered in splotches of pink, and a feather gently settled on his face.

"The gods are smiling at you today, Kazkal!" Ak'ten was elated.

Kazkal, on the other hand, was quite grumpy. "They smile, because I am painted pink and buried to the neck in fairy powder. They laugh at us."

Ak'ten looked up to see the bird flying as far away as it could from all of these strange goings on, and the fairy was laughing heartily, having shrunk back to her original size and shape. She waved and winked and flew away.

Ak'ten smiled. "Well, at least your mission was a success. What does it matter how? Did the gods not give you that feather to take back to your general?"

Kazkal breathed out a sigh, as he climbed out of the powder. "I suppose you are right, Ak'ten. Now let's get moving. If I remember correctly, and if the myths ring true, fairy powder glows randomly. It will be dark soon, and we will be quite a target as we glow brightly pink in the forest. No creature would hesitate to prey upon us."

Ak'ten considered that. "Yes. The myths do ring true." He removed himself from the powder and filled his empty pouch with some of it before they left.

Kazkal forced Ak'ten to move at a slow run in order to beat the sun. Warrior or no, he felt they'd had more than their share of harrowing adventures for one day.

2
The Techgnome's Close Encounter

Not very far away, there was a very different sort of gnome society from the one that Ak'ten was familiar with. This was a world within the human culture itself. This was the world that Pete knew. Pete was in his room, practicing on his electronic keyboard, when the phone rang. "Yeah?" Pete said, as he picked up the receiver.

"Hey, Pete! It's me," answered the voice of Pete's friend Retro.

"What's up, dude?"

"The humans are watching a bad ass movie, dude! You need to come see it!"

"What movie?"

"I don't know. Somethin' with Arnold Schwarzenegger."

"Kick-ass! I'm there, dude. I'll meet you on the way." Pete hung up, without waiting for a reply, and he bounded out of his home, leaving too fast for his parents to even ask where he was headed. Of course, he knew they would have stopped him, which is part of why he moved so quickly.

Pete met Retro at the entrance to the passage that led from their underground tunnel system, up into the walls of the human building itself. This was dangerous territory. Restricted territory. But Arnold was calling them to witness acts of mass destruction and coolness on the humans' giant TV screen. How could mere rules keep them from that?

Pete asked, "First or second story?"

"Second."

"Whoa!" Pete moaned. "What a climb." He shrugged and grinned. "Well, let's get goin'!"

Pete and Retro made the climb in record time through the walls and into the air ventilation system of the humans' apartment building. Once they were secure in the ventilation shaft, they could walk normally. "Are there any girls up here tonight?"

"No," Retro answered sadly. "I called a couple, but none of them could sneak out." He shrugged. "Their parents won't let them stay out long enough anyway."

Pete laughed, and he ran a hand over his short, blonde hair, as he shrugged. "Mine neither, dude."

Retro laughed. He knew they were likely to get in trouble if they stayed to watch the whole movie. He also knew that they were sure to do it anyway. That's the way things went, when he was hanging out with Pete. Pete wasn't a bad gnome by any means. He was just carefree. It never seemed to occur to Pete that the rules might also apply to him—no matter how many times he got in trouble for breaking them. Retro supposed that's why he loved hanging out with Pete so much. The fun they had made it worth all the trouble they found in the process.

The pair made their way to the air vent, just in time for a major explosion that sent police cars flying all over the screen. "Kick-ass!" This was Pete's general assessment of all Schwarzenegger films. He turned to Retro. "Why is the ventilation shaft restricted, anyway, dude? It's pretty bad ass up here."

Retro shrugged. "Well, pro'ly cause in the winter they turn on the heat."

"So? In the summer, like now, they turn on the AC."

"Yeah, but I guess it's not the temperature, so much as the wind. I mean, usually it's not so bad, but, sometimes …"

Pete rolled his big, blue eyes in amusement. "Oh, yeah! *Sometimes* if we were little babies, we could get blown right out through the vents and plummet to our deaths." He started laughing.

"Dude," Retro said solemnly. "It's not so funny. I heard it's actually happened to some kids."

"Yeah, but we're not kids, Retro. We're fourteen! We're practically grown."

"Is it hot in here to you?" one of the humans asked.

"Yeah, a little bit. I'll turn up the AC," came a second voice.

Pete and Retro exchanged a look, then they watched one of the humans get up off of the couch to turn up the air conditioner. Pete leaned out of the vents to get a better look.

"Pete, don't lean out so far, man. He's gonna send a wind any second. You'll fall out."

"Nah, I'm just tryin' to get a better look at things down there."

Just then, the wind came. Retro grabbed onto one of the grates, and his eyes widened in horror as he saw Pete fall. "Pete!"

Pete himself was feeling a bit panicked. He was too frightened even to breathe. How he had managed to hook his foot to the grate, he didn't know, but he had no faith that his hold was going to last. He finally managed, "Um … help?"

Retro heard the whispered plea and looked down at Pete's foot. "Dude!" He spread his own legs out, so that he wouldn't be blown out himself, and he leaned over and grabbed on to Pete's leg. "You're too heavy, dude. Give me your hand. Pull yourself up." Just then, Pete's foot gave out, and Retro was left holding the other gnome's full weight. "Hurry up!" He strained. "Give me your hand … and … lay off the Oreo crumbs for Pete sake!"

Pete managed to sit up and grab Retro's hand that was holding his leg. Retro almost dropped him then, but Pete's scream was drowned out by the sounds of things exploding on screen and Arnold's coarse one-liners. Something caught Pete's

eyes then. Something *not* on the TV. It was pink and flying towards him. The thing got right up in Pete's face, and he could see it was somewhat humanoid, but with wings and solid black eyes. The thing started muttering merry nonsense, and then it flew away.

Pete wigged out. "Dude! Pull me up! Hurry! I just had a close encounter of the third kind!" At that moment, Pete felt himself being lifted smoothly. "Dude, did you just eat a can of spinach, or …?" He stopped talking, as his feet were again planted on solid ventilation shaft ground. The wind had stopped, and it had not been Retro who'd saved him. Pete looked sheepishly into the face of the policegnome. "Hey. Thanks, man."

The policegnome shook his head. "Pete Davidson. Why am I not surprised? I should have expected to find you at the other end of this mess. Especially when I recognized young Percival trying to pull you back up."

"Dude, don't call me Percival!"

Pete laughed at Retro, then turned to the cop. "Yeah. He doesn't want everybody to know that his parents hate him."

"Shut up, Pete!" Retro rebuked.

"Well, boys. I hope you realize what a close call you had *this* time. The ventilation shaft is highly restricted. You are in a lot of trouble. Hm. I think I'll have to cuff you this time."

"Do what?" Pete asked in alarm. "Are we going to jail?"

"No. I just want your parents to see you in handcuffs is all."

"Dude," Retro shouted. "What a psycho! I bet you're from Garland!"

The cop and Pete both looked at Retro.

"You know. It's a human city near here. The copgnomes there are even crazier than you are. They pulled a gun on …"

The policegnome's glare was enough to shut Retro up. He put handcuffs on both boys without a word, and he started marching them forward. "Actually," he said at last, "I was born and raised in Garland."

Pete and Retro gave each other a look that made it clear they felt they'd reached the end.

3
The Tale of Prince Fenrir

Ak'ten slowly opened the creaking front door of Malík's hidden home, hoping that his master had already gone to bed. He really didn't want to be made to drink troll whiskey. He felt great relief wash over him, as he noticed that all the candles had been long since put out, and no sign of the old shaman was to be seen. Ak'ten closed the wooden door behind him. Then, to his surprise, a candle lit beside him, revealing Malík in a chair, waiting patiently for his apprentice to return.

"Well," came the old gnome's angry voice. "What's your excuse this time?"

"Malík! Um … good thing you're still up …"

"Ak'ten …"

"No, wait! I was with Kazkal on a mission! I had to rescue him from a snake. There was this bird … and some weird fairy … and a *fat* fairy … and I …" He noticed that Malík was unmoved. He took one of the two pouches from his belt, and he handed it over to the shaman. "I brought your fairy powder."

Malík rose, towering menacingly over the lad, and he took the pouch from his hand. "Go to bed, Ak'ten. We will discuss your lack of judgment in the morning, after we have taken Djreena No'tall her potion."

Ak'ten's heart fell. He nodded and began walking towards his room. He hesitated. There was something about that weird fairy that he felt compelled to ask Malík. He turned. "Who is Fenrir?"

Malík looked frightened then. His eyes widened. It was not a look Ak'ten was accustomed to seeing on his master's unflinching face. "Why … why do you ask, lad?"

Ak'ten was beginning to feel frightened himself, though he had no idea why. It was just the look on Malík's face. It was unnerving. "The fairy. The sick fairy that we saw. It said something about someone named Fenrir, and Kazkal was," he paused, searching for the best word to describe the warrior's demeanor "*disturbed* for our entire journey home."

Malík went to the wall and grabbed his staff, which had been leaning against it. Perhaps it was to make him feel safer, as he spoke of things he had lived in dread of for five years beyond a decade. "Fenrir," he said at last, "is the Darkgnome who killed Kazkal's father. Fifteen years ago. Before you were born. Kazkal was only a lad at the time." He shook his head, sorrowfully. Then he asked, "What do you mean that the fairy was 'sick'?"

"Well, she seemed … twisted. Almost *dark*. I don't know, Malík. I've never seen a fairy like that. She had an evil smile. Her rhymes were far from merry. She spoke of strange things. Baskets and death. Living with death. Fenrir. Then a bird ate her. Right before our eyes. That's right about when we fell off the tree trunk and were rescued by an exploding fat fairy."

"Ak'ten, can you remember, word for word, all the things you heard this sick fairy say? Can you do a recall exercise like I taught you?"

Ak'ten didn't know why it was such a big deal what some sick fairy had said, but he was eager to help Malík forget his anger. "Uh … sure, Malík."

Ak'ten grabbed a pen and a blank scroll. He dipped the pen into a little jar filled with black ink, as he went back in his mind to the very moment, and he wrote down, word for word, what the fairy had said. He handed it to Malík, who studied Ak'ten's glyphs with growing unease.

Malík muttered aloud, "Basket wet. Temple of the unknown god …"

"Malík, what is this? Why are you so afraid? You worry me."

The shaman looked to his apprentice and decided that he owed the lad *some* explanation. However, he was unsure how much to hold back. The gods would guide him. That's what he decided. "It's Fenrir. He is someone to be feared. Or at least he is a power to be respected."

"Why," Ak'ten asked. "Tell me, Malík. What makes him different than any other enemy? You don't speak of gremlins in this way … or of Darkgnomes in general."

Malík noted that the lad had failed to list Techgnomes among their enemies. This was a source of disagreement between them that had gone on for five years. However, that was not the issue at hand. "Very well, Ak'ten. I will tell you this tale. But it is a dark tale, and it may keep you awake. Are you sure you want to hear it?"

"Yes." Ak'ten was enthralled. "Tell me, Malík."

Malík sat down again, and he breathed out a heavy sigh. "Very well then. Fifteen years ago, as you know, Tribe Qadash lived in a different tunnel system outside of the gremlin territories. We were a strong and prosperous tribe back then. My latest apprentice … was called Fenrir."

"Oh! He was your apprentice!"

"Not quite, lad. He had been my apprentice, but by this time, the nineteen years of apprenticeship had ended, and we had already completed a fifth of our required ten years of partnership. He had taken a wife, and he was …" Malík hesitated to say it to the lad, but decided to be honest, "… a mighty warrior."

"He was a shaman *and* a warrior?"

"Yes. He was a special case. You see, Fenrir was not just Fenrir, but *Prince* Fenrir, the cousin of our present king Nesu. I saw the magic in him when he was born, and Clan Qadash and the Shaman Collective both agreed that I should teach him the ways of the shamans. Fenrir was a very apt pupil. However, he was somewhat like you are now in his disregard for authority and rules. And there was something else. He was obsessed with the dark arts. I had no idea that he'd been practicing dark magic, but I knew his interest in the subject was dangerous. That is why teaching on the dark arts for a shaman doesn't happen until his training has reached its second-to-last year. One must be well versed in the magic of light and truth first. Only then, should one seek to understand the dark magics, and then only to know one's enemies. Fenrir, unfortunately, would seek out the tomes on dark magic in my library. He would read them when I was not paying attention. I thought that I'd corrected him, of course. I thought that I had made him understand. But when he was twenty-one years old, expecting his first child, I learned, along with the rest of our tribe, that Fenrir had sold his soul to darkness.

"Fenrir emerged with an *army* of those Tech-affiliated Darkgnomes from the human city. He had pledged to some demon the destruction of his own tribe, in exchange for power that he would never have obtained on his own. It was a devil's pact. We were unprepared for such an assault. Even our greatest warriors were no match for their magic and Fenrir's skill. He was a Centenarian, you see."

"What?" Ak'ten was amazed. "I thought that the Centenarian Elves were all over one-hundred years old."

Malík shook his head. "No. That is a myth. They are only one-hundred in number. Never one more or less. Fenrir had been chosen to learn their ways. As you know, this goes beyond the magical training of a shaman, this goes beyond the martial training of the warriors. The Centenarian Elves are an unimaginably skilled group of hybrids—a cross between warrior and shaman. So, when Fenrir came face to face with Kinto No'tall, not even the No'tall Battleaxe could defeat him. He killed Kinto, and he nearly killed Kinto's father Meso. The older warrior managed to come through with his life intact, but he lost a leg and an eye in the process. He was forced into retirement."

A very sad look came over the old shaman then, and he went on. "What happened next, the reason Fenrir is to be so feared … I am afraid, I must take the blame for."

Ak'ten was amazed. It was impossible for him to imagine Malík doing anything wrong. "What happened? What did you do, Malík?"

"As you know, fairies are my specialty. I have studied their life cycle and their magic. I can interpret their gibberish. Very shortly before Fenrir's Uprising, I was out studying the nearby fairies. One of them spoke to me, revealing a tidbit about the future. Something quite profound. You must understand how difficult it is to put anything a fairy says on a timeline. They don't understand time. They see the past, the present, and the future all at once, and don't know which is which. But I can tell, and I interpreted the dark prophesy, that one of our own in Tribe Qadash would rise up against us, that ultimately, in years to come, he would be destroyed by his own son. My terrible mistake was that I did not suspect Fenrir. In fact, I trusted him completely. So excited was I at this prophesy I'd discovered, that I rushed home and shared it with Fenrir.

Fenrir, who was already planning our destruction. Quite unknowingly, I told him how to become unstoppable. And he did. Oh," Malík blinked back tears, "how he did."

"What do you mean?" Ak'ten asked. "I thought you said he hadn't had a son yet."

"Yes, but I also told you he was expecting his first child. I let him know that, were the child to be born, and born male, he would grow up to be Fenrir's undoing."

Malík cleared his throat. "Now, getting back to the invasion of the Darkgnomes …" Malík took a pause to sigh wearily, before he went on. "Many things were happening all at once. The king and most of Clan Qadash had been slaughtered. Prince Nesu remained alive, as did his son Ammu. His wife, Princess Atalanta I, had been wounded, but she survived, as you know, until the birth of her daughter years later. She died because of the wounds Fenrir had inflicted upon her. The birth was too much for her.

"But I must get to the point of this tale. The terror of it. Nesu and I led the gnomes who'd survived away from the old tunnels. Fenrir believed that we'd all been killed. We needed him to continue to think that. It soon came to my attention that Fenrir's wife and her sister were nowhere to be found. I told Nesu that I was going to find them, and he continued to lead his people into the gremlin territories, where Fenrir would never think to look, even if he'd known we still existed."

Ak'ten was on the edge of his seat. "Did you find her then, Malík? Did you?"

The most haunted look that Ak'ten had ever seen came over Malík's face then. "Yes, Ak'ten. I did. What I found, however, was something out of a nightmare. I had come too late. The squirrel she'd been riding was dead, and Maareta Maa-Na Qadash, Fenrir's beautiful wife, lay dead beside it, her belly ripped open. The child she had carried, the son who might have saved us all, had been ripped from her womb and … dashed against a stone until he was unrecognizable even as a gnome. The child was destroyed. Our hopes were destroyed. If Fenrir were to learn that we still existed, there was nothing to *guarantee* our survival. And it was all because I'd told him what I'd learned. It was all because I hadn't seen the signs. And *I'm* the very gnome who taught him how to wield his power."

Malík shook his head, then looked to the stricken face of Ak'ten. "So now you see why I am frightened by the mention of his name by a 'sick' fairy." He waved in the direction of Ak'ten's room. "Now get to bed. It is late, and we've an early morning. We will discuss your adventure with Kazkal after our chores … and what is to be done about it."

Again, Ak'ten nodded his head somberly. He made his way across the little home to his bedroom. He said nothing, because there were too many thoughts racing through his mind all at once.

After Ak'ten had gone, Malík stood up and went to his books. He pulled an ancient, magically preserved volume from its place on the shelf, and he blew the dust from its binding. The glyphs on the front identified this as *The Book of Secrets* written by Sheto Qadash nearly a millennium before. Malík opened the book to a page that had been dog-eared, and he read aloud, "Dark Fairy Powder: The Fifth Key." Malík felt a chill as he closed the book and considered the gnome who'd dog-eared that very page only a decade-and-a-half before.

4
Home in Handcuffs

Just outside of the door to Pete's home, the policegnome stopped and spoke sternly to the two handcuffed teenagers. "Now, I just want to give you boys a warning before I let you go. There's a reason that we've been patrolling the ventilation shafts more lately. In fact, just last week, I found a mutilated mouse in there. We think there's Darkgnome activity going on. And you know Darkgnomes, don't you, boys? They're associated with the Old World gnomes in the forest. Pagans. They perform animal and probably even *gnome* sacrifices. Much trouble as I get from you two, I don't want to see

either one of you mutilated by Darkgnomes. You boys just keep that in your tiny, little minds."

Pete and Retro just nodded their heads, as the officer knocked on the door of the Davidson residence.

Pete's mother opened the door.

"Good evening, Mrs. Davidson. Sorry to trouble you again," the policegnome offered.

Resna Davidson looked beside the policegnome to see Pete and Retro in handcuffs. She sighed and shook her head disappointedly. "Oh, no. What is it *this* time?" she asked.

"Found 'em playin' around in the ventilation shaft, second story. Pete almost took a nasty fall, but I got him back."

Pete looked miserable, as he lifted his hands to show her.

"Was it necessary to put them in handcuffs?" Resna asked.

The policegnome laughed. "No. I just wanted to show 'em what it felt like. These boys have quite a reputation. Handcuffs are probably in their future."

"Well, you can let him out now. He's not bad. He's just … lacking in judgment. I'll have a talk with him."

The officer looked at her as though she were an idiot, and he unlocked Pete's cuffs.

Pete ran inside and stood behind his mother. "He's crazy, Mom! He was born and raised in Garland!"

Resna turned and looked at her son. "Go to your room, Pete. Just wait till your father gets home. He went out looking for you, after you took off. Thank the … thank *goodness* he would never have thought to look in the air shafts!"

Pete frowned and went to his room.

Resna turned back to the officer and Retro. "Thank you, Officer. I'll call Retro's mother and let her know he's on his way home."

Retro looked sick.

Resna winked at him, offering a genuinely affectionate smile as she closed the door.

Pete sat in his room thinking about what he'd done for at least ten seconds, before he remembered the thing he'd seen while he was hanging onto Retro for dear life. The alien. Maybe the mouse the cop had found hadn't been mutilated by Darkgnomes after all. Maybe it was aliens!

After a few minutes, his mother came in, dashing his dreams of turning on the Gnometendo video game system and forgetting all about it. "Pete," she said. "We *need* to talk, Son."

"I know, Mom. I shouldn't have gone into the ventilation shafts. Are you gonna tell Dad?"

Resna nodded. "Of course, dear. He's going to ask where you were, and I'm not going to lie to him. Pete, what were you thinking?"

Pete suddenly came alive. "Well, the humans were just watching this kick-ass movie, and I just—"

"I know." She finished for him. "You just *had* to climb up the air shaft to watch, and you just *had* to get poor Retro involved. I just got off the phone with his mother, and I feel very sorry for him. I don't think she'll be as forgiving as I am. Maybe she's right, do you think? Why is it that you are always getting yourself into trouble? Pete, you came home to me in

handcuffs! Do you have any idea how a mother feels inside when she sees her only child in *handcuffs*?" She sat for a moment, then added, "And watch your mouth!"

"Sorry. It was a kick … a really cool movie though. Oh! I saw an alien!"

"Pete, you crawled all the way up there just to watch one of *those* awful movies?"

"No, dude! A *real* alien! When I was hanging on for dear life and about to kiss my sweet ass goodbye, this *alien* flew up to me, said a bunch of weird crap, then flew away."

"I'm not a 'dude.' Watch your mouth. And you've been watching *way* too many human movies, I think."

"No, woman! I'm serious! It was a real, live alien, right in my damn face!"

"Pete!"

"Sorry! I'm just wound up!" He grinned and started to giggle. Then he went on. "She was pink and had little bug wings and black eyes …" Pete noticed his mother's unusual expression. "What?"

Resna had gone pale. She stood abruptly. "Pete, you have an overactive imagination. I think I just heard your father drive up." With that, she turned and left.

Pete lay down on his bed, and he thought about aliens. Aliens and Darkgnomes.

5
In the Fortress of the Darkgnomes

Further into the human city, there stood an old church building long abandoned by the congregation that had built it. Forsaken by humans as it was, this building was still very much in use, for when light fades from a thing, the shadows are ever standing by, ready to replace it. Such had been the case with this building, when Fenrir had chosen it as the center of Darkgnome operations around the world.

The nine-and-a-half centimeter tall leader of the Darkgnome Legion paced in his study, which was located in a secret room at the top of the rotting bell tower. The room was filled with books. Mountains of books. Some of these books had been made by gnomes. Most, however, were giant books, larger than the Dark Prince himself, designed by humans, printed by human machines.

Fenrir had been long obsessed with occult knowledge. As a boy, he had haunted the forbidden tomes of his master's library. In the end, Fenrir's obsession had served him well. Those books had led him to Belial. Now, allied with Belial, these books would lead to greater things.

Fenrir had used magic to infiltrate the human world. He had many accounts in human banks, under a number of aliases. He had invested in human businesses and human archaeologists. He had invested in anything and everything that would further his search for the treasure Belial required.

Fenrir had used his vast resources to equip his Darkgnome fortress with the latest and most advanced human technology. He had the most elaborate computers that money could buy, the most powerful telescopes and spy equipment. He often found it ironic that he, a gnome born of the "Old World" had become the most technologically up to date citizen of this particular human city. Of course, that by no means meant that he had abandoned his shaman's training. Not in the least. In fact, Fenrir fancied himself the most powerful sorcerer in all the world. He had just recently destroyed Belial's human servant, a sorcerer by the name of Kurzan. Fenrir had murdered the man with relative ease.

Fenrir …

The gnome's ears perked, and he turned to the wall and viewed his own shadow. Two red slits appeared on the shadow, where Fenrir's eyes would have been. "Yes, master."

The demonic shadow seemed to smile. *You have done as I asked of you, my servant?*

Fenrir bristled at the condescending label, but he kept his thoughts focused, so that the old god wouldn't hear any of his secrets. "Yes, Belial. Kurzan is no more, and—"

And the coin?

Fenrir smiled malevolently. "The First Key is in our hands."

Fenrir's shadow began to laugh. *Excellent work, Fenrir. Excellent. And what of your quest for the others?*

"The other three keys are not yet in our grasp, but we grow ever closer to obtaining the Fifth Key." Fenrir grumbled, "There have been some episodes of *incompetence* among my people. They will be dealt with when they return."

Yes, yes. See to it. The shadow seemed to slump. *For now, I must … I choose to rest. You serve me well. We will speak again soon, my pet.*

Fenrir kept his fury in check, until the shadow flickered, and Belial had left it. Then he allowed his thoughts to flow freely. *Pet indeed!* Fenrir pushed one of the giant human tomes over in a rage, and he angrily forced it open. He growled to himself. He couldn't wait until his alliance with Belial was no longer a necessity. For now, however, there was no other way. Though he hated to admit it, Belial had been instrumental in locating the three keys that Fenrir had thus far acquired.

Fenrir had come face to face with Belial when he was twenty-one years old. The dark spirit had claimed to be a fallen god from the time of the First World. He had explained to Fenrir that he had grown weak and needed servants to bring him back to greatness. He had promised Fenrir power unimagined and had so far proved true to his word. He had led Fenrir to mastery over the local Darkgnome cult. A cult that was spread like a cancer throughout the gnome societies of the world but thoroughly unorganized. Fenrir had destroyed Damon, the leader of the local faction, and banished Sinistor, his second, then taken the reigns himself unopposed. He had reinvented the entire Darkgnome religion and eventually unified the scattered Darkgnome groups around the world into a mighty legion.

The Darkgnomes had always been focused on black magic, but they had also been comfortable with technology. They had accepted members from Old World and Techgnome societies alike. It was this philosophical cross-breeding that Fenrir had taken advantage of. There were enough former Techgnomes among these villains to allow him to build up the Darkgnomes' scientific prowess, just as there were enough former Old World Gnomes to allow him to build up their magical prowess. It was a combination that Fenrir believed invincible. He had combined the strengths of the Old World with the strengths of the Techgnomes and eliminated the weaknesses of both.

Belial had asked Fenrir to destroy his own Old World tribe as a show of his devotion. A sacrifice to his new god. Fenrir had done it. The promise of power had been too great.

There had been only one prophesy which had threatened him in all this time, and Fenrir had snuffed it out. Before his move to destroy Tribe Qadash, Fenrir had been informed by his master, Malík, that a gnome would rise up from within the tribe to try and destroy it. Malík also told him that this villain was cursed, in that his own son would grow up to be his undoing. The arrogant prince had shrugged the information off, until the day he'd incurred the wrath of the ancient gnome witch Zorha, who had set upon *him* that very curse, and he'd known it was he whom the fairies had told Malík about.

Wise enough to be cautious, Fenrir had hunted down his wife and her sister after his Darkgnomes had finished off the rest of the tribe. He had broken his sister-in-law's neck, which had been quite a task, for she, like himself, had been trained by the much feared Centenarian Elves. Then he had moved on his wife. He had torn the unborn child from her womb and smashed it into oblivion, leaving his entire family behind in death. And Fenrir had never regretted this action. He only ever looked back to the prophesy. He knew that he must never father another child. For that very reason, Fenrir had moved all the female members of his cult to other branches around the world. The Dark Prince had even considered particular acts of self-mutilation. Ultimately, Fenrir had been too vain for that. The *ability* to father a son made him appear stronger, even if he never intended to use it.

Fenrir considered the fact that Belial had never even been aware of this prophesy until he had let the old god know what he had learned. It was the first indication that Fenrir had seen of the level of Belial's weakness. Though the ancient spirit may have been a god at one time, he was clearly little more than an addle-minded ghost now. Belial was not all-knowing. Belial was not all-present. And Belial was very, very weak. Fenrir knew that the old god *needed* his rest. He couldn't help but notice how long it had taken for him to show up and ask after his encounter with Kurzan. And then there was the fact that this god had found it *necessary* to ask! Fenrir had no respect for Belial, but he did have need of him.

It was soon after Belial had given Fenrir dominion over the Darkgnomes, and shortly before Fenrir had used them to wipe out his tribe, that Belial had let Fenrir know what it was he truly sought. It was a mystical treasure long since passed into the realm of the mythic. A gnome bedtime story. It was a jewel known as the Devil's Pearl. Belial had insisted in the legitimacy of this pearl. Fenrir had been amazed, and he had set to work immediately looking up what he could on the matter in Malík's great library.

The Devil's Pearl had been hidden away nearly one thousand years before by Fenrir's own legendary ancestor Sheto Qadash. Sheto had defeated his sinister cousin Shi-Nook and taken the Pearl where none could find it.

And why hadn't Sheto simply destroyed the Pearl? The reason was simply that no gnome likely had the strength of will to do such a thing. At least, that's what Fenrir believed. He hadn't read the *entire* book that Sheto had written. He had mainly looked up the chapters on the power of the Pearl and the keys to uncovering it. Unfortunately, these keys were mostly hidden as well, or at least difficult to come by.

Once one had actually accumulated the six magical keys, however, one only needed to know where the Pearl was hidden. Then that gnome would be able to see all things, past, present, and future, for as long as he liked. And he would be granted one wish at the end of his time commanding the Pearl.

The catch was that whenever a gnome made his one wish, there was no turning back. The wish would be instantly granted. The gnome who'd made the wish would then be rendered dead to the Devil's Pearl and would no longer be able to use it in any way.

It was the wishing power of this pearl which Belial intended to use to regain his former stature. He needed Fenrir to help him, for it was a gnome's treasure, likely hidden where no human, such as Belial's late servant Kurzan, could get to it. Fenrir, of course, had other ideas for when he finally found the Pearl.

He walked some pages over in the book, and then he sprawled out on top of it to read. One of Fenrir's many sources of pride was that he had learned the human alphabet. There were not any other Old World gnomes, to Fenrir's knowledge, who could boast such a thing.

His concentration was broken by the creaking of a door. Without looking up, the Dark Prince asked, "What is it, Necros?"

"Lord Fenrir, Bast and Moloch have returned from their meeting with the humans."

Fenrir stood up quickly and went to a crack in the wall. Through a series of strategically placed mirrors, Fenrir could see all the way into the front chamber of the building. He noticed two suits tailored to fit humans, lying in heaps on the floor, and he smiled. It was a trick which no shaman in the Old World would have even considered—using magic to make gnomes grow to human size, thus allowing them to infiltrate the human world. The shamans would have considered it blasphemous. Fenrir only saw it as pragmatic, and the single challenge was covering the points of their ears. He turned to Necros. "Bring them in."

Necros bowed and went to collect them. When Necros returned, he was accompanied by the other two Darkgnomes, who had returned to their original sizes upon entering the church.

"Well, how did it go?" Fenrir asked.

Bast and Moloch both smiled. Bast spoke first. "Very well, my lord. Very well. The secrets we seek will not elude us for much longer."

"Yes," Moloch added. "We have obtained complete economic control of the archaeological expedition in Egypt. This is the closest we've been able to come to the prophesy about the Sphinx's paws."

"And were our Egyptian agents there in disguise as well?" Fenrir asked.

"Yes," said Bast. "They know what to do. As soon as they have access to get beneath the paws, they will."

"Of course," Moloch added, "there are still a great many details to be worked out. The dates are not yet set. It could even be a few years before our human archaeologists are allowed to start their work. And then, it would only be for a certain length of time, as usual."

"Yes, yes," Fenrir said with a grin. "I'm just happy that we've finally gotten the ball rolling. We need that human equipment to be working for us over there. This is excellent news." He turned back to Necros. "Necros, bring in our newest captive."

Again, Necros nodded and left the room. When he returned, he held a fairy in magical chains. Fenrir regarded the horrified creature, and he offered a most predatory smile. "You may all leave us now. I feel like celebrating, and it's high time we started to work on this one. She doesn't look to have been worked on at all." He glanced up at his Darkgnomes, silent laughter painted on his lips. "No interruptions."

The other gnomes, knowing Fenrir's intentions, bowed and backed out of the room, closing the door behind them. The rest of the night was filled with the sounds of a fairy screaming.

6
A Visit from the General

The morning was still early when Ak'ten and Malík returned home from visiting Djreena No'tall. So far, Malík had not forced Ak'ten to drink troll whiskey, but he had made Ak'ten explain to Djreena why her potion was so late in coming. That was punishment enough, as far as Ak'ten was concerned. Djreena was in so much pain, and Ak'ten knew she had suffered a day longer just because of him. He tried to console himself with the fact that Kazkal would have been eaten by a snake, had he obeyed Malík's orders. It worked to some extent, but he still felt bad about Djreena. He hated that there hadn't been a way to help them both at once.

When Malík had closed the door of their home behind them, Ak'ten asked nervously, "So what now?"

Malík answered, "Now, we eat our breakfast and prepare to go see King Nesu."

"King Nesu? Has he summoned us?"

"No," Malík went to his work table and set to preparing their meal. "I simply wish to discuss some things with him."

Ak'ten perked up. "It's about the fairies isn't it? I was thinking about it all night!"

"Don't concern yourself with it, lad."

"But, Malík! Don't you think the sick fairy was trying to tell us that Fenrir has been capturing fairies? That she escaped, but he still has some held prisoner in the human city?"

Malík stopped what he was doing, and regarded Ak'ten with wonder. He hadn't really focused on teaching Ak'ten to translate fairy gibberish. Those were teachings for later years, if Ak'ten chose to specialize in fairies. "My goodness, lad. You are so much trouble at times, but I never have doubted that I chose you well. How is it possible that I am a specialist and you a mere apprentice, yet you have come untrained to the same conclusions as I have? How did you get so good at translating fairy gibberish?"

Ak'ten shrugged. "I just watch you is all."

Malík shook his head. "Amazing." He met Ak'ten's stare. "Well, yes. If you must know, that is exactly what I intend to share with Nesu." He lifted a finger. "But you must keep this business quiet. No one must learn that we have any reason to fear from our old enemy just yet. It would bring too much unnecessary angst to our tribe. So guard your tongue."

Ak'ten nodded.

Just then, there was a knocking at the door. "I'll get it," Ak'ten said, as he walked across the room. He opened the door to see the striking features of Tribe Qadash's highest ranking warrior. "General Argon!"

"Ak'ten. Just the gnome I was looking for." The general glared down at the young shaman's apprentice. His dark skin and dark eyes made Argon look imposing enough, but the tattoos on his unusually *bald* scalp made him look absolutely menacing.

Argon had lost his hair, after rising to the rank of General, and as a result, he was constantly out to prove his rank to the other gnomes; though few now dared to challenge him. He was the fiercest warrior in all of Tribe Qadash.

"Um … we were just about to go see—"

"I would like to come in." The general leaned forward, letting his shadow cover the youth.

"Um … sure. Come on in, General Argon."

Malík stopped what he was doing and greeted the general. "Welcome, Argon. Would you like to join us? We were just about to have breakfast."

"No," said Argon, without even taking his eyes off of Ak'ten. "Warriors eat at the break of dawn. We never dally the day away."

Ak'ten was defensive. "We've actually just returned from our first errand of the day, ourselves. We had to take a—"

"Sit down, Ak'ten." The general's eyes made it clear that this was no request. Ak'ten found a chair and took a seat.

The general pulled another chair up and sat right in front of Ak'ten.

"What's the matter, General?" Malík asked with concern.

Argon looked over to Malík. "Ak'ten and An'sep had another fight yesterday afternoon, it seems. Were you aware?"

Anger colored Malík's cheeks. "No. He left that part out of his excuses last night, I'm afraid."

"Yes," Argon said with a sarcastic smile. "I figured he might." He looked back at Ak'ten. "Boy, you have been *told*! I don't know what it's going to take to get it through your thick skull, but you cannot be a warrior, and it is against the rules for An'sep to spar with you. You are *not* to encourage him. It will do you no good."

Ak'ten was wounded, as always, and he refused to accept the things he was being told. He stood up and looked down to the general. "But I'm a better fighter than any of your warrior apprentices! You only forbid them to spar with me, because it embarrasses you to have trained fighters lose to a stray! It embarrasses them too. Just ask An'sep."

At that, the general was on his feet, and he pushed Ak'ten down in his seat very forcefully. "Upstart! This is the *last* time I'll let you get off with a warning, stray." He put a finger right in Ak'ten's face, almost touching him. "You are to stay away from An'sep. He is a good apprentice to Kazkal, but when he gets around you, he lets anger and jealousy cloud his judgment. I'll admit he deserves every trimming you've given him, but you should *not* go unpunished."

The general composed himself, and he walked over to the door. He turned before leaving, for emphasis. "Stay away from An'sep, Ak'ten. Or I'll be talking to King Nesu about arranging proper punishment for a stray who won't mind." He looked to Malík, and he bowed his head slightly. "Malík." Then General Argon left, closing the door behind him.

Ak'ten sat trembling in rage and hurt.

Malík didn't know whether to be angry or sympathetic. Argon had been harsh, after all. Malík was even a bit offended himself. "Ak'ten, do you want to tell me just what that was all about?"

Ak'ten looked to Malík with desperate eyes. "It was An'sep's fault, Malík! He started it! He drew his sword!"

"Ak'ten, it doesn't matter who starts or finishes a fight. When a fight occurs, all parties are to blame. Why do you and An'sep do this, when you know how much trouble you will get into in the end?"

"Because I … hate him, Malík." A tear rolled down the young gnome's cheek.

"Ak'ten! How sad for you. How I pity you. Hatred is such a terrible thing. Why would you let him fill your heart with it? Do you truly give An'sep such power over your spirit?"

Though they made sense, Ak'ten did not enjoy hearing Malík's words. "No, I just don't understand why a peezwizz like An'sep gets to do whatever he wants in life, just because of his family. And I have no choices. No matter how much talent I have. Fenrir got to be a shaman *and* a warrior! He got to do whatever he wanted, because of who *his* family was. I have no

choices, and most gnomes don't even like that I am training to be a shaman, all because I'm a stray! And I hate that word. I'm no stray. Strays have no one, but I have you at least. And I have a purpose."

Malík was moved by Ak'ten's pain, and he went and knelt in front of him, taking his hand. "Yes, Ak'ten. You certainly do have a purpose. One day, I promise you, all who speak against you now will choke on their cruel words. You may be without a clan, but I will always be your family, Ak'ten. You will always have a home."

Ak'ten sniffled.

Malík rose and said, "Now let's get moving. We must get our news to King Nesu, before the morning grows too late."

"What about . . .?"

"Oh, let's not waste our efforts with breakfast here today. Whatever we come up with, surely Nesu will offer us better when we arrive in the Royal Caverns."

Ak'ten lit up at the notion. King Nesu certainly did know how to feed a gnome, after all.

"I must tell you now, though, lad. When we arrive, although you do know part of my business, there are other matters which I must discuss alone with King Nesu. I know it frustrates you, but I will have to ask you to wait outside the room. There will be plenty to occupy you there. Oh, and do try to stay out of trouble." Malík offered the lad a smile born of affection and good humor.

Ak'ten shrugged and laughed shortly, wondering if such a thing were at all possible.

7
The Royal Caverns

There were two ways to enter the caverns of Tribe Qadash from Malík's home. One was a secret passage from inside Malík's bedchamber that led directly to the Royal Cavern itself. By necessity, very few gnomes ever learned of this tunnel's existence, and it was only ever used in dire circumstances. That is why Malík and Ak'ten went to the caverns by way of the main entrance.

The pair left their little home and walked the short distance to the secret entrance beneath another of the mighty tree's thick roots. The great stone was rolled aside, as usual, and two guards stood watch just inside the entrance. Knowing Malík and Ak'ten, they allowed the two gnomes to enter without question. The shaman and his apprentice then began the long descent down the dim, torch-lit stairway carved into the ground beneath their feet. Deep beneath the earth that nurtured their tribe's great tree, the stairs came to an end, and Malík and Ak'ten arrived in a vast open cavern known as Qadash Commonground.

Commonground was the center of the tribal caverns and was the place where all clans came together as a tribe. Circular in its parameters, the cavern was filled with torchlight and gnomes from every clan in the tribe selling their wares and practicing their trades.

The entire western wall was carved, top to bottom, into a glorious work of architectural artistry that served as the face of the Royal Caverns. The wall was decorated with figures of gods and legendary gnomes of days gone by, a great central balcony from which the king would often address the tribe, a myriad of grand, colored windows, and glyphs that spoke of ancient truths that served as the foundation of gnome society. There were also many mysterious symbols that, it was said, only the gnomes of the royal clan itself truly understood. A grand archway at the very center of the "ground" level, containing two gigantic, crimson doors, was the entrance to the Royal Caverns.

Along the northern, eastern, and southern walls were carved much smaller entrances. These were for the other twelve clans of the tribe, each of which had cavern territories of their own. Malík and Ak'ten headed to the west, where they were questioned by the royal guards as to the nature of their visit, before being granted entrance to see the king.

Within the Royal Caverns, the pair was given as warm a welcome as usual. King Nesu invited them to have breakfast with him and his eleven-year-old daughter Princess Atalanta II. The food was very good and very filling. Still, it didn't manage to fill the void in Ak'ten's heart. He remained very down over General Argon's visit.

Malík noticed this, of course, and he was very concerned, but he had to put the morning's business first for now. He patted Ak'ten on the shoulder, then turned to Nesu, who sat beside him at the great wooden table. "And now, my king, I must speak with you in private about the business which brings me here in the first place."

A serious look shadowed the great king's face. Nesu was a strong king, who had been through more than most in his time. He had come to the throne at an early age, due to the vile deeds of his cousin Fenrir. He knew that for Malík to leave his apprentice out of a matter meant that it was concerned with only a handful of possible things. Very serious things. "Of course, Malík. We'll adjourn to my private study at once." He rose and led the way.

Malík followed, turning once, before he went, to give Ak'ten a reassuring smile.

When the adults had gone, Ak'ten brooded, almost forgetting that he was not alone.

"What's the matter, Ak'ten?" Atalanta asked.

Ak'ten looked across the table at her. "Oh, nothing. I'm just … tired."

Atalanta seemed to see right through him. She got up and went around the table, taking the seat beside him. "What are you so tired of?"

Ak'ten regarded her with surprise, but only shook his head.

"Come on, Ak'ten. Don't be such a peezwizz. It's clear that something troubles you. Am I not your princess? You must tell me the truth."

Ak'ten studied Atalanta's sincere, blue eyes; the long yellow hair that framed her face so elegantly. Yes, she was certainly his princess, but more importantly, she was his friend. She and Ak'ten would always talk when he and Malík visited the Royal Caverns. Ak'ten decided to be honest with her. "I am tired of being a stray is all. Some days, it just gets to me. I get angry at gnomes whose affiliation with a clan gives them choices. I get angry with my parents for abandoning me. I get angry with myself, because I can't just be the gnome that I was born to be. Or at least, the gnome that everyone seems to *think* I was born to be." He shook his head and got up. "You wouldn't understand. You couldn't possibly know what it's like to be stuck like this. You're a princess after all, as you only just said." He walked over to three large stone stairs that marked the entrance to one of the many corridors in the Royal Caverns. He sat on the stairs and pouted to himself.

Once again, Atalanta went to him. She sat down beside him and put a hand on his shoulder. She smiled. "Ak'ten, you are very wrong. Do you think a princess has choices? Do you think my life's dream is to exist in this stuffy cavern, growing up to rule the tribe, making laws, passing judgments? Don't you think I'd rather be …" she looked down at her feet, and was surprised at the tears which came to her eyes, "… playing Seek with you and your friends? Slug wrestling until my fancy dress is unsalvageable? Perhaps even going to visit other gnomes, when they are sick, as you and Malík get to do? But I am here. I am a princess, which means my only choice is to grow up and become a queen. I am the sole heir to my father's throne now, even if he won't believe it. My brother has been missing for ten years. My father is the only gnome in the tribe who refuses to believe what that means. So I have no choices. I am like you. Never assume that I wouldn't understand. Perhaps it is you who fails to understand." She wiped the tears from her eyes and smiled again.

Ak'ten sat dumbfounded. He'd never really thought about that. "I'm sorry, Princess. It was wrong of me to assume."

Atalanta smiled still. "It's all right, Ak'ten. And for what it's worth, I never think of you as a stray. I only see you as a friend. A friend who gets to do things I cannot. But then, I at least get to hear about them. And I must acknowledge that I have some privileges, being a princess, that you do not. And we each have burdens. We both lack certain choices, if we are to remain in everyone's good graces. So let's just resolve to look out for one another. If nothing else, we can have each other's understanding."

Ak'ten finally smiled, thankful for the wisdom of his beautiful friend. "That's a deal." He reached down and took her hand. "These talks of ours always do me good."

8
King Nesu

In the king's private study, Malík prepared to tell Nesu what he had learned from Ak'ten's report. He noticed, however, that Nesu's attention had been drawn to a scroll on his desk.

"What is it, Majesty?"

Nesu went over and picked up the scroll. He unrolled it and scanned the glyphs that were painted there. "Hm. My advisors want to meet with me. I grow tired of this. I know what they mean to say to me. The ten-year mark is upon us after all."

Malík spoke tenderly. "You speak of your missing son."

"Yes." Nesu shook his head sadly. "And it pleases me to hear you refer to him as 'missing,' old friend, and not 'dead,' as my advisors and perhaps all of Tribe Qadash would have us believe."

Malík nodded his bearded head. "Ammu may be alive yet, I cannot see. The fact that I cannot find Ammu at all, alive or dead, leads me to suspect that sorcery is to blame. Someone powerful doesn't *want* us to find him."

A determined look came over Nesu. "We *will* find him, Malík. Only, I do not know if we will find him in time, or if he'll still be fit to rule. That would be the concern of my advisors, if they were not so sure he had been killed."

Malík considered. It was indeed a concern, if Nesu's dying clan were to maintain rulership of the tribe. Prince Ammu had gone missing in a battle with gremlins a decade before. There was nothing to suggest that he'd been killed, other than the fact that he had been seen going into that fateful battle. The warriors there with him had all been killed, but of young Prince Ammu, no body was left on the battlefield. Not even his crown.

The trouble now was due to the fact that Nesu required a male heir to pass the crown to, and no male heir now existed. The ruling Clan Qadash had almost died completely. Now only three remained: Nesu, Atalanta, and Fenrir. Fenrir would have been next in line for the throne legally, by imposed marriage to the princess, but Nesu doubted that would happen, considering the villain believed them all dead. As for young Atalanta, her only hope of ascending the throne was to marry a royal

cousin, of which there were none left within the tribe. If there were no heir to the throne, the various heads of the clans would resort to murder and perhaps even civil war to decide which clan should rule the tribe. That is why Nesu's advisors frequently urged Nesu to remarry, to father another son. But Nesu was stubborn. His love was more powerful than his reason, when it came to his late wife and his missing son. Were he to remarry, he would be accepting their loss as final.

As if reading Malík's thoughts, Nesu said, "I will die before I give up hope that my son is alive. My advisors need not be so worried. After all, I am still in my prime." He turned to Malík with a solemn smile. "But what business brings you here, old friend? I don't mean to keep you from it."

Malík hesitated only for a moment, torn between wanting to comfort his friend and needing to get on with more urgent business. In situations such as these, it was the shaman's usual way to get to the matter at hand. "Ak'ten encountered a … sick fairy yesterday afternoon. Or, I should say, a twisted fairy. Fairies do not get sick naturally."

Nesu stroked his red whiskers, as he considered. "You are the expert, old friend. So what was so troublesome? Was it her sickness?"

"No." Malík gripped his staff harder, growing tense as he spoke. "It was what the fairy said. You see, in order for a fairy to grow twisted, there must be someone to cause it. Someone must torture her. Otherwise, fairies are a carefree and happy people. And you know well my expertise, and that I have been able to interpret their gibberish. Well, what this twisted fairy spoke were frightening words. For she revealed that our old enemy, your sinister cousin Fenrir, is still very near. He has perhaps even entered our forest to gather his specimens."

"What? Are you certain?"

Malík nodded gravely. "Very. And it was clear from the fairy's gibberish that he's been abducting her people … torturing them. And there is only one reason that I can think of that Fenrir would be torturing fairies."

Nesu felt cold, for he suspected he knew. "And what is that?"

"He seeks to produce *dark* fairy powder. It is the Fifth Key to obtaining the lost Devil's Pearl. Fenrir marked the pages in a book of mine before his insurrection. I have long feared the reason why."

"But, even if he had all six of the keys, he would have to know where the Pearl was hidden. Do you think that he has found it?"

"I do not know. It is doubtful. For surely the shamans would have sensed such a disturbance. They would have called a convocation. But even we do not know the location of the Pearl. No one does. I have the book that your ancestor Sheto wrote himself, and he does not say where he hid it. He does not even hint at it. He only lists the keys. Though I do not know their identities, I do know that four of these keys have been entrusted to shamans of my order, and I can assure you that I would have heard news of their disturbance. So we need not worry yet about Fenrir using such a horror as the Pearl, so much as we must be on full alert. We must be cautious, for he has entered our forest to abduct fairies. He is clearly seeking the six magical keys to releasing the Devil's Pearl. Our tribe is in danger of discovery."

"Yes," Nesu said in a haunted tone. "The Dark Prince must never learn that his tribe still lives. Our resources are all tied up fighting the gremlins. If he found us, I have little doubt that he would destroy us. Our warriors are fierce … but Fenrir is fiercer."

9
The Tale of Shi-Nook

Princess Atalanta entered the Cavern of Blood promptly after the guards had delivered her father's request to meet him there. It was rare that she had seen this particular chamber of the Royal Caverns. It was a room of secrets, now sparsely lit. She saw her father's silhouette standing beside the altar of the Blood Stones, in front of the enormous family tree that covered the wall on the western side of every level of the cavern. The princess knelt and bowed her head. "You sent for me, Father?"

Nesu walked into the light and motioned subtly with his hand for her to rise. He lit another torch and smiled broadly. "No need for such formalities, Ati. There are no guards here."

The princess gracefully rose from her humbled position and smiled at her father. "What is it?"

The king looked to the western wall. "I have a story to tell you. This is the best place for its telling."

"Is this an epic recently acquired from our neighbors? Or something humorous?" Atalanta probed.

"It is something … true," the king answered. "Something from the distant past, nearly a thousand years before our day. Come with me to the Great Wall."

Atalanta followed her father to the rail at the edge of the upper level. She looked at the great genealogy which flowed from the ceiling down to every level below. She had seen this before, but not often. This was the lineage of the whole of Tribe Qadash. As it grew over the years, new levels were carved out to accommodate the generations.

Nesu spoke reverently. "You should have seen the wall in our original caverns, before the Darkgnomes drove us here. It was so beautiful. Every name was etched in gold, and the most brilliant detail was used in the carving of the glyphs. This one was hurried, copied from scrolls, though it is still so very humbling. It is humbling to see how every clan within our tribe is descended from the same source. We are all cousins, in effect. All blood. Every gnome in our kingdom is a kinsman, and it is the purpose of the king to remember it and treat them as his children. Oh, but I would love for you to see the first tree, now surely overgrown in the Ruins on the other side of the Plains of Sebau. To stare at the first generations, and to know that their names were carved in their own time, the time of King Aleph Qadash himself. The very gnome who founded our tribe more than a thousand years ago.

"But this story I am going to tell you now has to do with the days of his grandson King Saret, son of King Adama.

The princess considered. "Not much time is spent by my tutors delving into such ancient things, Father. They say that most of these tales are myths."

The king laughed softly. "Well, Ati, that would certainly be the easiest thing to believe. There were many strange events in those days. Perhaps your tutors refer to the First Time. Those tales may never be substantiated. Still, I have come to see the truth in myth. For every allegory exposes something true. But this genealogy is documented, there on the wall. Most of your tutors have never even seen this wall." Nesu rarely brought gnomes here. It was a sacred place to kings. One day, Nesu knew, his bones would lie within the walls of this very cavern. He only ever brought gnomes here when it seemed appropriate. When there was a conflict between clans, for instance, or, like today, when some terrible enemy sought to unearth the Devil's Pearl of legend.

The king considered. "I suppose there are those who would laugh if they knew I meant to tell you the tale of the Devil's Pearl. For nothing from our history is so much regarded as myth."

Atalanta's eyes narrowed. "The Devil's Pearl? I have never heard of such a thing."

"As I said," the king went on, "it is mostly thought of as myth, for how could such a powerful thing exist? But I am telling you, it does. I am telling you that it was once present in our very tribe."

"What *is* it, Father?"

"That's what I brought you here to learn. This is a secret, Ati, like all the ones before. There are certain things an heir to the throne should know that would only trouble all of his … her tribesgnomes."

Atalanta nodded, understanding.

Nesu began the tale. "As I said, this is something that happened in the time of King Saret. However, the story takes place in the last days of his reign, and it is more about three younger gnomes: Nekhet, Shi-Nook, and Sheto. These three cousins were the grandsons of King Adama. Nekhet was the heir to the throne of Saret. Shi-Nook, son of Kain, was jealous of the crown and plotted to exterminate Saret's line."

Atalanta interrupted. "Was this the same Kain known as the Prince of Serpents?"

"Yes, it was. He was a tremendous sorcerer, and so was his son Shi-Nook. So too was the third cousin in this tale: Sheto, son of Jess-Thera. Sheto, I have heard, was something of a square peg in a round hole—curious of everything. As I said, he was a great sorcerer, but it was not known. He toyed with the magical arts without any teacher save for himself and the scrolls in the Royal Library. Malík could tell you of the danger in such studies. After a time, however, he was trying to hide the fact that he'd grown more powerful than even the tribe's own shaman, Kroshaq the Mystifier.

"You were not born until our clan was nearly extinct, but at most times, there have always been royal cousins. Some of these become like one's own brothers. So, as these gnomes grew up, Sheto and Nekhet became very close. Shi-Nook, on the other hand, became distant.

"Like Sheto, and like his father Kain, Shi-Nook had also grown adept in the magical arts. All the more unheard of, because he was a fearsome warrior. Shi-Nook's expertise differed from Sheto's, however, in that his power came from delving in the dark arts. He used his powers to forge a great, black sword. When wielded in battle, this sword was said to emit an ominous green light. Some said it was a veil of green smoke. No one knows for sure, since the Sword of Shi-Nook has been hidden away now for centuries. This sword could allegedly defeat any foe. Even spirits were susceptible to its blade. Shi-Nook used the sword to become even more respected as a warrior than he already was, and very few knew its secret."

Atalanta considered. "That sounds similar to the No'tall Battleaxe."

"Similar, I suppose," Nesu agreed. "But still *quite* different. The No'tall Battleaxe can never be used for evil. That's the strongest part of its magic. The Sword of Shi-Nook was forged in darkness, its killing power open to any who wielded it.

"But it was not this sword that ultimately made Shi-Nook a terror to his own tribe. Instead, it was an ancient, black pearl. Actually, accounts of the Pearl's appearance vary. What matters is the power of the Pearl. The Devil's Pearl. It is unknown how this ancient jewel ever found its way to our region of the world. It is only known that Shi-Nook found it. This pearl gave the one who held it great powers. One could see anything, anywhere, any *time*, simply by gazing into the Pearl with intent to see it. It worked to Shi-Nook's advantage that all soon learned of his supernatural ability to see them wherever they were, that all knew he'd uncovered this menace from the First Time. No one dared keep secrets from Shi-Nook. No one aside from his cousins, who feared the power had gone to his head. Their suspicions proved true, on the day that Shi-Nook entered the king's throne room and declared himself the new king of Tribe Qadash.

"King Saret's outrage fell on deaf ears. No one dared oppose the mighty Shi-Nook. Not even to defend their rightful king. Prince Nekhet knew that his father would be killed, and in little time Shi-Nook would have him killed as well. No one could hide from Shi-Nook's pearl. Before Shi-Nook had even noticed him in the shadows, Nekhet snuck out through a secret passage and went to find his cousin Sheto. They conspired together quickly, before any had time to notice the heir's absence. They made plans to destroy Shi-Nook, before he could set the Pearl to finding him.

"King Saret was imprisoned and urged to abdicate the throne legally. When the king refused, and Shi-Nook grew irritated enough, Saret was put to death. Shi-Nook took the crown from the old king's head and placed it on his own. He sat on the throne immediately thereafter and demanded that Prince Nekhet be brought before him to officially relinquish his birthright.

"What Shi-Nook had failed to take into consideration was that his own father, Kain the Prince of Serpents, was still in line before him for the throne and had been devoted to his brother Saret. Prince Kain wouldn't hesitate to stand against his son.

"Kain found his nephews as soon as Shi-Nook had ordered the young heir be brought to him. He conspired along with them, and a plan was put into motion. The cousins had decided to use a magical artifact that Sheto had created, called the Cloak of Winds, to sneak up on Shi-Nook and kill him. Kain, eager to spare his son's life, suggested they strip him of his power by using the Cloak to steal the Pearl. In the meantime, Kain would provide a distraction. What he didn't tell his nephews was that he expected to lose his own life in the process.

"Kain entered the throne room with a great show of power, openly declaring himself opposed to his son's coup. He told Shi-Nook that he had just come from slaying the crown prince and had come for the throne which was now rightfully his own. What followed was perhaps the most legendary shamans' duel in all of gnome history.

"During this epic clash of powers, while all the guards had abandoned their posts to watch, and the doors to the great chamber stood open, Sheto and Nekhet made their way to the throne beneath the Cloak of Winds. The power of this cloak was that it transfigured the wearer, or wearers, into the very wind itself—invisible and unhindered by gravity or form. Save for the inability to pass through solid objects, they were like ghosts beneath this magical garb.

"It was only the obstacles created by the shamans' duel, ironically, that hindered the pair's approach to the throne, where the Devil's Pearl rested. Ultimately, tragically, Kain was defeated and destroyed by his power mad offspring. Fortunately, this happened just as Shi-Nook's cousins managed to take hold of the villain's treasure.

Sheto threw the cloak aside, revealing himself and the crown prince. He vowed to use the Pearl's wishing power to remove the object itself from existence. According to the Legends from the First Time, one could make a wish on the Pearl only once, and then its power would abandon the holder forever.

"Enraged, Shi-Nook drew his sword and threw it, unexpectedly, straight into the heart of Nekhet, who fell instantly. 'You can wish the Devil's Pearl out of existence,' he taunted. 'Or you can revive the heir of Saret and perhaps save yourself the shame of losing in combat with me over the throne.'

"Sheto weighed his options. He realized that the Pearl would be dead to him if he revived Nekhet, but he also realized that if he revived his beloved cousin, he could hand the Pearl to him, and Nekhet could wish it out of existence. It was with this knowledge that Sheto chose to save the life of his crown prince. As soon as the Pearl had revived Nekhet, Sheto tossed it to him, telling him what to do. Unfortunately, the Pearl fell short, and the still dazed prince had to scramble after it.

"Shi-Nook wasted no time in retrieving his sword and decapitating Sheto while the young sorcerer was too stunned to react, having dropped the terrible jewel. Shi-Nook knew that there could be no political motive in restoring Sheto to life, but he was counting on the love of Nekhet for Sheto to take the power out of the crown prince's hands. Then, he could kill them both again without much effort. He knew that Sheto was the only weakness in Nekhet's strong heart. He believed that Nekhet loved Sheto enough to forfeit everything to bring him back. 'Wish the Pearl out of existence, Nekhet,' he said. 'Or use its power to restore noble Sheto, who deserves no less after doing the same for you.' Shi-Nook predicted his cousin's choice perfectly. Now Nekhet and Sheto both lived, but the Pearl was useless in their hands. Only Shi-Nook would still have the power … if he retrieved the Pearl.

"Sheto told Nekhet to hold fast to the Pearl, then he set himself in Shi-Nook's path. Yet another shaman's duel was about to begin. Despite Nekhet's horrified protestations, Sheto revealed his power to all. Shi-Nook blocked the blow, and the battle was begun. To the astonishment of all, Sheto arose victorious, destroying Shi-Nook and the line of Kain with him."

Nesu sighed with relief at having gotten through the whole tale from memory. "And that is the story of Shi-Nook."

Atalanta was amazed. "But what happened to the Pearl then?"

Nesu nodded. "A point I must come to, or the tale was told in vain. None besides Sheto and Nekhet ever had the heart to wish such a powerful thing out of existence. So, Sheto took the Devil's Pearl to a secret land and hid it within a labyrinth filled with traps. He made sure that the keys to

overcoming these obstacles were hidden as well, so that none with evil intent could ever find the Pearl."

"But why tell me all of this, Father? What makes the telling of this tale so urgent?"

Nesu paused, then met his daughter's eyes. "Tell no one what I say."

Atalanta nodded soberly.

Her father continued. "One of our enemies seems to be searching for the keys to get past Sheto's defenses. If he finds the Devil's Pearl, and something happens to me, you must know what we face as a people, and you must do everything within your power to stop this evil once and for all. Remember the tale of Sheto and Nekhet. Keep it always close to your heart, until this threat has been put back to rest."

"Father, who is this enemy you speak of?" the princess asked.

Nesu answered plainly. "It is none other than my own cousin, the Dark Prince Fenrir."

Princess Atalanta gasped, as her blood ran cold, and her heart threatened to fail within her.

"He has quite a few traits in common with Shi-Nook, I suppose. Fenrir, now Lord of the Darkgnomes, is the one who nearly destroyed us all several years before you were born."

"He's the reason I never knew Mother," Atalanta said quietly. Prince Fenrir had often been the subject of her nightmares.

"Yes," answered Nesu distantly. "The greatest traitor in all the history of our tribe. None are as hated, or as feared, as Prince Fenrir."

10
Ak'ten's Quest

Late that night, long after his meeting with King Nesu, and having just sent Ak'ten to bed, Malík's mind was still unsettled. He perused the many bookshelves which filled his tiny home until he found again *The Book of Secrets*. He took it from the shelf and immediately sought out his most comfortable chair, intent on reading by candlelight until the sun rose, if he must. He needed to find any clues at all, if they existed within the book, as to where the Devil's Pearl had been hidden so many centuries before.

Malík situated himself and breathed a great sigh, before opening the book. It had been a long day, and there were many things on his mind even in addition to the activities of his former apprentice. He was worried about his current pupil just as well. He felt so badly for the lad. He was frustrated by the fact there was little he could do; for Ak'ten's need to prove himself stemmed from his being orphaned without ever having known his parents. Malík mused to himself. "If in fact such gnomes ever did exist." He chuckled quietly, but it was a nervous chuckle. All this business with Fenrir was coming sooner than he would have liked. He wanted nothing more than to keep Ak'ten innocent for just a few more years.

Malík opened the book to Sheto's handwritten introduction, then his ears cocked at the sound of a door creaking quietly. He closed the book and covered it underneath his beard awkwardly. "Ak'ten. What's the matter, lad?"

The boy's shadow fell over him, and he replied from behind him, "I can't sleep." The shadow shrugged.

Malík chuckled, then suddenly went cold. There was something about a shadow he'd forgotten. Something he'd dismissed again and again, but Ak'ten's shadow reminded him, and he wanted to forget. He turned slightly, careful not to uncover the ancient tome beneath his flowing whiskers. "Well, that much is clear. Try telling me something I *don't* know. Such as why."

Ak'ten came around in front of the old shaman, and he sat before him in the candlelight. His face was sad and almost grim. This had been a rough day for him. The words of General Argon wouldn't leave him any peace. Ak'ten burned to prove himself now more than ever before. The more he was told he could not do a thing, the more he strove to prove the world wrong. "I was just thinking about that fairy is all."

Malík studied the boy. "*Is* that all? I don't think so."

Not for the first time, Ak'ten was irritated by the fact that nothing got past a shaman. Especially Malík, it seemed. "Well, I was also bothered by Argon's … visit. I guess. But I was mostly thinking about the fairy." He looked up, a spark of determination in his eyes, as they glistened in the candlelight. "If Fenrir *is* abducting fairies, as we suspect, and I do not doubt that he is, then might we go after them? A rescue, Malík. *Shouldn't* we?"

Malík did not respond right away. This moment was playing on his fears most terribly. He hated that this matter had come to the lad's attention. He wanted only for Ak'ten to remain ignorant and uninvolved where the Dark Prince was concerned. Just for a little while longer. Now he feared the gods had other ideas, and Malík was not above making the gods work for their ends, when they directly contradicted his own. "No. That is not an option, lad. It wouldn't be prudent."

Ak'ten was incensed. "*Prudent*? Malík, are you serious? Fenrir is torturing those fairies to the gods know what terrible end! How can we, knowing this—you an expert on fairies—simply let it continue! You told me yourself how dangerous Fenrir is! Is it not our obligation to put an end to his dark plans before they fully bloom?"

It was true. All that Ak'ten said. Still, Malík was far more concerned with keeping Ak'ten safe than worrying over any other matter of virtue. "Ak'ten. We are shamans, not warriors.

It is not our place to go on quests and rescue fairies or anyone else for that matter. Our place is here, within the tribe that we serve." The words tasted viler than troll whisky on his tongue. Malík consoled himself. It was best for Ak'ten to be denied this quest.

Ak'ten could not believe his ears. "But, Malík ... what about the time you went into the deep forest with the shaman Xersek to drive out the Demons of the Blood? What of the tale I've heard about your quest with Meso No'tall decades past, to free the captive Patriarchs of our clans when the Darkgnome Sinistor held them all for ransom? Did you not, on your own, set out to vanquish the sorceress Gwenllian when she became a threat to the warriors on the battlefield? And what of—?"

"Enough, Ak'ten." Malík was at once surprised that Ak'ten even knew of these events, for he had never bragged, and he was unsettled all the more for what an argument his apprentice had made. "Those were different times. Different situations. You must trust me now. Rescuing those fairies is no quest for you." He sighed, then amended, "Or myself."

Ak'ten was undeterred. "But we could get Kazkal to go with us. If it is a warrior's quest. Surely together, a shaman and a warrior—"

"Ak'ten," Malík rose from the chair, still clutching the book beneath his beard, "I have made myself clear. We will *not* be going after those fairies. With or without any such warrior. It is not for shamans to command the army. Now forget this foolish notion, and get some sleep."

Ak'ten eyed Malík curiously. "What's under your beard?"

Malík looked down, feeling foolish, and he pulled it from beneath his whiskers, still obscuring the title glyphs from Ak'ten's eyes. "Just a book. I *was* going to do some reading. Now, I think I'll just go to bed. Perhaps I can make you see things differently over breakfast in the morning." He smiled down at his confused apprentice. "For now, however, please let these thoughts go, and get some sleep." Malík walked away and entered his room, closing the door behind him.

Ak'ten was utterly puzzled by Malík's behavior. He blew out the candle by Malík's favorite chair, and he went back to his own bed. Sleep did not come.

More than an hour passed.

When Ak'ten heard Malík's gentle snoring, he decided it was time to do what must be done. For even if Malík himself lacked the courage, Ak'ten did not. If Ak'ten could rescue the fairies, the general would have no choice but to recognize his skills. Undoing the plans of the Darkgnomes was a far greater test than sparring even with gnomes as skilled in the war arts as An'sep.

Ak'ten dressed himself quietly, all the while keeping his ears tuned to Malík's snoring. He made sure to take along his flute and a small bag of fairy powder. When it was clear by the depth of Malík's snores that he had it made, Ak'ten set out into the night, determined to put his plan into action.

After a great deal of walking, Ak'ten found his way to the warrior camp. One of the perks to being the only shaman's apprentice in the entire tribe was that everybody knew him, and he could pretty much come and go as he pleased anywhere he liked. If he wasn't on an errand for his master, gnomes often assumed that he was. So the guards at the camp, not seeing why else Ak'ten would approach in the dead of night lest he were on such an errand, simply waved him in.

Practicing great stealth, Ak'ten found his way to the hammocks of the sleeping warriors. He recognized Kazkal right away, whose hammock hung beside that of An'sep. Ak'ten grinned mischievously. It would be so satisfying to just sneak up on An'sep and scalp him completely as he slept. He suppressed a laugh, seeing that there would be no honor in it. Ak'ten crept up to Kazkal's side and nudged him softly, whispering his name. "Kazkal."

The warrior, knowing this was no call to arms, opened just one eye to see who it was. When he recognized Ak'ten, he opened his other eye and whispered, "Ak'ten. What is it? Is there trouble?"

Ak'ten nodded. "Yes. Do you remember the fairy we saw?"

"The fat one, or the scary one?"

"The scary one."

Kazkal grimaced. "Yes … though I'd like to forget. What of it?"

"Malík can translate their gibberish, as I said. Do you remember her rhymes?"

Kazkal did. He thought of the gnome who'd murdered his father. "Vaguely."

"Well, what it meant was that Prince Fenrir has been abducting fairies. He's been torturing them. He's been in our very forest to collect them, most likely."

Kazkal sat up. "Fenrir? By the gods …" He looked at Ak'ten somberly. "Do you know why the mention of that name by the mad fairy so disturbed me, Ak'ten?"

Ak'ten nodded.

"Malík told you? About my father?"

"Yes. That's why I thought you would want to help me."

Kazkal gave Ak'ten a suspicious look. "What do you mean?"

"I'm off to free the fairies from Fenrir. I hoped to have a warrior's aid."

"This is no mission from Malík. Have you told him what you're planning?"

Ak'ten looked away. "Yes. But … he didn't seem interested in doing the right thing."

Kazkal leaned over, closer to Ak'ten. "Malík is right, Ak'ten. It's not about whether or not to do the right thing, it's about planning. What would you have us do? We can't just get up in the middle of the night and somehow find the Darkgnome fortress, rescue the fairies, escape with our lives intact, and come home the heroes of the day. A quest requires preparation, lad."

"But, Kazkal! If we don't go now, who knows how soon Fenrir's plot will come to fruition? Perhaps we can stop it before it's too late. But if we wait and plan and think and think and think, it may be too late by the time we've set out."

"Ak'ten, for one thing, we don't even *know* that there is a plot of any sort. I'm still not convinced that fairies speak anything but utter nonsense. That being the case, the mention of Fenrir's name had no meaning. It was simply a very strange looking fairy who'd buzzed past someone that spoke the name and felt the need to repeat it. We don't *know* anything. This matter *requires* planning and research. Warriors do not embrace an empty quest. We must have patience."

Ak'ten looked at Kazkal in frustration. "I suppose I am the only gnome in Tribe Qadash who still has any courage at all."

"Ak'ten, that's not the case. Keep your head, lad. Go home for now. I promise we'll discuss this later … with Malík. Go now, before you wake the general, or worse … An'sep." He turned to spare a cautious glance in the direction of his apprentice's hammock. When he returned his attention to Ak'ten, he spoke in a serious tone. "Promise me, Ak'ten."

"Promise you what?"

"Promise me you'll go home."

Ak'ten hesitated, then nodded his head unconvincingly.

Kazkal was not comfortable with that. He resolved that he would check up on the youth in the morning and make sure he'd gone home. He *would* have to discuss this matter with Malík. "I will be in touch about this, Ak'ten. Now get on home."

Ak'ten hesitated only for a moment, then he nodded his head, with a determination that Kazkal was afraid to interpret, and left the camp.

"I promise to go home, Kazkal," he said to himself, as he looked back on the warrior camp. "I promise to go home just as soon as I've rescued those fairies." With that, Ak'ten turned his eyes to the horizon, where the unnatural lights of the human world glowed through the treetops, and he set forth on his quest.

11
Meetings Along the Way

Not long into his journey, Ak'ten's courage started, ever so slightly, to wane. The night was so dark and full of such strange noises. About half way to the edge of the forest, Ak'ten was frightened by the strangest sound yet. It was the sound of someone humming, he thought. Yet at the same time, it might have been a great gnome-eating toad, or a screech owl. He wasn't sure, and so he froze. There was a rustling in the tall grass beside him, and then an ungodly squawk. Ak'ten shouted in fear as the creature sprang forth from the grass, cackling wildly and pointing.

"Awe, she really had you goin' there, didn't she, lad! Morrha did!" The thing cackled some more and wheezed a bit.

Ak'ten got his bearings and dared to study this creature of the night, with her frizzy gray hair and gray skin, her bulging yellow eyes, only to see that she was a very old *gnome* herself. "I'm sorry, who is Morrha?" he asked.

The old gnome stopped her cackling and looked to space, as though she'd just been asked the most perplexing question. "Well, you know what?" She turned to Ak'ten with a dazed expression. "I think …" She looked to either side of them, as if she feared someone might be listening in. Then she shouted, "I am!" Again came her cronish laughter, and she punched Ak'ten in the arm. "She had you goin' again, din' she lad! He he he! Morrha's a tricky one. Hm, I wouldn't trust her, if I were you. Eh … confidentially speakin' o' course." She stopped again, struck by an inspirational thought. "Say, you wouldn' be interested in some tea, would'ja, lad?"

Ak'ten stammered, unsure what to make of the old gnome. "Uh … no. Not really. I have a lot to get—"

"Ak'ten!" she shouted with glee. "Your name is Ak'ten! Well, would you like some tea then, Ak'ten?"

Ak'ten was growing more frightened by the second. Was this some mad spirit of the wood? Would she eat him? "How did you know my name?"

She looked at him as though he were less than intelligent. She reached up and knocked on his head. "Well, you just said your name was Ak'ten, didn'ya?"

"No, I—"

"Yes, you did!" She pointed a knobby, gray finger right in his face, and he couldn't help but moan at the sight of her gnarly yellow nail. "I heard'ja plain as the night!" She laughed some more. "Oh! I know! You won't take tea with strangers, eh? Well …" She extended her hand in a more friendly manner than before, then grabbed Ak'ten's own hand and shook it mightily. "Morrha the Moon Witch at your service! Pleased to meet'cha! Now how 'bout that tea?" She smiled wildly, exposing her long, crooked, yellow and brown teeth with merry pride.

Ak'ten recoiled. "The moon witch! I know about you! M—"

"Malík? Malík indeed!"

"But I never said—"

"Yes, you did! I heard you! You said Malík! And let me tell you somethin' about that old fart Malík! Don't ask me that! Be quiet! Any gnome don't know what a fart is oughtta spen' some time with them Techies! Learn a thing or two 'bout funny names of bad air! But that particular *fart* Malík! I'll have you know, he has always had the biggest crush on me. Jus' jealous 'cause I jilted him. He is." She muttered a bit, then shouted, "Fart!"

Ak'ten decided he had to get away. "Well, Morrha, it was nice meeting you. I really must be g—"

"Say, ducklin'! Why don't you come home with me! You are a pretty young gnome, aren't you?" She cackled, then a look of genuine concern came over her. "You're on a quest, eh? Be careful, my little fishy. My guppy! Ducklin'! There's Meefs about. And you know what weirdies them Meefs are!"

She looked cross. " 'Course them Meefs drink Morrha's tea, don't they?" She nodded her head joyously. "That they do!" She laughed some more. She laughed until she couldn't open her teary eyes.

Ak'ten took the opportunity to slip away.

Morrha noticed and ceased her merriment. She shouted into the shadows. "Well, just ya be careful of the city then, my little tug boat!" At that she laughed some more and walked with a bit of a limp back to wherever it was that she had been going.

Ak'ten was glad to be rid of her. Malík had warned him about the mad moon witch of the forest. He just never expected he would run into her in person. The moon witch had once studied to be a shaman, but went mad and abandoned her training. She had her own ideas about the uses of magic, and she had been banished to the forest; disowned by the shaman collective at a convocation with the Great Ghost. Ak'ten himself had never been to the Great Ghost. He dreaded the day he would have to go before the collective and be either confirmed or denied in the order of the gnome shamans. He shuddered. From what little he knew about the Great Ghost, it was no wonder Morrha had gone mad. But then, Malík had said she'd gone mad before the convocation. Ak'ten tried to put his mind on other things. His hour before the Ghost was still four years away.

As Ak'ten neared the very edge of the forest, he heard two young gnome voices. He wondered if they were Techgnomes. Techgnomes were a society of gnomes that lived in a completely opposite way from the lifestyle that Ak'ten knew. They were godless. According to Malík, they were even soulless. It was said that the Darkgnomes were associated with the Techgnomes too. But Ak'ten disagreed.

Many years before, when Ak'ten was still a child, he had met a Techgnome near the very spot in which he now stood. Each of them had had a musical instrument that they played. Ak'ten had his flute, and the other had played some strange Techgnome instrument which Ak'ten had never imagined. Together, they had harmonized and soothed the birds, who then joined in with their song. Alone, they had been unable to accomplish this feat. Ak'ten had since wondered what his own society and the Techgnomes would be capable of if they ever let go of their fear of each other and lived as friends. As far as Ak'ten was concerned, Techgnomes were nothing to be feared.

Ak'ten crept closer, and he could hear them more clearly.

"Dude! You have to help me get that key chain! It's too cool!"

"No, Pete! It's too late, dude. The cat's gonna be out soon. I don't want to die!"

"You won't die! We'll just go get it real fast and then you can go home. Come on, Retro! Don't be a girl!"

"No way, Pete! I'm outa here! You can stay and get eaten by the damn cat if you want to, but I'm goin' home!"

"But I can't lift it by myself! It's too big."

"Too damn bad, dude!" With that, Retro retreated beneath the gigantic building; the building Ak'ten had seen so many years ago. The building which was surely a human structure.

He heard the gnome that was left muttering to himself. "Fine, dude! I'll just get it myself!" With that, the young gnome started heading right towards him.

Ak'ten decided to be bold. He walked out from the shadows and intercepted the young Techgnome. "Excuse me," he said.

Pete froze in his tracks and regarded Ak'ten. "Whoa! What the hell?" Pete's eyes narrowed. "Hey, waitaminute. I know you!" He studied Ak'ten's attire, his long hair, his serious demeanor. "You're that Old World gnome that plays the flute!"

Ak'ten was startled. Could this be the very Techgnome he'd met years before? He studied the other gnome head to toe; his strange attire, his oddly cut blonde hair, his fair complexion. Suddenly he smiled. "You! You played that … that thing!"

Pete laughed. "It's a keyboard. Wow! You're still a dork, huh? That's cool though. Especially if you help me get this key chain. A human lost it. I want to hang it on my bedroom wall."

Ak'ten didn't know what a dork was, but he didn't want to show his ignorance either. He didn't want this Techgnome to think less of him. "Uh … yes. Of course."

Pete breathed an overly dramatic sigh of relief. "Whew! Thanks a lot! That reject Retro is too much of a woman sometimes, you know? He's such a wimp!"

Ak'ten was beginning to get the picture. "A real peezwizz, eh?"

Pete didn't know what a peezwizz was, but the Old World gnome didn't need to know that. He hesitated for a second, then said, "Yeah. Exactly, dude! He's a *total* peezwizz!" The two gnomes walked together to the key chain Pete had scoped out. "My name's Pete by the way. What's yours?"

"I'm Ak'ten."

Pete stopped. Was this guy clearing his throat, or was that really his name? He decided not to be totally rude, which was hard for him, but he was really intrigued by this Old World gnome. "Ak'ten? That is a funky name! I like it." Pete's mother had warned him about Old World gnomes, and so had his father, and so had every teacher he'd ever had in school. Old World gnomes were allegedly evil pagans who hated technology and everything to do with the human world. Pete's experience with Ak'ten years before hadn't shown that, but that's what he'd been told. It was also said that the Darkgnomes were associated with the Old World gnomes. Darkgnomes freaked Pete out, even though Pete never condemned anybody without a personal reason. He had enjoyed his time with Ak'ten, before he'd been dragged away by his mother, and Ak'ten had been dragged away by some gnarly looking old dude. Probably his great, great, great grandfather or something.

Pete ventured further. "Wow, your hair is really long! That's pretty kick-ass! Do you still play the flute?"

Ak'ten nodded enthusiastically, pointing to the instrument strapped at his belt. "I do. And do you still play that … um …" he remembered suddenly, "*keyboard*?"

"Yeah, dude!" Pete was getting excited. "We should get together and play again sometime! That was pretty bad ass! Too bad we're forbidden to hang out and all."

Ak'ten considered. "It's only wrong if we get caught."

Pete grinned boyishly. "Hell yeah! You're pretty cool for a guy who runs around almost naked most of the time and probably *still* hasn't seen a movie ever." He laughed at this. "What brings you out of the forest anyway, after all this time? I thought you were gone for good after that old guy with the Santa Claus getup dragged you back into the forest."

"Malík. He's my master."

Pete was astounded. "Master? Are you a slave?"

"No, I'm his apprentice. He is the master shaman. He teaches me."

"Oh, I get it. Like he's the Jedi master and you're the Padawan, right?"

Ak'ten really had no idea what the other boy had just said, and his face made it plain.

"Oh, that's right. No movies. Dude! You have to see some movies! You've never seen *Star Wars*? Or anything, right? Not one movie!"

Ak'ten nodded, afraid he was in trouble. He remembered Pete had had a problem with this before. "I'm still not sure even what that is."

Pete was amazed. "I still don't believe it! I love to watch movies, play video games! I have to get you up to speed! What do you do?"

"Mostly I study magic and do shaman tasks with Malík. He studies fairies. I'm on a quest."

"What? Magic and fairies? Dude! You are so weird! There's no such thing!"

"Are you serious? You mean you've never done magic of any kind? Never seen a fairy? Not one?"

Pete felt defeated. "Well, no. I mean, how could I? They don't exist." He lit up. "But I did see an alien once! I kid you not! Right in my damned face, dude!"

Ak'ten laughed. "Well, I'm going to have to show you some magic sometime. I can't imagine a *gnome* who has never known magic."

"Dude! Do you think your *master* will mind if you stay out? I mean, 'cause you should spend the night! My mom won't mind!"

"Oh, I was planning on staying out. I'm on a quest remember. That reminds me. Do you know where the Darkgnomes are?"

Pete jumped back. "Ah! Why? Are you one of them?"

"No!" Just as Ak'ten was thinking how absurd it was for Pete to ask this, he realized that it might be a valid question for him to ask Pete. "Are you?"

"Hell no!" Pete laughed. "Why do you wanna know where the Darkgnomes are?"

Ak'ten knew he shouldn't trust his secrets to just any gnome, but he studied the youth before him. Pete had honest eyes. Ak'ten decided to explain. "The Darkgnome Fenrir has been abducting fairies and torturing them. I am the only gnome who was willing to leave the forest and rescue them. No one else would come." Ak'ten looked sad. "But Fenrir is a powerful sorcerer, and he must be stopped from hurting the fairies before his unknown plan is fulfilled."

"Weird!" Pete said. "Dude, really! Come over! My dad had to work late, so we haven't even had dinner yet. I can help you on your *quest*! This is gonna kick ass! 'Course, I still don't believe in fairies, and I think you're pretty crazy. But good crazy, you know. Like … different."

Ak'ten smiled. "I will need food and rest. I'm beginning to see what Kazkal was trying to tell me about preparation."

"Cool. Of course, we'll have to disguise you. You can't let anybody figure out that you're an Old World gnome. My parents would probably kill you on sight."

Ak'ten looked frightened.

"Don't worry though. I'll take care of it. I have just the thing."

12
A Night with the Techgnomes

After taking hold of Pete's treasure, the two young gnomes managed to drag the human-made key chain to a small opening at the side of the human building. Pete led Ak'ten underground, through an elaborate tunnel system very much like the tunnels of Ak'ten's own tribe. There were differences though. For one, instead of torches of fire to light the corridors, there were small globes which shone with a silent light. Ak'ten was amazed by these. He dropped his end of the key chain and went to get a closer look at one. "What magic is this?"

Pete snickered, and he dropped his own side of the key chain and went to join his new friend. "It's not magic … um …" he couldn't remember the other gnome's strange name, "… uh … guy. It's electricity."

Ak'ten gave Pete a most inquisitive look.

"Oh, that's right. How do I explain?" He scratched his head. "Well," he offered at last, "you know lightning, right?"

Ak'ten nodded his head.

"Good! 'Cause that's what it is. Electricity is the same thing as lightning. It's just we learned to harness it."

"You capture lightning in these little spheres, and that's not magic?"

"Trust me," Pete said. "Go to enough science classes and there's nothing you can't explain. Those little round things are light bulbs. Some human invented them."

"Oh." Ak'ten backed away from the light bulb, as if suddenly seeing a danger there. He had easily forgotten that the Techgnomes were heretics. He'd forgotten that they held humans in such high esteem. Ak'ten looked down at the metal key chain. He studied it. It was round, painted yellow on one side with what Pete had described as a smiley face drawn onto it. Ak'ten had laughed at it at first, thinking it sublime. But now he began to realize what it really was. It was a ring for holding keys, and it was nearly as wide as he was tall. This was by no means an abominable thing, for key chains he had seen in his own world. The terror of this key chain lay only in its size. It was a reminder of just how far away he'd strayed from home, and no one even knew yet that he'd gone, nor would they ever know where, if he failed to return.

"What's up? You looked pissed off."

Again, Ak'ten didn't want to let on that he had no idea what Pete had just said, so he simply smiled nervously and picked up his end of the key chain. "I am just eager to find food and rest. How long till we reach your home?"

Pete shrugged. "Not too far, dude. It's just around that bend." He grabbed his end of the human thing then, and the pair resumed their dragging and pushing.

After a brief silence, Ak'ten asked, "What is the name of your clan?"

"My *what*?"

"Your clan. You know." Judging by the blank look on Pete's face, Ak'ten began to realize that Pete did not. He tried to think of another way of putting it. "You are Pete, but is there not a name for your clan? A name that you were given by your father and his father?"

"Oh! You mean my last name! I get it. It's Davidson. Pete Davidson. What about you?"

A troubled look came over Ak'ten then. "I have no clan. I am a … stray. That's what I am called anyway. Malík took me in when I was an infant. They say that the gods had mercy on me, and I'm to repay them by living the life of a shaman."

"Is that a good thing?"

"It is good, because I would otherwise be a servant … a slave. Strays have no rights in our world." He looked at Pete. "I do not know if it is the same in yours."

"Well, if you're saying that people without last names become slaves, then no. Hell no, dude. That's nuts! We put those kinds of kids up for adoption and they get to take the name of the parents that choose them. I mean, kind of like what Malík did for you, I guess, except that they become an official member of the family … er, clan. Whatever."

This concept was alien to Ak'ten, but it set his heart to longing. Oh to be able to wear Malík's name and have all the rights of a gnome with a clan. It had always seemed such madness to Ak'ten, the way his people treated strays.

"Here we are, dude." Pete dropped his end and brushed his clothes off. "Okay, wait here a minute. I don't want my mom and dad to see you until we make you look like less of a freak. I'll be right back." With that, Pete went in through the small door and closed it behind him.

When Pete entered the house, he found his mother heating up their dinner. His father must have finally gotten home from work. "Hey, Mom, where's Dad?"

Without turning from the oven she was checking, Pete's mom answered, "He's in our room changing into some more comfortable clothes."

"Oh. Can I have a friend over for dinner tonight?"

Pete's mother rose and faced him. It was summer, and there was nothing planned for the morning, but she really didn't want Retro over just yet. It was still too soon after the pair of them had been brought back in handcuffs. "Well … who is it?"

"Who is what?"

Resna put a hand to her forehead. Pete sometimes appeared to have the attention span of a fly. His teachers had urged her to put him on medication for it, but Resna had always refused. Pete's mind only wandered from one thing to the next at such an amazing pace, because he had so many things to think about. He was very smart. She refused to see it as something to be corrected. His teachers had called it ADD, and they considered it a serious disability. Resna had learned to live with it though. "Pete, who is it that you want to have over for dinner?"

"Oh yeah! Um … some new kid."

"Oh." Resna was relieved momentarily. "Sure, Pete." She smiled. "What's his name?"

Pete shrugged and looked at his mother as if she'd just asked the most unreasonable thing. "Idunno." He grinned and bounced off to his room.

Resna only shook her head, fascinated as always by the inner workings of her son's mind.

Pete quickly sifted through his wardrobe. He went to the back of the closet, where everything his crazy Aunt Zola had ever given him eventually ended up. It was important that his parents not recognize his own clothes on the new kid, and he had never worn any of these particular gifts. At last he spotted just the outfit, and he began to giggle uncontrollably.

When Pete finally got back outside to Ak'ten, he handed him the bundle of clothes. "Sorry, dude, this is the best I could do."

Ak'ten took the bundle and unfolded the items. There was a yellow tie-dyed T-shirt and the largest pair of pants Ak'ten had ever seen.

"They're fat pants. And I don't mean phat, as in pretty hot and tempting. I mean FAT! As in monstrously obese! My nutty Aunt Zola always gives me weird clothes for Christmas. She saw some raver gnome wearing these in a magazine once and decided that's what all the kids were wearing. Well, not me. I understand I'm her favorite nephew and all, but I'm her *only* nephew too, so there is no escape." He began to giggle.

Ak'ten puzzled over the outfit briefly, but figured it out without help by looking at Pete and getting the approximation. When he'd gotten the clothes on over his own pants, he said, "I look ridiculous."

"That you do," Pete said. "Here, this'll make it better." He then put a backwards visor on Ak'ten's head and began to laugh.

Ak'ten was not even slightly comfortable. "Do I look that bad?"

"Oh, no. You just look totally … not Old World is all. It's so not you. It's perfect. Besides, I laugh at everything. Don't take it personally." He looked down at the key chain. "Now let's get this thing up on its side and take it in."

With that, Ak'ten gathered his own shirt and vest, stuffing them easily into the massive pockets of his enormous borrowed pants, and the young pair hoisted the key chain up onto its side.

Pete opened the door to his home to make way for his treasure. He pulled, and Ak'ten pushed.

It was only a few seconds before Ak'ten heard the sound of Pete's mother's voice for the first time. "Pete Davidson! What on earth is that *thing* doing in my living room!?"

Pete whispered to Ak'ten, "Just keep coming. Trust me." Then, in a louder voice, he said, "Just passing through, dude!"

"Pete!" His mother was not happy.

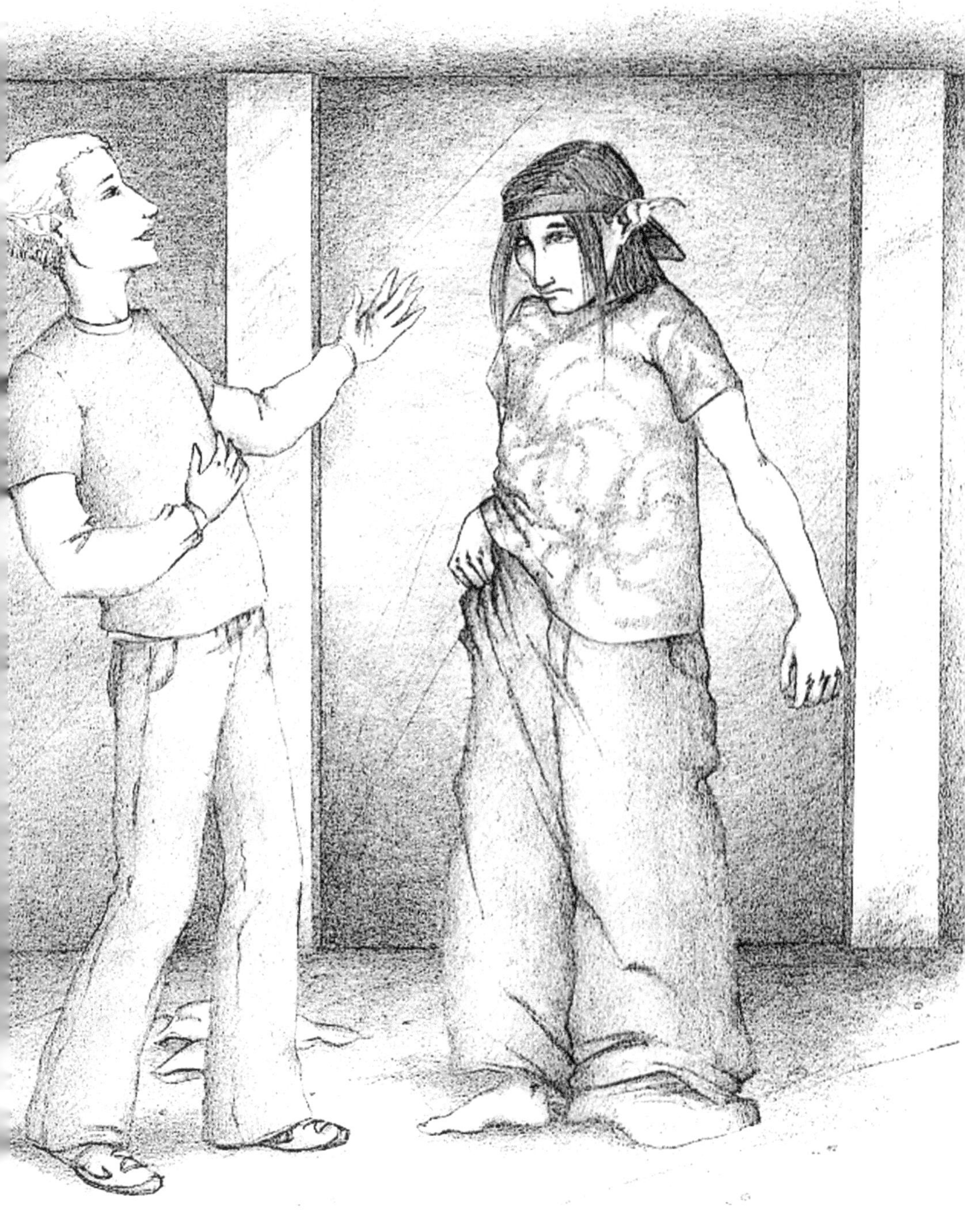

"I meant Mom, dude! Sheesh! Sorry!" At that, Pete backed right into his father. He stopped and turned around.

Ak'ten looked around to see what was happening.

"Hey, Dad. What's up?"

"Nothing much, Son. What's this?" His father spoke in a calm voice, regarding the giant key chain that had left a great streak in the carpet as far as it had been dragged.

"Key chain," Pete answered.

"Oh," His father replied. "Be sure and wash your hands before you come to the table."

"Okay, Dad." Pete nodded to Ak'ten, as his father went to the table. "Okay, let's go," he whispered.

They got the key chain into Pete's room and propped it up against a wall in the dark. Pete saw no reason to turn on the lights, since they were just coming right back out again anyway. He then led Ak'ten to the dinner table.

Everything in this place was strange and confusing to Ak'ten. He was glad at least to see that tables and chairs were no different for Techgnomes than they were for his own people. Still, once he'd taken a seat, it was difficult for Ak'ten to keep his eyes from wandering all over the room.

Everyone served themselves and began to eat without a word. Ak'ten thought that these people of Clan Davidson must have been hungrier than he was. At last, Pete's mother spoke. "So," she looked directly at Ak'ten, "my son doesn't seem to want to introduce you to us. He really does have better manners than that." She looked pointedly at her Pete.

"Oh …" Pete's eyes went wide, "… right. This is … um …" at the same time as Pete said, "Bill," Ak'ten answered more honestly.

"Ak'ten." He and Pete looked at each other fearfully.

Pete's father looked up from his food. "Gesundheit."

Pete's mother was not so easily fooled. "Well," she looked back at Ak'ten. "Is it Ak'ten, or Bill? Surely it's not both."

"No!" Pete said, wondering how his mother could have possibly identified *Ak'ten* as a name. "Um … Bill … is his father. That's what I was about to say."

"Strange way to introduce a friend, Pete." She smiled, but there was something going on behind her eyes that Pete did not like. He feared the jig would soon be up, and Ak'ten would be dealt with terribly. What if his mom called the police? He had been expressly forbidden to associate with Ak'ten five years ago, after all. He'd been told the Old World gnomes were dangerous.

"So, Ak'ten. Do you have a last name?"

"No," Ak'ten answered without thinking. "I'm a st— I mean … I have no cl— fa— … um … last name."

Resna regarded the stranger at her table quizzically.

Pete jumped to explain Ak'ten's trouble speaking. "Oh, I forgot to tell you, he has Tourette's syndrome. Makes him talk all weird sometimes." He leaned over to Ak'ten's ear and whispered quickly, "Look at my dad and say 'ass.' "

Ak'ten turned to Pete's father and said quite calmly, "Ass."

"See?" Pete exclaimed, pointing. "He's crazy!"

Pete's father regarded Ak'ten with dry humor. "Oh. Well that's unfortunate." He went back to his meal, and he picked up a copy of the paper and began unfolding it indifferently.

"You don't *have* a last name?" Pete's mother asked Ak'ten, unbelieving.

"Oh," Pete cut in, before Ak'ten could answer on his own. "Sure he does. It's … uh …" He thought back to a movie he'd seen recently about a magical quest that reminded him of Ak'ten, and a fitting surname came to mind. "Underhill. Ak'ten Underhill. Son of Bill Underhill. You know him?"

"No," Pete's mother replied.

"Well of course you don't know him! He's new! So, Dad, long day at the office?" Pete was desperate to change the subject.

"That's right, Son. Long day."

"Mr. Q.?"

"Mr. Q."

"He's gotta be pretty rich to always hire you to put together all those elaborate computer systems! What was it this time? Did he want to be able to zoom in on a fly anywhere on earth by satellite and watch from the comfort of his own home?"

"No. Only in Egypt."

"Oh." Pete suddenly actually heard what his father had said. "What? Are you serious?"

"Yep. He's a strange gnome." He looked at Ak'ten. "I've never met the guy, but he's my most lucrative client." He chuckled happily.

Things were quiet for a few moments, and Ak'ten and Pete took the opportunity to quickly fill their bellies.

"So." Pete's mother asked at last, "Where did you two meet?"

They answered in unison. "Outside." Then Pete cut off any further questioning. "Can Ak'ten spend the night?"

"Well . . ." Resna began.

"Well," his father repeated without looking up from his copy of *Gnome World News*. "He is kind of rude, but I guess I won't be *too* insulted if he stays just one night."

His father's dry humor was so constant that no one laughed at it anymore. They just went along, and Pete's father was believed to laugh at it all in his head, though no one knew for sure.

"Yeah. He is pretty rude," Pete said. He looked at Ak'ten scathingly, then grinned to show Ak'ten he was kidding. "Well, I've had enough. Thanks for the grub." He stood up from the table, and Ak'ten followed in a daze.

Ak'ten stopped and turned back quickly to say, "Thank you for that very filling meal, good woman."

Pete's mother continued to work on the puzzle of Ak'ten Underhill long after he'd left the room. She started by saying to her husband, "Scott, what do you think of this Ak'ten Underhill?"

"He seems all right."

She pondered the name. "Ak'ten sounds like an Old World name, don't you think? I mean, it doesn't sound like a name one would receive from a father named *Bill* does it?"

"I don't know, Resna. I haven't read as much as you have on *anything*, let alone Old World gnomes."

"I don't know. I've just been worried ever since I found him with that Old World gnome so long ago. You know how Pete is. He'll take in anybody. He's just so accepting of the differences in other gnomes."

"That's true," Scott said. "But Ak'ten is not an Old World gnome."

"How can you be sure?"

Scott put down his paper and looked at his wife as though she were a child. She was always so clever, but she had managed to overlook the most obvious thing. "Because, no Old World gnome would *ever* dress like that." He went back to his paper. "Those gnomes would likely just kill someone before they went to all the trouble of dressing like them just to blend in."

The words of her husband failed to comfort Resna in the least.

In Pete's room, once the lights were turned on, Ak'ten was shocked and amazed once more. There were things all over that Ak'ten had never even dreamed of.

"I'll show you around in a sec. I just need to call Retro real fast." Pete then picked up a strange device, hit a small pad, and began speaking into it. "Retro! Dude! You won't believe what I found after you left!"

Again, Ak'ten could swear Pete was using magic, but it would have to be the most powerful magic he'd ever seen. No shaman he'd met had the power to speak with someone through a strange device like that. And he knew it was really happening, because he heard another muffled voice coming from the other side, in response to Pete's words.

As Ak'ten looked around, he suddenly realized how thirsty he was. He had neglected his drink at the table, because he'd been so distracted and nervous.

"Yes, dude! A real Old World gnome! And get this! He's the same one I met a long time ago, when my mom got all pissed off! He's here right now! They just don't know 'cause he's in disguise!" He suddenly noticed the sulking look on Ak'ten's face. "What's wrong?"

"I didn't drink anything at the table. I am still thirsty."

"Oh, well, there's water in the bathroom." Pete pointed to a room that branched off from his own, a closet of sorts covered in tiles.

Ak'ten nodded gratefully and left Pete to his unusual conversation. In the bathroom, Ak'ten found water in a large white bowl. It looked fresh and clean. Cleaner than he was used to. There was no ladle around, so Ak'ten got down on his knees and scooped as much water up as he could drink. He drank handful upon handful.

Pete walked in and shouted aloud, "Whoa! Dude! Le'me call you back!" He touched a pad on the talking device again and threw it into the other room. "No! Dude! Stop! I meant the sink!"

"Oh." Ak'ten stood up, embarrassed. "Is this water for some special purpose?" He looked to the large white bowl. "I am so sorry, Pete. I didn't know." He wiped a dribble from his chin, and Pete cringed in disgust.

"Well, dude, I suppose you could say that. Yeah … special use." He giggled. "I hate to tell you now that you've already …" He couldn't say it. "Well, see, we use the water there … in the toilet … to piss and crap in."

Nothing changed in Ak'ten's expression.

"You understand?"

Ak'ten admitted, "No." The words "piss" and "crap" were completely lost on him.

"Take a leak?" Pete tried. "No?"

Ak'ten shook his head. "I'm sorry, Pete. I don't understand."

Pete grinned. "Aw, what the hell! I'll just show you." He nudged Ak'ten out of the way and stood in front of the toilet. "Okay. Here ya go. *This* is what we use the water in there for." With that, Pete unzipped his pants and proceeded to take a leak in the water from which Ak'ten had just been drinking.

A look of stunned disbelief came over Ak'ten then.

Pete finished and zipped his pants back up. "Now do you understand why you shouldn't drink out of there?" He giggled.

Suddenly, Ak'ten bent over double, grabbed his stomach, and threw up everything he'd just eaten all over the tile floor.

"Oh," Pete said, as he grabbed a towel and threw it over Ak'ten's chunder. "I guess I should have told you." He looked over to the toilet. "We throw up in there too."

13
Magic and Technology

As the night went on, Ak'ten learned a great deal about Pete's world. He learned what video games and movies were. He learned how faucets worked and what a phone was. After Pete's parents went to bed, his stomach had improved, and Pete led him to the kitchen for a midnight snack, where Ak'ten learned about refrigerators. It was still quite beyond Ak'ten that the Techgnomes did not consider any of these things to be magical. He was beginning to see that Techgnomes were not without magic, as he'd always been told they were. They simply had a different word for it, and that word was "Technology." So great was Ak'ten's fascination, that he almost forgot his quest.

When the boys finally decided that it was time to get some sleep, Pete turned out the light in his room, and Ak'ten again marveled at the magic of light bulbs.

Pete made Ak'ten a pallet on the floor, keeping the bed for himself. As he lay down and his mind began to drift, Pete realized he had spent the entire evening bringing Ak'ten up to speed on himself, or at least his stuff, and he hadn't asked a single question of his guest. Pete sat up. "You still awake?" The pair had adapted to a quieter voice since Pete's parents had announced it was bed time.

"Yes," came Ak'ten's reply. "We just went to bed a brief moment ago. Why?"

"Well … I just was wondering what it's like where you come from is all. I mean … why do my parents say that Old World gnomes are dangerous?"

Ak'ten shrugged on his pallet and propped himself up on a shoulder. "I suppose it's because we have different ideas about things. My people tell me that Techgnomes are heretics. That you have no gods and no magic. No souls. They say you could take my soul from me by changing my ideas."

"But we *don't* have any gods, dude. We don't have any magic. Neither do you. You just think you do."

Ak'ten smiled, finding he understood the situation better than any of his elders back at the tribe. "No. That's just it. You just think that you *don't*. Perhaps your technology *is* magic. Powerful magic. But you call it something else. I suppose it *is* a different *kind* of magic. But it *is* magic. And perhaps you

simply don't *recognize* the gods. Maybe the gods are just as active in your world as in ours, but your people don't have a name for it."

"You mean like luck? And when chance brings retribution to gnomes who've hurt other gnomes? Would you call that the will of the gods?"

"Yes. Exactly!"

Pete wasn't so sure about that. His mother had warned him long ago that talking to Old World gnomes was dangerous. That they could make him feel like he was missing something that he could never actually have. But it seemed to Pete that Ak'ten wasn't doing that at all. He was actually trying to convince Pete that he *did* have all of these things. Not that he was missing them. "I never thought about it. Of course, I really don't believe in gods, but it's kind of cool to think about. I mean, my parents say that religion is the one great flaw in the human world. It causes wars. People are willing to kill and be killed over metaphors. It's insane, if you think about it. I mean, have you ever actually *seen* a god?"

The realization was unsettling. "No. I guess not. I have only seen the evidence of their work."

"Or have you seen the evidence of chance and coincidence? And as for your magic, maybe it isn't magic at all, but just another form of Technology."

"No. I'd say there was definitely a spiritual force behind all magic," Ak'ten said.

"And I'm telling you that there is only a scientific force behind technology. But I guess it shouldn't matter is the thing. I mean, who cares? What difference does it make? I mean, one of us has to be wrong, right? I mean, we couldn't *both* be right. Right?"

"I suppose. But then … maybe we could. Maybe we both truly lack the knowledge of each other's cultures. I was just thinking it would be easier if that weren't the way of it. If we really were the same and just had different names for all of the same things."

"Yeah. I know. So … what's the deal with fairies?"

"What do you mean?"

"Well, you said you saw one. That makes it different than magic and gods, because, if you could see it, then that means your culture just misunderstands something that's real. Like you were saying you wished it was."

Ak'ten sat up. "It's not a misunderstanding. Fairies are magical beings. They have nothing to do with your world."

"How do you know?"

"Malík is an expert on them. It's his specialty. Fairies never stray into the human world. They remain among the trees and rivers. And magical things. Things that the human world seeks to destroy."

"Well, if they're magic, then they aren't real. We don't believe in fairies around here, dude. Maybe it was a poodle."

"A poodle?" Ak'ten considered, thinking back to Malík's lessons on all of the human-serving monsters that roamed near the edge of the forest. He shook his head thoughtfully. "No. Those things don't fly. You've been into the forest though, haven't you? Surely you've seen a fairy!"

"No, dude. There's no such thing. Of course, I haven't been very *far* into the forest. Only as far as where we met those times before." Pete was beginning to feel like Ak'ten had won a point. He went quiet for a fraction of a moment, then lit up anew when he realized he could even the score. "I *have* seen an alien though!"

"You told me. But … what do you mean? What's the big deal? I've encountered many gnomes from other regions. It's part of being a shaman."

"When we talk about aliens, though, dude, we aren't talking about being from just another *region*! We're talking about being from another *planet*! A space alien, you know! Like in *E.T.* … which you haven't seen, duh! I forgot! Well, it didn't look like that anyway! It was like all pink and had bug wings and a little dress. And it was *way* crazy! I could tell by its pitch black eyes and goofy expression! It would have laid eggs inside of me if I hadn't been so swift and clever and gotten away!"

Ak'ten was riveted by Pete's description. "Pete! That's a fairy! That's exactly what they look like! Where did you see it?"

"I saw it up in the vents. Well, I was technically not *in* the vents at the time. It was in the humans' apartment, flying right at me."

"*What*? Pete, fairies don't fly around in humans' apartments!"

"No duh, dude! That's 'cause there's no such thing! But *aliens* do! I saw it!"

"Remember how I told you that the Darkgnomes have been abducting fairies?"

"No." Pete remembered then. "Yes."

"Well this fai— *alien* you saw must have escaped like the one I saw in the woods who was all screwed up. She must have been trying to find her way out."

"Dude, I thought you said they were kidnapping fairies! Not aliens!"

"Whatever. Can you take me to where you saw it?"

Pete scratched his head and considered, as he put his feet on the floor. "I dunno, dude. I'm not allowed, and I got in *huge* trouble last time I went there, and Mom and Dad are sleeping and wouldn't have a clue where I'd gone, so …" His face lit with a grin. "Sure!" He got up and started to put on his shoes, which he absolutely never untied, and he threw on his favorite ball cap.

Ak'ten stood up eagerly, returning to his disguise, and the pair of them set out into the night, quietly, not daring to wake Pete's parents. For, if there was one thing their cultures seemed to have in common, it was that adults had no sense of adventure.

The human air shaft was yet another wonder. The walls were all metallic and shined all around them wherever Pete's amazing flashlight pointed. Pete had warned Ak'ten that it was quite a climb to the second story, but by the time they'd reached their destination, neither of them was winded. To Ak'ten, the climb had been as nothing compared to the climb he'd made with Kazkal days before. As for Pete, he was just as much a creature of mischief as Ak'ten himself, and had made this very climb countless times before.

Pete shined his flashlight on the vents that led to the human dwelling. "This is the spot." He remembered how he'd gotten into his nightmarish predicament the time before. "Um … if the air starts blowing, grab hold of those vents. It'll stop eventually, but it can be strong."

Ak'ten studied the vents. "This is where you saw her? Your alien?"

"Yep. This is the place."

Ak'ten noticed something from the corner of his eye and turned to study it. He bent down and breathed out in wonder. "There really *was* a fairy here!"

Pete saw what Ak'ten was looking at and made a face which only the dark could see. "What the hell is that?"

Ak'ten lifted some of the glowing, pink substance on the tip of his index finger and smiled in the glow. "Fairy powder!"

"You mean like *pixie dust*? So like if you think a happy thought, can you fly?" He started laughing out loud.

Ak'ten frowned, a little confused. "Well … no. I don't know of any such properties in fairy powder. Maybe Malík does."

"Dude, I'm just kidding! I know it won't make you fly. Besides. That's not pixie dust. It's space poop."

"*What*?" Ak'ten wondered if it *were* something other than fairy powder. This was a very strange place after all.

"You know! *Space* poop! Poop from an alien, dude! That alien must have crapped all over the place to mark her territory after I left!"

Ak'ten was relieved, as he rolled his eyes and said, "Oh! Space poop. Right. I get it." Suddenly his ears cocked, and as

Pete opened his mouth to reply, Ak'ten raised a finger to his lips. "Shhh. Someone's nearby. I can hear voices."

"What? I don't hear any—" Pete was suddenly silenced when Ak'ten leapt up and put a hand over his mouth, then dragged him around the corner.

Ak'ten looked at Pete's flashlight. "Turn it off. Now," he whispered.

Pete obliged, still with Ak'ten's hand over his mouth, and he motioned upwards with his expressive, blue eyes.

Ak'ten noticed that Pete had lost his hat. "Sorry. I didn't mean to be so forceful. But I recognized a name and suspect—Shhh!"

Pete eyed the older gnome grumpily, speaking very plainly with his eyes, as if to say that *he* wasn't saying *anything*, and how could he with his mouth covered? Ak'ten released Pete timidly, hoping he could trust the other gnome to keep quiet. Pete didn't make a sound, and Ak'ten shrugged apologetically. Then the voices were right next to them.

"We've already been over all this a hundred times! Oh, look, now it's glowing," one of the voices said.

Ak'ten's eyes went wide as he remembered the fairy powder still stuck to the tip of his finger, and he stuck his hand in his pants quickly, so the glow would not give away their hiding place.

Another voice answered, "Yeah, so? It does that sometimes. Still ain't no fairy. Just her dust."

"I thought fairies had to be fat in order to burst and leave dust."

"Well, this fairy's been through a lot. Things might be different after the torture. Maybe it's like she's bleeding."

"Do fairies even *have* blood?"

"I don't know, Fenrir's the expert!"

Ak'ten gasped in spite of himself. That was the name he'd thought he heard mentioned before. He leaned right into Pete's ear and whispered in his tiniest voice, "Darkgnomes."

Pete gasped, and Ak'ten's hand was instantly back over his mouth.

The Darkgnomes' conversation continued. The first voice whined, "What are we going to do? This is the end! We can't just lose *two* fairies! Fenrir will have our heads … or *worse*! I think we should run away."

"And do what? This is our life! And where would we hide? You know Fenrir has eyes and ears everywhere. If he had to look for us, we'd be destroyed for sure! If we just go back and tell him what happened, there's at least a *chance* he'll show mercy."

"A *chance*? Not much of one. Once he calls us into the steeple, it's over. We'll burn in Hell after only a moment with him. In case you haven't noticed, he isn't exactly the nicest guy." Something caught the Darkgnome's eyes. "What's that?"

"Aw, it's just some kid's hat. Kids come up here all the time."

Ak'ten's and Pete's hearts were racing.

"How do you know? I'll bet there's someone here!"

"Don't be stupid, Rimmon. I grew up here, remember? I'm telling you some kid just dropped it here, or it got blown

up here. Happens all the time. Nothing to get the jitters over. Save that for Fenrir."

"You're right, Jack. I just don't like the idea of someone listening in. So what are we going to do?"

Jack considered broodingly, arms crossed. "We have to go back to Fenrir. We'll just tell him that the fairies got away, and we looked *everywhere*. By now, if they survived, they're already back in the forest. Frankly I don't know what he's so worried about. Nobody listens to fairies. Not even in the Old World, right?"

"More or less. Nobody quite gets their gibberish."

"See? So Fenrir will *have* to be understanding. We can just capture two *new* fairies and no harm will be done."

"Right. Let's go back and get it over with."

Ak'ten leaned in to Pete's ear again. "We'll follow them."

Pete nodded his head.

"What was that?" Jack's head spun around.

"See! I told you! Someone's here!"

Ak'ten thought his heart was going to beat right out of his chest. He'd thought no one could have heard that whisper. No one other than Pete, whose ear his lips had practically been inside of when he'd done it.

"No, the shaft carries voices from all over. Besides, it doesn't matter. We're leaving."

Ak'ten and Pete prepared to follow the Darkgnomes. They dared a glance around the corner, Pete ducking down on his hands and knees, squeezing between Ak'ten's legs and the wall to get a look. They saw the Darkgnome who'd just spoken lift his hand. A great shadow came right out of the wall behind him and enveloped the two Darkgnomes. It formed into a ball then and carried them out right through the wall.

When it was clear that the Darkgnomes were gone, Pete stood up. "Oh wow! That's … not … *possible*! What they just did!"

Ak'ten nodded grimly. "Darkgnome magic."

"Magic! Kick ass!" Pete was exhilarated. "And … and … did you *hear* them? One of them grew up *here*! He was a Techgnome!"

"Yes." Ak'ten had been equally troubled by the implications of the conversation. "And the other was an Old World gnome. I thought the only one of us to go to the Darkgnomes had been Fenrir. It seems there is much about the Darkgnomes we do not understand."

"Like how in the hell they pass through walls in a big fricking shadow! That was *so* kick ass! Can you do that?"

Ak'ten smiled. "No. That's Darkgnome magic. I don't know it. I can do other things. But I'm still an apprentice. Teleportation is not one of my skills." He looked defeated then. "How will we ever find them now? There's no telling where they went."

Pete's brain was already working on that. "Do fairies teleport?"

Ak'ten looked at his strange new friend, wondering where he was going with this. "No."

Pete lit up. "Well then, I bet I know where they went! The fairy escaped from somewhere with a steeple! That means a church. And the fact that they can't teleport means a *nearby* church! So the Darkgnomes would have been looking relatively near. Right? And so I know the place. There's a church the humans don't use anymore. It's a pretty far walk. Could take days. *But*, I do have an alternative solution."

Ak'ten was thrilled. "What? Tell me."

Pete's face scrunched up in thought. How could he explain it to such an uneducated gnome? "Well … let's just say that Techgnomes have a way of getting from place to place pretty fast. But we'll have to wait till tomorrow. You'll have to spend the night again."

"I will then." Ak'ten was happy to. Besides, it would give him more time to learn about the Techgnome world.

"Kick ass! So for now we'll go back to my place, and I can teach you how to play that video game I was showing you. We can put it on two-player!"

Ak'ten thought for a moment. This was heresy, for sure, but he just couldn't see the harm in it. Besides, it had looked like fun when Pete was doing it. It was just a game. "Sure!" he answered. And for the rest of the night, the quest was forgotten completely.

14
Fenrir's Plot

In the Darkgnomes' stronghold, one of the order's most prominent members strode towards Fenrir's chamber, followed by two new initiates.

"Hold, Mephistopheles. The master is busy."

The tall, sleek-looking gnome regarded the one who'd just spoken. "Too busy for *me*, Necros?" He turned and offered a smug smirk to the new members behind him. When he returned his attention to Necros, he said haughtily, "Surely not."

Necros grumpily warned him. "I tell you he is *busy*, Mephistopheles. I dare not allow any interruption."

The arrogant Darkgnome made a melodramatic sigh and threw his head back as if he were on a stage. "Oh, Necros! *What* is he doing then? I'm sure he wouldn't mind help from his greatest pupil—whatever he's doing."

Necros rolled his eyes. "Jack and Rimmon have returned empty handed from their task. Fenrir has them waiting. He wants to maximize their fear."

"So he's not even there?"

"Oh, he's in there. They just don't know it."

Mephistopheles laughed a bit too much. "Just like our dear master! So clever!" He turned to the new members again. "Why else do you think I've taken after him so! I won't try and hide the fact that I'm more like our master than *any*," he nudged Necros, "of the other Darkgnomes. You follow *my* lead if you want to excel in the organization."

Necros wanted to vomit. "Keep it down, you prancing idiot! You'll—"

"*What?*" Mephistopheles turned on Necros savagely, still as though he were on a stage. "How *dare* you speak to me in such a way? You know I'm Fenrir's favorite! You know I have more power in the tip of my finger than you have in your entire body!"

"You may be his most *adept* disciple, Mephisto, but *I* am surely his most trusted. Fenrir has too keen an eye, I'll wager, to trust in the likes of you."

"Why you …!"

Just then, the doors to Fenrir's chamber opened, and the Dark Prince stood there, smiling menacingly.

The new initiates were both frightened and relieved.

"Won't you all come in?"

Mephistopheles and Necros exchanged a glance, then turned and bowed to Fenrir, entering the chamber without a word.

Fenrir looked the new initiates up and down as though they were meat, then smiled and said, "You too. I want you to see this."

The pair exchanged a look of terror, then did as they were told.

"Necros. The door."

Necros closed the door behind them all, and the four Darkgnomes who'd just entered all stood to the side of the room, as Fenrir crossed it, passing right by a very pale-looking Jack and Rimmon.

Fenrir took a seat atop a pile of human-made books. He spoke to the frightened pair of Darkgnomes. "Well?"

Jack spoke. "I … um … well. You see … we looked *every-where*! The fairies have escaped. By now they've returned to the forest."

"But," Rimmon interrupted, "we can get you two more, Lord! We can easily do that. It doesn't matter *which* fairies!"

"Right," Jack said. "Not that we didn't try *very* hard to find those two fairies, but really it doesn't matter too much that they escaped. Er … not at all … actually."

"Really?" Fenrir asked. "How interesting. And *why* do you say this?"

"Well …" Jack looked to Rimmon, then back to Fenrir. "Well, Rimmon says that no one in the Old World tribes even understands fairy gibberish. It's nonsense. So it's not like anyone could learn what we're up to from an escaped fairy. No one pays them any mind. Um. Sir."

Fenrir reached down beside the stack of books and raised something up which caused the two gnomes to swoon with fear, as sweat from their own bodies threatened to freeze them. It was the Dark Prince's own shaman's staff, carved from ebony in the shape of an enraged cobra, containing three jewels instead of the usual *one* at the top of the staff. Two jewels served as the viper's eyes, and one, the largest of the three, was seated in its mouth. All of these were blood red against the sleek blackness of the staff's body. "So, *no one* in the Old World can possibly understand fairy gibberish. Is that what you're telling me?"

The two gnomes only trembled.

"Tell me," Fenrir continued. "Have you not heard of the shaman Malík?" He waited only a moment, then turned on them in fury. "*Tell me!*"

"Yes, master!" they blurted out together.

"But, Lord!" Rimmon pleaded. "We all know that the old shaman was killed *years* ago! Did you not kill him yourself? Along with his entire tribe! *Your* tribe, sir!"

"Ah, Rimmon! Your loyalty touches me. So you let the fairies go, because you were so confident in my ability to defeat Malík—a shaman many *centuries* my senior. I am touched. So why do you seem so hot under the collar, Rimmon?"

The Darkgnome looked into Fenrir's eyes and saw not the usual sparkling brown corneas and piercing black pupils, but fire. A fire seemed to blaze right on the surface of the Dark Prince's eyes. "Master, no!" Smoke started to rise from

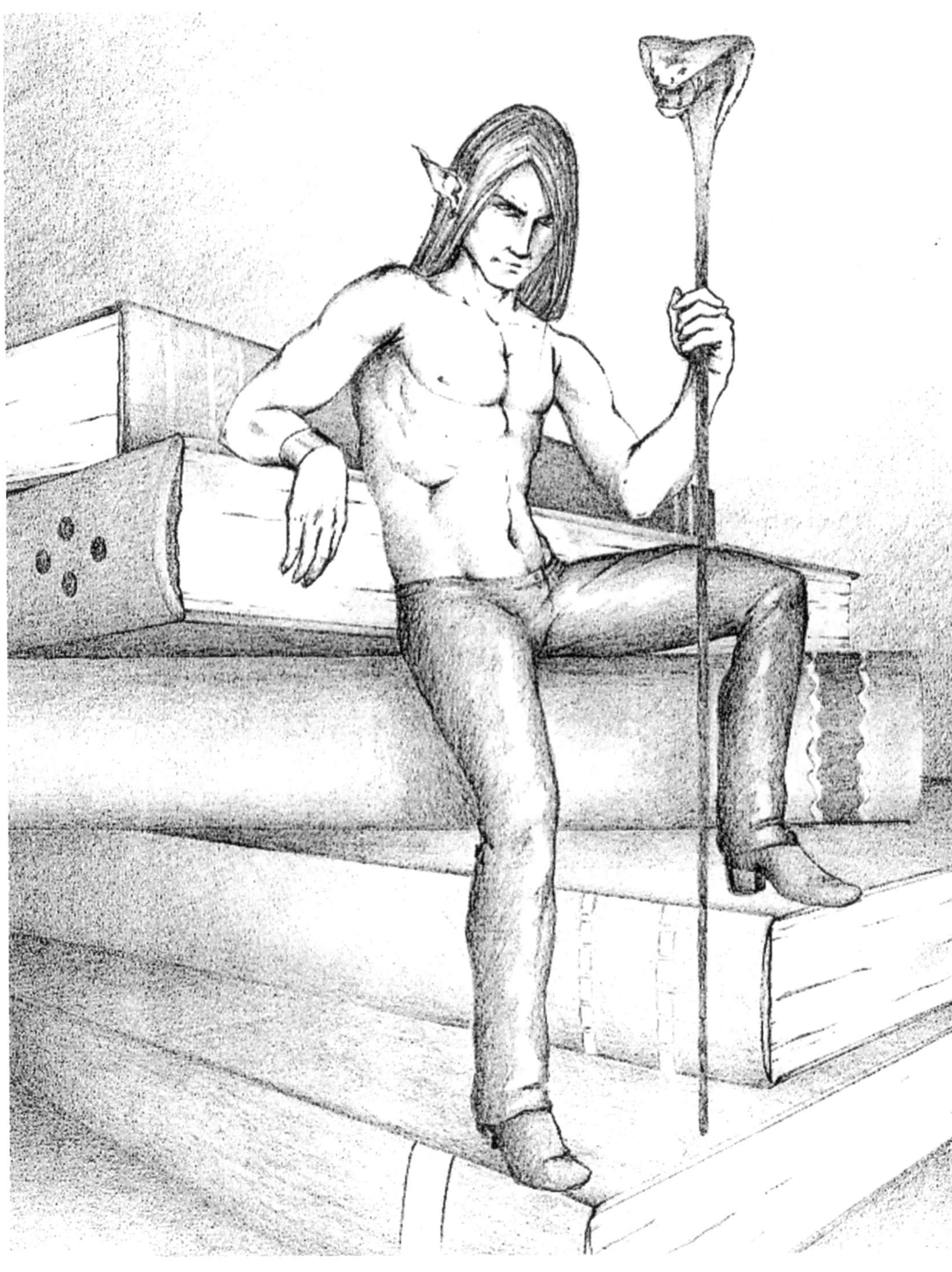

Rimmon's clothes, from *beneath* his clothes. He batted at it, as Fenrir continued.

"I am touched, but I am afraid that failure cannot be tolerated. For, while you have had every confidence in my success, I have *always* had my doubts. I never saw a body. I never *destroyed* his body directly. Our duel ended strangely, and amidst much commotion. You were but a child at the time, I know." He laughed as Rimmon started whimpering, and the smoke began to give way to flames. "But you've heard the tale a thousand times at least from those who were there, Rimmon. And even if the old shaman *was* destroyed as we like to think, do you really believe only *one* gnome in all the region can understand fairies? Wouldn't he have taught some others even just a little of what he knew? He taught me, didn't he? I understand the fairy tongue all too well. But …"

He stopped, noticing that the flames had started to go wild. Rimmon was screaming now, as Jack looked on in terror. Fenrir rolled his eyes. "But you're not even listening to me, Rimmon! Why do I even try?"

He waved his staff, and the flames tore through the younger Darkgnome with an unrelenting intensity, burning him quickly into ash.

"So, Jack. You seemed to think it was a good idea to listen to Rimmon. Tell me, do you always do what little piles of ash tell you to do?"

Jack looked sidelong at the smoking remnants of his fellow Darkgnome. "No, sir. I … I only thought it would be better to come to you directly than to run. It would have been stupid to run!"

"And right you were, Jack. For when you come to me to report your failure directly, you die *quickly*!"

Fenrir tapped his staff on the ground, and Jack's skin began to tingle. He gasped in horror, turning his head from side to side, looking for smoke. There was none, he looked down at his sleeve and saw that it was moving, that it had changed color … that it was not a sleeve any longer at all. He looked to his shirt, his pants, his shoes, and he screamed out in horror, frantically batting at the great fire ants that, through Fenrir's malevolent power, had taken the place of his clothing. The ants bit down, all poking him with their many legs as they ripped flesh from bone with venomous pinchers. Jack's desperate tears mingled with his blood as his screams abruptly ended. It was a quick death, as the Dark Prince had promised.

When naught was left but bone and hair, Fenrir tapped his staff one last time, and the ants vanished without a trace, not even leaving behind the clothes they'd once been or the flesh they'd torn away.

Fenrir turned to regard the new initiates. "Now you know. I do not accept failure. This is the way to true power. This is the power you could one day wield over others. Is that what you want? Do you want to spread fear and terror? Do you want to control all who would cross you and live without mercy or regret?"

The two young gnomes nodded.

"Good. Then this is where you belong. I asked Mephistopheles to bring you here so that I could let you in on our great agenda. Our goals. I wanted to let you see what we're doing, so that you can be of more use to us. Don't feel at all special. I offer this explanation to all of our local initiates. It's entirely self-serving."

The two gnomes looked at each other, fear and wonder in their eyes.

Fenrir noticed this and chuckled quietly to himself. "I can see you're eager for me to get on with it. I can tell by the way you carry yourselves that you're both from the city. So I can assume without doubt that you've heard of the pyramids of Egypt, the Sphinx, and magic though you view it as a myth. But I can also assume that you've *never* heard of the Devil's Pearl. That's a gnome legend; and the Techgnomes have lost all the old legends of their grand heritage. It's sad, but useful." Fenrir gestured with an apathetic wave to a particular stack of human-made books. "Most human sorcerers who know of our existence haven't picked up on the differences that keep gnomes divided into two distinct cultures. They lump *all* gnomes who live in and around their cities together under the label of *metrognomes*. They are blind to our realities. They don't know, for instance, that in the absence of magic and mythology, *your* people have delved in science, bringing gnomes to a state of technological advancement never dared by the gnomes of the Old World. You'll find nothing but appreciation for that here. However, you must be willing to embrace the culture that your ancestors left behind just as well, for the key to our ultimate victory is to join the strengths of both gnome cultures into one power. This is how we will finally locate the Devil's Pearl."

When he saw the perplexed looks on the new initiates' faces, Fenrir went on with a smug grin. "Follow me." He led the group through the mountains of human books to a small, gnome-sized door.

What lay beyond the door amazed even the two young Techgnomes who'd grown up with computers and all manner of technology. The room was enormous by gnome standards; full of monitors and equipment. The room was so entirely computerized, in fact, that the young gnomes couldn't even begin to take in all of its facets. Tiny lights looked back at them like eyes in the soft, blue glow that filled the room, the hum of electronics sang in their ears. The monitors all showed different places, most of which appeared to be Darkgnome strongholds in other parts of the world. Still others showed buildings and other images the gnomes were unfamiliar with. On one monitor in particular, they recognized a pair of lesser Egyptian pyramids.

One of the two initiates dared to ask, "Lord Fenrir … what is all this? What power could you still need to find? How could a simple pearl or an ancient human monolith offer you any power that you don't already possess?"

Fenrir offered a predatory smile in response. "The Devil's Pearl is *anything* but simple. I will tell you the story. The Cliff's Notes version. The Devil's Pearl was first known in what the Old World legends refer to as The First World. Whether this weapon was created by humans or gnomes is unknown; for the two species existed side by side in the First World. But what *is* known are the powers of the Pearl. Known to me, because the Pearl was in the possession of my own tribe less than one thousand years ago, and a record was kept by my ancestor Sheto of the events that ensued as a result of it. This *simple* pearl, as you called it, had the power of the very gods." He noted the skepticism in their eyes. "Yes, I know a belief in the gods is anathema to the Techgnome mind, but so is belief in sorcery, and you've seen enough of that by now …" He offered a menacing glare. "*Haven't* you?"

The two gnomes both shouted, "Yes!" and they offered assurances that they were without doubt as to anything the Dark Prince had to say.

Fenrir went on, as if there had been no interruption to his tale. "The Pearl was infused with the power to project images from anywhere in Creation. With this artifact in your hands, you could see anything from the dustiest corner of the most distant galaxy to the very room beside you. No enemy could defeat the gnome who held such a tool. And that wasn't even the best of it. Perhaps the most potent power of the Pearl, and what it has ever been sought for, was that the Pearl could grant it's holder a single wish. Any wish at all. Be it for an end to the very universe, or for their hiccups to go away. The Devil's Pearl could grant it. *Would* grant it. Yes, even if its holder were to wish the Pearl itself out of existence, the wish would be granted." The Dark Prince smiled. "But none have yet been capable of making such a wish. And so the Pearl has endured.

"The only catch to this ultimate power was, of course, that once a holder of the Pearl used it to grant any wish, great or small, they could no longer use it for *anything*. The Pearl was dead to them. No longer could they see across the untold billions of worlds, no longer could they look into the past or future on a whim. You see, the power of the Pearl is rife with pitfalls. One must use the very best of one's judgment. And so the Pearl was kept within the circles of the First World's most elite … until the end.

"Countless millennia ago, when the First World was annihilated in a terrible global tempest that drowned nearly every living thing, the Pearl was lost. As far as we know, it was not unearthed from its once watery grave until around 1012 C.E. It was then that a member of my own Clan-and-Tribe Qadash came upon it right here, in the part of the world that the humans now refer to as Texas. Of course this land was very different then, and any speculation on how the Pearl made its way here has nothing do with my point. This is not the story of how the Pearl came to Texas. This is the story of how it was lost, and how I intend to find it.

"You see, there was a powerful gnome named Shi-Nook, who found the Devil's Pearl and used its powers of sight to take over my tribe. Unfortunately, powerful as he was, he was defeated by my ancestors, Sheto and Nekhet, when Shi-Nook was distracted and away from the Pearl. Sheto defeated him in a shamans' duel, but only after he and Nekhet had both been rendered incapable of wielding the Pearl's power."

At this, Mephisto interrupted. "Of course, I'm sure the outcome of the battle would have been much different had Shi-Nook not just engaged in another duel only moments before. His powers were weakened from the battle with his father."

"Don't interrupt, you fool," Necros scolded.

Fenrir only smiled. "Don't worry, Necros. I choose to take it as a sign that he was paying attention, as all Darkgnomes should when I speak. For, having slaughtered my entire tribe, I am the last living heir of the Qadash throne. And the Devil's Pearl *will* be mine."

He turned to the new initiates. "Look here." He turned to a computer terminal and brought a three-dimensional map up on the screen. It appeared to be some sort of labyrinth. "Sheto took it upon himself to hide the Pearl where no corrupt gnome would ever again find it. He went into exile for many years. He built *this*." Fenrir indicated the map on the screen. "This is a reconstruction of Sheto's Labyrinth, in which is buried the Devil's Pearl. "What Sheto did was quite elaborate. He allied himself with an ancient guardian spirit from the First World, he raised a number of dead warriors from their graves as the walking dead and brought them to a secret location, where he'd constructed this maze. He placed enchantments all about the underground structure that could only be undone by six magical keys.

"Obstacle one, the guardian spirit," Fenrir manipulated the image to focus on specific parts of the maze as he went, "will only allow gnomes to pass the threshold of the labyrinth who offer him a coin from the First World. Something I assure you can't even be found on the Internet. Human culture has forgotten the First World." He turned with a grin. "I recently acquired such a coin from a human sorcerer named Kurzan."

Returning his attention to the computer terminal, Fenrir moved them through the CG image, to just past the entrance. A mass of oddly animated skeletons popped up on the screen. "To take things in order, and to let you know how we created this simulation, the second obstacle is finding one's way through the labyrinth. This can be done only with the Map of

Sheto, which is rolled into a scroll that can only be opened in the presence of the five other keys." He anticipated their question. "No. We don't have all the keys yet, but we *do* have the map. This simulation is simply an educated guess at how the maze is set up, based on the order that the keys are listed in Sheto's book and some of the other things he wrote. I had to slay a shaman in order to get it. That was the first of two gnome shamans this year." He amended, "So far."

"The obstacles on screen now are Sheto's enchanted dead. These guardians can only be felled by the Sword of Shi-Nook, which Sheto took with him into exile after the crowning of King Nekhet." He smiled. "I have that too. Hence shaman number two."

Again Mephistopheles interrupted. "And don't get any ambitious ideas of your own. He keeps them *very* well guarded."

Ignoring the interruption, Fenrir went on, scrolling through the elaborate cyber-maze. "And once we've found our way through the maze itself, we come to obstacle number four, a lock on a great stone door. This lock is also enchanted and can only be turned by a magical key, which Sheto himself forged and gave to yet another shaman to be protected when he returned. You see, when Sheto came out of exile, he stopped along the way to visit shamans from four other tribes, leaving them each with one of the mystic keys, which they have passed along as need be over the centuries. But shamans tend to live a long time. For all I know, the original shamans still guard the remaining keys. But I have found two and will find the other two yet, whoever they may be.

"The fifth obstacle is the stone door itself. Immovable without the aid of a very rare substance: dark fairy powder. Now in order to create dark fairy powder, one must first come by a dark fairy." He thought back to the previous night's torture session. "We're working on that."

The two new Darkgnomes followed the computer image through the door and to the Devil's Pearl itself.

"Having found the Pearl," Fenrir explained, "we must get back out of the maze. We have to get by a second wave of the enchanted dead, much larger than the first. And this time, not even the Sword of Shi-Nook can help us, simply because there are too many of them. We would be smothered before we could even begin to hack through them all. This is where the sixth key comes in. It's the cloak that Sheto and Nekhet used to steal the Pearl in the first place. The Cloak of Winds that makes the wearer a part of the very air—invisible, ungraspable, even to the enchanted dead."

Fenrir closed the program and turned his full attention to the four Darkgnomes in the room with him. "Then of course, we leave with the Pearl and annihilate the human race, making room for a new Gnome Empire. No longer will our kind be forced to hide, living under trees and buildings. We will be free to walk the earth wherever we choose. We will tell our …" He rephrased, "You will tell your children tales of the giant monsters who once ruled the earth and how you helped to destroy them." His thoughts seemed to drift. "It will be a red dawn."

He hit a button, and a secret panel slid up on the wall, revealing six glass cases. Three were empty, but what the others contained widened all eyes in the room. Even Fenrir's, who never grew tired of gazing upon them. There was the ancient coin, the time-reddened, unopened scroll, and the black, jagged steel of the Sword of Shi-Nook.

The two new initiates then bombarded Fenrir with excited questions, wanting to know how he had gained such knowledge, such power.

Flattered, and with an air of success, Fenrir ignored their questions. "As for how the ancient monoliths of Egypt tie in with all of this, that brings us to the greatest obstacle of all: finding the location of the labyrinth.

"During his self-imposed exile, Sheto could have gone anywhere on the planet, and he left no such details in his book when he returned. Not long ago, however, we encountered a prophesy—a prophesy that stated the secret of Sheto would be found beneath the paws of the Sphinx. Of course this could have been a fantasy, but we had to look into it none the less. Just in case.

"What we have discovered so far is more than encouraging. It speaks of a gnome presence in the age-old structures of the Giza necropolis." He again turned to the computer and brought up an image of a human sitting on a chest, holding a mechanical device labeled with letters from the human alphabet. Fenrir translated. "The machine on this man's lap is a robot called *Upuaut.* About nine years ago, *Upuaut* was sent to explore the shafts in the Queen's chamber of the Great Pyramid. What it discovered, and incidentally photographed, was, by human standards, a very small door." Fenrir brought up an image of the alleged door. "The human Director of the

Giza Pyramid Plateau for Egypt's Supreme Council of Antiquities," he brought up yet another picture, "has allowed no further exploration to be done. Perhaps if he knew of the gnome species' presence in the world, he would change his mind.

"It is obvious that the time of Sheto was long after the time in which the Sphinx and the Great Pyramid were constructed. However, it seems very likely, with Sheto's knowledge of the occult, that he may have known of the hidden gnome chambers at Giza. He certainly had time to travel there. And what better place to hide a secret than Egypt? It seems every grain of Egyptian sand holds a secret.

"Even if it doesn't pan out, this is the best lead we've had. And we know from Sheto's book that he left the secret of the Pearl's location somewhere, in case of some extreme circumstance when it was actually needed by those who serve the gods. Our theory is that the maze itself is beneath the Sphinx's paws, where seismographic tests have already revealed a possible underground tunnel system. If the door in the Great Pyramid is of any value to us, it is because it holds a map of the passageways beneath the Sphinx, leading to Sheto's labyrinth. I must repeat, this is only a theory at present, but it is the closest we've come to finding the Pearl. We have just managed to gain complete financial control of Egypt's Supreme Council of Antiquities. It's been done so quietly that not even the director himself is aware of it. It may take some time, but we will eventually have *gnomes* excavating the secret shafts and tunnels there."

Fenrir made a gesture with his hand, indicating that he was finished.

Necros and Mephistopheles ushered the new recruits out of the command center.

Fenrir left the computer room and, when he was alone at last in his chamber, he felt a sudden coldness in the air. He turned and studied his shadow.

Red slits again appeared as eyes. *Fenrir …* The voice seemed stronger than the last time, but not by much. Belial had taken his place once more in Fenrir's shadow. *I am concerned.*

"My lord, Belial. There is no need."

Do not be overconfident. I have existed for ages and seen overconfidence destroy many powerful beings. Overconfidence is a symptom of unreason. Never presume to have all the answers, my servant. I am concerned that the failure of Rimmon and Jack has cost us. It puts our plans in jeopardy. If the escaped fairies are discovered by someone else …

"Then we will deal with it. But truly, who is there to find them? And who would make the assumption that we're trying to make dark fairy powder? Who but Malík?"

Precisely.

"Malík is dead!"

You are not so sure. I've seen your dreams …

Fenrir went pale. The old shadow had never revealed this power before. How much had he seen? Fenrir guarded his thoughts, making a note to guard his dreams as well.

You never saw the body. You fear your old master's power. You think he may have survived.

"Well … *did* he?" Fenrir struggled to keep the smugness from his voice. "Surely you *know*."

What I know is that you should exercise caution at every turn. Let your uncertainty over the fate of Malík remind you of this. We must be cautious.

"Our plans go well, Belial. I have dealt with the failure of Rimmon and Jack, and the escaped fairies will likely not live very long in their condition. We have only *possibilities* to fear. I will hold my confidence."

After waiting for a response for an appropriate amount of time, Fenrir realized that Belial had left him. His shadow was simply his shadow again. He laughed to himself. Belial had not answered his question about Malík, because Belial didn't know. His doubts were only there because of what he'd seen in Fenrir's dreams. A power to be careful of, yes, but also the revelation of a weakness. There were things Belial did not know. This fallen god would yet be the pawn of his own servant.

15
A Secret Mission

The following morning, Malík awoke to find Ak'ten's bed empty. While this was not in itself unusual, his feelings urged him towards the conclusion that something was amiss. Malík opened up Sheto Qadash's ancient *Book of Secrets* and tried to read as he ate his lonely breakfast. However, it became harder and harder to concentrate. While it was true that Ak'ten had often risen and gone directly outside, the lad never missed a meal, if he could help it.

Malík closed the book and began to go over the possibilities in his mind. Just then, a knock at his door drew his ponderings to a halt. Malík went to the door and opened it to a messenger from the warrior camp.

"Good morning, Malík. I have a message from Commander Kazkal No'tall." The messenger handed Malík a scroll.

"Thank you, my friend." Malík opened the scroll right there, and read the glyphs within:

> The Most Revered and Powerful Shaman Malík,
>
> I had a visit from your apprentice last night which left me concerned. I simply write to enquire whether the lad got home. He wanted to go off rescuing fairies. I believe you know the situation to which I make reference. I promised to come and discuss it with both of you in hopes of setting him straight. However, knowing the lad so well, I cannot help but worry until I hear back that he is home safely.
>
> Commander Kazkal
> Clan No'tall

Malík rolled the scroll back up and tucked it into his belt, as he thankfully dismissed the messenger and locked up his home, setting out to speak with the king.

The royal guards led Malík into the main chamber of the Royal Caverns, where sat the throne of King Nesu Qadash. One of the shaman's two heavily armored escorts spoke, before noticing the king was not on his throne. "My King, Shaman Malík …" He looked around until he found the king on the floor level, looking away at him from a conversation he appeared to be having with a fierce-looking girl of about fourteen. If the guard hadn't known better, he would have sworn the girl was a warrior. The broadsword strapped to her back looked battle worn, her very demeanor suggested that she knew no fear, and, most troubling of all, the guard knew he had never admitted this girl to see his king. "My king! Is everything all right?" He regarded the girl with suspicion.

"Yes, yes." He noticed the look in the guards' eyes. "Zephyr is an old friend."

She smirked at the guards, noticed Malík. "And I was just leaving."

Nesu addressed the shaman. "Malík, what's the matter? You look as if you've seen an angry god."

"Forgive me, my king. I must speak with you alone."

Nesu nodded towards the guards, but they didn't leave right away. They looked at each other, then sternly back to the girl, unsure of what to do.

Zephyr snickered. "I can find my way, without your help, boys." The pleasure in her eyes was undeniable. "I saw myself in here, didn't I?"

Nesu knew she was trying to ruffle their proverbial feathers. He smiled uncomfortably, trying to maintain a serious face, and he nodded at the guards once more and motioned towards the door with his hand.

Reluctantly, the guards bowed and made as though to take their leave. To the king's gratified irritation, however, they stood at the open door and waited. He sighed. "They say good help is hard to find. The thing is, when one finds it, it never seems to let up."

Malík turned towards the great, thick doors of the main chamber, and he pointed wordlessly with his gnarled wooden staff. The jewel at the top, which somehow resembled a great, crystal eye, lit up, and the doors swung closed violently. The guards barely had time to shout and move out of the way on the other side.

Nesu put a hand to his forehead. "I'm going to be lectured over this, I'm sure."

Zephyr laughed, and she looked Malík over head to toe. "Hm." She grinned once more with that mischievous curl of her lips. "I like his style." She turned to Nesu. "I'll leave you boys to your business." She bowed, then headed for the shadows, where she easily seemed to vanish without a trace.

When Malík got no sense of the girl's presence in the room, he spoke knowingly. "A Centenarian."

Nesu, knowing he could have no secrets from this great old shaman, simply nodded and said, "Yes." Nesu then met Malík's urgent stare, and asked, "What is it, Malík? Dare I ask? Has something happened with the situation you recently brought to my attention?" Nesu then noticed the absence of Ak'ten, and began to suspect. His eyes narrowed. "Where is your apprentice this morning? Off running errands?"

Malík shook his head gravely and spoke to the point, "To answer your questions in order, nothing has happened with the

Fenrir situation … yet. However, my apprentice may have set out to change that, by no errand of mine."

Nesu's eyes went wide. "Go on."

"Ak'ten burns to meet his destiny. He is a brave and virtuous gnome, despite all the trouble he causes me. He feels strongly that we should be rescuing these fairies. He can't stomach the notion of just letting the torture continue, especially when we suspect the dark ends to which it is being carried out. He vanished in the night, but not before stopping by the warrior camp to try and get help." Malík removed Kazkal's scroll from his belt then and handed it to the king.

Nesu read the message and handed it back to Malík. "This is dire."

"Yes. It *could* be. He is only a youth, and he does not see the consequences that his actions may bring. Fortunately for us, he does not know where Fenrir *is*. He is on a blind quest. I only fear his success, because he has a knack for getting into things. And there is …" Malík trailed off, only thinking the conclusion to his statement … *the rest of his story.*

At this, Nesu turned from his dark contemplation and asked, "Does he know?"

Malík shrugged, feigning ignorance. "What do you mean?"

"Don't, old friend. We haven't time for games. Everything is dependent on us finding Ak'ten before he find's Fenrir. The shamans are not the only ones who have been watching out for the lad all these years. So please, answer me, Malík. Does he know the *circumstances* of his adoption by our tribe?"

"I have told him none of it. He knows only that we do not know of his parents and that the shaman collective allowed me to take him in as my apprentice."

Nesu nodded, satisfied. "I agree with your decision to keep it from him thus far. Now, matters are precarious, and we two must be frank with one another. We must not be deceptive. I have known all these years how Ak'ten came to us … to you. That is why I have been so supportive of your pairing, in spite of his reckless nature. I think the gods are testing you. They are giving you an opportunity to make amends for Fenrir with yet another wild apprentice."

Malík looked hurt by the king's words.

Nesu smiled. "No, I don't mean to blame you for Fenrir's own decisions. I mean only that I think the gods have given you Ak'ten, so that you will *know* that you were not to blame. You will have great success with this second wild youth. That is my conviction. I believe in your success with Ak'ten as whole-heartedly as I believe that my son will one day be found alive."

Nesu's tone returned to brooding then. "Now, in the matter of our frankness, I believe that you also have known my secret for some time."

Now it was Malík's turn to smile. "Well, I did *raise* a Centenarian Elf, didn't I? How could I miss one in a crowd? Am I not a shaman?" He chuckled. Malík had long ago concluded that all the crown princes of Tribe Qadash had been taken into training among the Centenarian Elves at the age of twelve. It was fitting that the ruler of a tribe should be so prepared. "And Prince Ammu …"

"Yes." Nesu smiled broadly. "Why else do you think I am so convinced of his survival." Nesu laughed, and Malík joined him, catching the joke. "You see, old friend? We have wasted so many years pretending to have our secrets from each other, and here we find it has done us no good at all! We will be better for having confessed. We will be better able to solve this problem as it grows. The first step, for now, will be to get your apprentice back and somehow convince him not to go looking for Fenrir on his own ever again."

Malík nodded. "I have given the matter some thought. A large group of hunters would more likely attract attention. I request the aid of one warrior, with whom I shall go into the forest and track my young pupil."

"It is a sound enough plan. Need I ask which warrior you would choose?"

"Probably not. I request the aid of Kazkal No'tall."

Nesu nodded. "Granted. Of course I knew you would want to take our best. I'll send for him immediately. I will tell him that you are awaiting him at the home of Meso No'tall. He will need to leave An'sep behind, after all, and it must appear that the both of them are on leave. I will also arrange to have a squirrel ready for you from my own stables. We can't have anyone asking about this mission."

Malík bowed. "Thank you, Majesty. We will find him." The shaman turned to leave, then a question came to mind. He turned back to King Nesu. "On the matter of us dissolving all secrecy between us, I find I am curious about the young Centenarian you were speaking with when I arrived. Was her errand related to mine?"

Nesu nodded. "It is because of your visit here yesterday that I requested a messenger. The Centenarians will begin their own quest to find the Devil's Pearl. Not to uncover it of *course.* Only to find it. That way, if Fenrir manages the same, they will be waiting for him, guarding his sinister prize with their lives."

Malík nodded, satisfied with the plan. He was prevented from leaving then, when the king asked him a question.

"How long, Malík, do you think we can keep it from him?"

"Majesty?"

"No more games, Malík. I know old habits die hard. You know what I meant. How long, with the gods tugging at his heart against our will, can we keep Ak'ten from knowing how he came to us?"

Malík pondered the shadows of the room, not wanting to meet the king's gaze. At last he looked up, and gravely he spoke. "I do not know." The shaman turned then and set out on his quest.

An'sep No'tall relaxed on his hammock and gave in to daydreaming beneath the shade of his tent. His friends Ras'kaal Set and Jared Davahd had joined him, lying now in two of the tent's other hammocks in similar states of mind. It was during down times like these that apprentices could gather their thoughts and ponder the course of their lives.

"So," Jared's voice broke the silence, "who's you're favorite, Ras'kaal?"

An'sep propped himself up at this, as did Jared, to see the other apprentice's answer.

Ras'kaal grinned a silly grin, and propped himself up to meet their expectant gazes. "I'd have to say … Keela, Clan Jinto. She has the greatest smile, I think. The loveliest in all of Tribe Qadash."

An'sep laughed. "Really? I'd never have known it!"

"Nor I," agreed Jared. "Keela. Yes … she does have a smile on her. And eyes to match."

An'sep picked up on the dreaminess in Jared's voice. "So who is *your* favorite, Jared? Not the same, I hope, for Ras'kaal's sake." He laughed merrily.

"Oh, no!" protested Jared. "My favorite's not Keela at all!"

"What's wrong with her?" Ras'kaal asked defensively.

"Not a thing, my brother! Relax!" Jared giggled. "It's only that, I don't really know my favorite just yet. I mean, on the one hand, there is Jono Jinto. So lovely, with skin so soft and eyes so deep. I could simply fall in love."

The other two gnomes snickered at this, feeling for the youth. "But Jono is already taken, poor Jared! What are you to do?" asked Ras'kaal.

Unperturbed, Jared answered with a smile in his voice. "Then, on the other hand, there is Sarai Set, the most perfect-ly—"

"That's my sister, you peezwizz!" Ras'kaal shouted as he bolted to his feet.

Jared and An'sep laughed heartily at their friend's reaction, and the other only snarled.

"Still, she is a lovely one. Her figure has taken form quite nicely. Perfect for giving birth to my many strong sons." Jared continued to laugh.

Ras'kaal looked helplessly over to An'sep. "Is he serious, or is he trying to find his death on my blade for idle amusement?"

"I'm sure he means it, Ras'kaal. I have seen him with her. At the king's last feast, I thought he was in love."

"Yes, I am quite serious. Your sister is the very sunlight." Jared beamed.

Ras'kaal was exasperated. "Taken or no, I suggest you stick to mooning over Jono. He was your *first* favorite after all."

"Then, on yet *another* hand, there's—" Jared began.

"Now wait, Jared! You've only got two hands!" Ras'kaal interrupted. He turned to An'sep. "Rescue us, An'sep. Who is *your* favorite?"

At this, Jared began laughing uncontrollably.

"What?" the other two asked in unison.

"Why do you bother to ask, Ras'kaal? We *all* know who An'sep's first and only favorite is," Jared answered once he'd gained control.

"Do you?" asked An'sep skeptically.

Ras'kaal was beginning to laugh now. "Very true. We do. For how many songs have you written, An'sep, about your very own cousin and mentor?"

"Yes," added Jared. "It's quite disgusting. And you keep us up nights with your dreaming!"

Ras'kaal laughed. "Truly! And you pine at all hours, deafening us with your silly verses about his magnificent beard and his powerful arms. You are love sick, my friend."

"So what if I am?" An'sep asked haughtily. "I have far better taste than the both of you when it comes to favorites. One day, Kazkal and I will be no different than Fraternus and Jono. After all, they were once mentor and apprentice. Look at them now."

"Well, I suppose you'd be right, except for one thing," Ras'kaal said. "Kazkal's favorite is your grandfather's servant girl Kyana!" Ras'kaal and Jared both began to laugh.

All the color left An'sep's face then, and he stared murder at the both of them. Before he could respond, however, a gnome in the traditional garb of a royal messenger strode into the tent and asked, "Where is Commander Kazkal, Clan No'tall?"

"Um … he's practicing his swordsmanship with some of the others, I think, in the—" An'sep didn't even get to finish.

"I know the place. Thank you."

"Weird," said Jared.

"Do you think Kazkal is being summoned by the king again?" asked Ras'kaal.

An'sep shrugged.

Just then, Kazkal came under the tent, holding a scroll. "An'sep." He motioned with a jerk of his head, and the young apprentice went quickly to his side, well aware of the eyes of his friends following him. Kazkal read over the scroll from the royal messenger. He rolled it up quickly. "Come on," he said to An'sep.

The pair went immediately into General Argon's tent and showed him the scroll. "King Nesu has a secret mission for me. It must appear that I have been given personal leave," Kazkal explained.

Argon read over the scroll and nodded.

An'sep reached for the scroll then, and Argon fixed him with a stern glare, as he handed the scroll back to Kazkal. "Let me guess," An'sep said. "Too dangerous for a mere apprentice."

Kazkal put a hand on An'sep's shoulder.

Argon spoke. "The only danger you may find, young An'sep, is in your grandfather's bottles of brew. You are going on leave, and for the *record*, so is your cousin Kazkal. The king has ordered this to be a secret mission, so you must do us the favor of pretending that Kazkal is out relaxing, when your clansgnomes ask after him."

Disappointed, An'sep nodded.

Argon looked to Kazkal. "May your mission be a successful one."

The No'talls then left Argon's tent. They were approached immediately by the dark-featured archer Jono. "Royal summons?" He smiled broadly. "Must be a fine quest then. Need a pair of bowmen?" He held his bow aloft and laughed lightly. Jono was always laughing.

At this, Jono's partner Fraternus approached. "Yes. We had no part in your adventure with the mud troll. You owe us some sport, I think."

Jono looked at Fraternus and laughed.

Kazkal shook his head with a smile. "That quest was also by royal summons. I was commanded to go alone. This time," he tried to repress the sound of amusement in his voice, "I am going on leave."

"Oh! I get it. *Leave*!" Jono laughed quietly, looking around to see that none were listening in.

"How interesting," Fraternus added. "Strange the king has never ordered *us* on a vacation."

Jono winked at An'sep. "Well, then, No'talls. May your *vacation* be … a successful one." He snickered, and the others could not help but join him.

An'sep's young friend Ras'kaal ran up to the group. "Was that a royal summons? Are you going on a quest?"

Jono and Fraternus turned on the young gnome and shouted in unison, "No!" Then Jono added with an amused grin, "That was a messenger from Clan No'tall in a costume. He was making sure Kazkal and An'sep knew where the costume party was."

"They're on leave," Fraternus explained.

"Yeah," Jono said, holding back more laughter. "Kazkal's going dressed as a glowing pile of pink fairy powder." At this all the warriors laughed out loud.

"We'll see you soon," Kazkal said as he started to walk away. He shook his head and muttered to An'sep, "I'm never going to live that one down."

An'sep laughed all the more.

***

The knock on the door finally came, and Malík was greatly relieved. The need to find his headstrong apprentice had filled him with the eagerness and impatience of a youth. "That's them," he said to Meso, who sat beside him at the table.

"Sheza!" Meso called from where he sat. Meso did not want to waste the time it would take to pull himself out of his chair, drunk and old as he was, and hobble to the door on his wooden leg, and the servants had been sent away, in light of Malík's request for secrecy.

Sheza No'tall, Meso's wife, was already on her way. "I've got it, Dear." She opened the door and beamed. "Well! How are my fine, young grandsons? She hugged them both shamelessly as she ushered them into her home, and both warrior and apprentice were glad that they were far from the eyes of their fellows in arms.

When she'd released them, they both greeted her in unison. "Hello, Grandmother."

"How about some of my famous blueberry muffins?"

Meso managed to rise to his foot and balance just barely on his wooden peg of a prosthetic. "Woman, what these gnomes need is some of my special—"

She interrupted crossly. "No drinking! The day is young yet. If you hadn't bribed Dentoo into spiking your blackberry juice this morning—"

"Bah!" Meso waved a hand at her dismissively. "I gave my tribe an eye and a leg! I'll drink as I like!"

An'sep laughed at the bickering of his grandparents. He found it all the more funny, because both knew he and Kazkal never drank anything aside from water and fresh, unfermented juices. It was clear to the young gnome that his grandfather was just pushing his wife's buttons by offering spirits.

Malík rose beside Meso. "Thank you for coming so quickly, my friends. I am uncertain how much King Nesu made known in his message."

Kazkal began to lighten his load, so that he could take a seat at the table. Malík was, as ever, awestruck when Kazkal unstrapped the ancient and legendary No'tall Battleaxe from his back and set it down by his side. The axe was enormous; the double bladed head generally spread behind Kazkal's back like a pair of great iron wings. In fact, no gnome could lift the axe at all, unless they were worthy. The axe had a way of knowing who was a hero, and who was a villain. With a magical glow, it could even reveal a gnome's innocence if wielded against them.

The magical axe had been forged by a shaman long ago, and it had been passed down through the generations. It had once belonged to Meso, who passed it down to his son Kinto. After Kinto's fall in battle with the Darkgnomes, Meso had hung the axe on the wall in his war room, having been crippled himself in the very same battle. Only recently had the Battleaxe returned to its purpose, when Meso had given it to Kazkal, Kinto's only son. It was an honor that Kazkal was trying to grow into. He was humbled by the gift, but he alone had ever questioned whether or not the mighty battleaxe would allow itself to be carried by him.

He released a great sigh as he sat, and An'sep was quick to settle down in the seat beside him, across from the two much older gnomes. "I was told the bare minimum, but I take it this has something to do with your apprentice, Malík. I take his absence here, in conjunction with his visit to me last night, as evidence of this."

An'sep gasped and looked at Kazkal, who decided to ignore him. He was deeply bothered that Ak'ten had been paying his mentor visits in the night, all the more because Kazkal had not mentioned it to him before now.

When Malík nodded, Kazkal went on. "The scroll I received from King Nesu only explained that there was an urgent situation, a mission, that I was to meet you here, and that it was to appear that An'sep and I were going on leave. General Argon knows just as much." He grimaced. "Jono caught on and, to explain the royal messenger, told one of the apprentices that I was going to a costume party. I *suppose* that was helpful."

An'sep couldn't help snickering, as his grandmother came back into the room to empty her tray of muffins and blackberry juice in front of the men. He looked at her with a twinkle in his eyes and added, "Jono also said that Kazkal would be going dressed as a pile of fairy powder."

All the gnomes in the room laughed at this, and Kazkal felt his face warming, as he frowned. Meso laughed loudest of all, slapping the table like thunder as he guffawed. Malík spoke through his more subtle laughter. "Ah, yes. Ak'ten told me about your … *episode* with the exploding fairy."

Kazkal fixed his apprentice with a sneer that failed to look sincere as he fought back his own amusement, then he turned back to the others and said, "It was a harrowing escape from the very jaws of death."

The other gnomes only laughed harder. Sheza had to sit down and catch her breath.

Malík spoke then, as he summoned his staff from a nearby wall, and it floated into his hand. "Well, my glowing pink warrior, let us be about our quest. I shall explain more as we go. The bottom line is that we must find Ak'ten, before he finds …" He regarded the other gnomes in the room. He looked to Kazkal and finished his statement cautiously, "… what he's looking for."

Kazkal stood, and An'sep made to lift the No'tall Battleaxe from the floor to hand to him. It wouldn't budge. Frustrated, An'sep returned to his seat and folded his arms. On the night the axe had been given to Kazkal, An'sep had wanted to prove his own worth by lifting the axe as his cousin and grandfather had done. While Meso had laughed and explained that he would grow worthy with experience and time, it had done little to comfort the young gnome.

As before, Meso laughed at his youngest grandson, when Kazkal lifted the axe as though it were the very air itself and strapped it to his back. Having taken his seat again, Meso didn't bother to rise. He took a great swig from his mug and grumbled with a grin, "Be patient, young An'sep. The axe knows you still have much to learn. Your day will come."

A thought occurred to Kazkal. "Where are the servants?"

Sheza answered, "We sent them on some errands, so that you could discuss your business with Malík without prying ears."

"Um … and …"

Sheza beamed, as she answered Kazkal's inarticulate question. "Kyana is with them, and she is very well. Looking more beautiful by the day."

An'sep rolled his eyes. No one had ever openly said that Kazkal had feelings for Kyana, but it was more than obvious. It sickened An'sep. He felt that it was foolish for Kazkal to waste his time on some servant girl. As a warrior, his attention should be focused on his apprentice. It disgusted him even further that his grandmother seemed eager to encourage Kazkal's attraction, and his grandfather said nothing to dissuade her.

Sheza went to An'sep, as if sensing his turmoil, and she put her hands on his shoulders. "I'm so pleased that you'll be staying with us until your parents and brothers return from their trading venture with Tribe Nebu-Ki."

"Yes, lad!" Meso bellowed from his seat at the table. "We can share strong drink and tales of war!"

Sheza glared at her husband. "Tales of war, I will tolerate, but you will not share your *afflictions* with any gnomes under the age of nineteen!"

"Bah!" was all Meso could say in his defense.

Kazkal laughed lightly, as he made to follow Malík out the door. "Take care, An'sep. I will hurry back to rescue you."

"Thank you for your hospitality, my friends," Malík offered. He paused and considered. "Mainly for the muffins, of course. May the gods smile upon you and all of Clan No'tall." He smiled through his beard, as he turned and, followed now by Kazkal, set forth once again on his quest.

16
An Unexpected Battle

"I don't get it," Kazkal said, as he buckled the saddle onto the squirrel the king had lent them. "How do you expect to track him, if he didn't leave any footprints?"

Malík pulled a small sack from his robe and reached inside. "Fairy powder has many uses, son of Kinto." He sprinkled some on the ground near the warrior camp and said, "Take me to Ak'ten." As soon as he'd said it, pink footprints appeared on the ground, right before their eyes.

"Impressive," Kazkal said. "This is going to be easier than I thought."

As soon as Kazkal had finished loading provisions into their squirrel's saddle bags, he grabbed it by the reins and led the skittish creature along, as the pair of gnomes walked on, following the fairy powder footprints. Malík dropped more of the magical substance whenever the trail ended.

Kazkal commented on their beast of burden, as it jerked at a sound in the leaves, yanking the warrior's arm harshly. "Fine specimen, this one," he scoffed. "Seems afraid of its own shadow. And to think he came from the Royal Caverns."

"Mind your manners, my friend. The royal squirrels receive special training. Perhaps he knows something we do not about the sounds of the forest."

At that moment, the two gnomes were interrupted by a familiar voice. "Pst! Kazkal!"

The warrior turned to regard a nearby bush. He narrowed his eyes. "Jono?"

Quiet laughter answered his question. "In here! Quickly!"

Kazkal and Malík followed the voice and found Jono and Fraternus poised and alert. "What is it?" Kazkal asked.

"We were scouting the area," Fraternus answered. "We came upon about ten gremlins, including their medicine man Streptos."

"Streptos?" Kazkal asked. "What's that old wizard doing this far from his tribe's settlement?"

Jono laughed. "That's what we wanted to know. So we followed them."

"And lost them," Fraternus added. "They just disappeared."

Jono nodded his head. "We think they caught on to us. So we're waiting it out until—"

At that instant, a twig snapped somewhere behind them. The quartet turned to find themselves surrounded by gremlin warriors aiming spears and crossbows. The sight of even a single, unarmed gremlin was enough to keep most gnomes awake for a month from fear. The creatures were gnome-sized, and even gnome-shaped. But their skin was pitch black, covered with white stripes like an inverse zebra. Their eyes were totally red, their hair a shock of white that stood straight up on their heads, and their nails and teeth, revealed in devilish smiles, were all sharpened to a point.

A hissing laughter filled the air, followed by heavily accented English. "Thought you sneak up! No such loock!"

Malík turned to the gremlins' twisted imitation of a shaman and tapped his staff on the ground two times, causing the jewel to light up. "Streptos! I've often wondered when we'd meet on the battlefield!"

The gremlin warriors fell back, baffled. Streptos scolded them in the gremlin tongue. "[Do not fall back! These monsters have no power! Not while I am standing! Do you think I cannot defeat this aged fool? Kill them. Now!]"

This was a command that the three gnome warriors were far too accustomed to hearing on the battlefield. Though they did not understand the precise words of the gremlin tongue, they had come to learn the gist of them. They raised their weapons and prepared for combat.

Soon the air was filled with arrows and spears. Kazkal watched in disbelief as the king's squirrel ran off into the forest, all of their supplies still strapped snugly into its saddle bags. "You see, shaman? I told you it was a cowardly creature!" Kazkal shouted grumpily.

Malík did not have time to reply before he saw Streptos running from the scene. He gave chase without hesitation. Outside the cover of the shrubbery, the magical footprints were still visible. "Hold, Streptos! We have business!" He aimed his staff at the terrified gremlin. "What are you doing this far from your tribe?"

"I owe nothing! You *all* steal this land from us!"

"Who taught you the human tongue? Some child?"

Streptos lifted his hand to his face, palm up, and blew black powder into Malík's eyes. Then he shouted in his own language, "[Kill the shaman!]"

At this point, only five of the gremlin warriors were left alive, but they fled the battle within the bush and fell on blinded Malík. The disoriented shaman dug his staff into the ground and twisted it to the right, unleashing a great explosion of red light that blasted the gremlins backwards.

One of the gremlins rose to his feet, removing a dagger from the belt above his loin cloth. Before he could get to Malík, however, Kazkal decapitated him with a sure blow from the No'tall Battleaxe. "Malík's been blinded!" he shouted. "Dispatch them quickly!"

Fraternus and Jono were swift to answer the call. While the gremlins were regaining their feet, the mighty archers each targeted two, killing them without further combat.

Kazkal ran to Malík, who was feeling all over his robes. "Malík! Are you all right? What are you looking for?"

"Fairy powder—to restore my sight! I can't find my pouch!"

Fraternus bent down and retrieved a small, nearly empty pouch from the ground. "Is this it, Malík?"

"How by the Red God should *I* know, you fool! I've been blinded!"

Jono laughed.

"That's it," Kazkal confirmed. "Bring it."

Fraternus handed the pouch to the grumpy shaman and stepped back by his partner Jono.

Malík reached into the pouch and sighed. "It's been spilled. But there's still enough, I think, to track our quarry for some distance. First let me—" Just then Malík was knocked over by something very large and hairy, pouncing from the shadows.

Kazkal shouted, "Arachnis!" The great tarantula held Malík to the ground, eager to sink its horrific fangs into his chest. Jono and Fraternus both shot an arrow into the creature's abdomen. It turned from Malík, raging. Kazkal gave it no further time to react, slicing it cleanly in half with his axe.

A rustling in the leaves caught all their ears.

"What happened to Streptos?" Jono asked.

Malík grumbled, as he staggered to his feet, "Cowardly beast probably ran off."

"But not before leaving us with a parting curse, I fear," Fraternus said shakily.

Somehow, glancing at the spiders closing in around them, Jono still managed to laugh. "It seems Nubus seeks to put us to the test this day."

Kazkal surveyed their surroundings, praying to that very god for might. "Let us prove ourselves then. And this will not be the day that he collects his debt!"

The shaman went on in blind frustration. "I can't find my pouch *or* my staff! I dropped it all when that *thing* attacked me!"

"Hold, Malík," Kazkal said. "I believe you would not truly appreciate restored sight at this moment."

"Oh, don't tell me—" Malík never finished his sentence before another spider leapt at him, knocking him down. As Malík hit the ground, he heard more spiders pouncing, the whistle of arrows, the splat of a battleaxe finding its mark, and he felt his staff. He grabbed it and blindly blasted at the monster above him. He heard it squeal and felt it lift off of him. He heard the splat of Kazkal's battleaxe once more. Then only the panting of three warriors trying to catch their breath.

"It's this horrid stuff that wizard blew in my eyes! It's some sort of spider spell. It keeps me from hearing them, and it draws them to me! Find my pouch!"

Again, Fraternus found the pouch. He lifted it and frowned. "There's barely any left." He handed it to Malík.

"Just enough to restore my sight." He pinched out the last of the fairy powder and rubbed it into his eyes. He blinked for a moment, then breathed a sigh of relief. "That was an evil substance indeed."

Good blood. Good blood.

"And now I can hear them. There are more on the way, and I suppose none of us has tainted blood, or I'd hear them say so, and they'd turn away." It was a known fact in the shaman community that great spiders like these refused to feast on tainted blood. They much preferred the blood of the pure. This is why, many ages ago, the shamans had made it a priority to learn to hear the thoughts of such creatures.

Jono grabbed a leaf and scrubbed at Malík's eyes aggressively, trying to remove the last traces of the substance Streptos had used.

Malík then burnt the leaf with a blast from his staff. He cocked his head and listened. "I don't hear them anymore. They've lost interest."

"Then I suppose we must part company," Fraternus said. "We must report Streptos' activity to General Argon."

"And we didn't see you here," Jono added.

"Thank you for your discretion, Jono," Malík said. "May the Gods guide you on your way, free from danger."

Fraternus saluted. "May the gods guide us all." He and Jono turned then and left.

Malík surveyed their surroundings. Ak'ten's trail had been trampled in the commotion. The fairy powder was depleted. There was no way now of following the young gnome's steps. He spoke somberly, "May they guide us all indeed."

17
Sneaking Out

"All right, Dude! We're on!" Pete whispered loudly in the dark, quietly jingling a pair of keys in front of Ak'ten. The young gnomes had lain in the dark, waiting for the sounds of his parents' gentle snoring, before Pete had ventured out to acquire transportation.

"Keys?" Ak'ten asked. "I don't understand. Have we been locked in?"

"No," Pete giggled. "You're *crazy*, dude! C'mon. I'll show you."

With that, Ak'ten rose from his pallet, still wearing his ridiculous disguise, and followed Pete out of the room, into the living room, and through a back door that Ak'ten hadn't really noticed before. The room that it led to was far different from any other room in the Techgnome abode. It was bland, gray, cold, sparsely lit, and it reeked with a stench Ak'ten had *never* encountered. He made a mental note not to drink from anything in this room.

Pete closed the door quietly behind them, then, still whispering, said, "This is our garage. It's where we keep the car." With a sideways nod from his head, Pete indicated the thing in the middle of the room.

"This is how Techgnomes travel quickly across great distances? It's a … *machine*, isn't it?" The reservation in Ak'ten's voice was unquestionable.

"Dude! You're in the Techgnome world now! If you want to save those fairies, you have to play by our rules!"

"We could always go on foot."

"But it would take *days*! By then those fairies will be goners! You know how nasty Darkgnomes are! Besides, I didn't hear you complaining about machines when we were playing video games last night."

Ak'ten nodded somberly. "I guess I *wasn't* thinking about it. It just seemed so … magical to me. But you're right. We must get to the Darkgnome lair with all speed. It's easier for me, I guess, if I just think of your technology as magic." He smiled at Pete. "And even if I don't understand this magic, at least I know that you know how to work it."

Pete shrugged, making an uncomfortable face. "Well … I'm not … technically I mean. Er …" He laughed and shrugged again, this time throwing his uncertainty aside. "I've never driven before, to be honest. I'm not old enough, well, legally. But I've seen my parents drive lots of times. Well, my dad, I mean. Mom hates driving. But anyway, how hard could it be?" Pete got into the car and turned the keys half way in the ignition, he put the top down with the flip of a switch, then put the car in neutral. "Okay, now we have to push it outside before we start it, 'cause it could be kind of loud, and if the folks wake up, we're screwed. Go turn the latch on the garage door, then lift it up."

Ak'ten was deeply worried about this. He looked at the metallic, yellow beast that Pete wanted them to push out into the night. The beast that, by his own confession, Pete was not even sure he could control. He shook his head and smiled, as he made his way to the garage door. Pete was certainly a brave gnome. As brave as Ak'ten himself. Surely the gods would be with them. He found the obvious latch on the garage door and turned it until it clicked, then he lifted the door. It was the simplest new thing he'd encountered in this strange place.

"Good. Now get in front and push. The car should just roll out. Then close the door behind us." Pete bounced in the seat, playing with the steering wheel and making car sounds with his mouth.

Ak'ten, of course, never having heard car sounds before, was suddenly concerned. "Are you well, Pete?"

"Huh?" Suddenly Pete realized. It was getting easier to understand this Old World gnome by the hour. "Sorry. I was just playin' around. Let's go."

Ak'ten moved to the front of the vehicle and pushed. It moved easily enough, rolling on rubber wheels. Soon, he didn't need to push it at all, as the slope of the driveway carried it down to the little road below. Ak'ten closed the door, bothered by the fact that he couldn't lock it down from outside. He left it hovering slightly above the hard ground and made his way to the car.

"Hop in, dude!" Pete patted the seat next to his. Ak'ten leaped over the side of the car and took his place. "Now, open up that compartment there."

Ak'ten followed Pete's finger to a latch on a small square door. He turned it, and the door fell open, revealing something that resembled a large key.

"We have to wind it up," Pete explained. "Plug it into the keyhole at the back of the car, then turn it to the right until it won't turn anymore. We don't want to have to make too many stops." Ak'ten got back out and found the keyhole easily. As he wound the car, Pete continued to explain. "Dad's usually pretty tight-fisted when it comes to money, but this car's pretty cool. It's a Tonka. Actually, our cars are human toys that we have our mechanics convert, so that they're drivable. They run mostly on wind-up technology, but the keys run all the electronics. We figure it's cheaper than gasoline, which is the stuff the humans use. Yet another pointless thing they like to have wars over. But Tonka's a good brand for conversion, because

they make *really* tough toys. It can take a lot of damage and still keep going."

"It's all wound up," Ak'ten said.

"Kick-ass! Let's go!" Once Ak'ten was back in the passenger seat, Pete turned the keys and put the car in drive. It jerked forward. Pete hit the brakes. "Whoa! Whiplash!" He tried again, repeating the process several more times, squealing the tires as he went. At last, Pete sort of got the hang of it, and they began to pick up speed.

Ak'ten was terrified and amazed. "We're going so fast! This is incredible! I've never seen such magic!"

"You keep saying that, but you haven't seen the half of it, dude!" Pete reached up and pulled a CD from the visor at the top of the windshield. "All my dad ever listens to is cheesy 80s music, but some of it's okay. That's all Retro listens to as well. It's 'cause he's poor and only ever gets hand-me-downs. His parents have a plastic car, dude! Even the *wheels* are plastic! That's okay though. He likes it that way." Pete skipped track after track, until he found the 80s song of choice. A tune by The Cars, which seemed to apply.

Ak'ten was lost in awe. Awe for the speed at which they traveled. Awe for the amazing music that Pete had just made fill the air without instruments. Awe for Pete himself. What a strange gnome this was. Strange, but so far not in the least bit dangerous. That is, aside from his obvious lack of driving skills.

The car swerved, and tires shrieked, as Ak'ten and Pete made their way to the Gnome Freeway, even farther below the human world than the rest of the Techgnome settlement.

18
Meef

Malík came out of his trance to find Kazkal No'tall pacing uneasily. He cleared his throat to announce that he was back.

"Well?" Kazkal asked.

Malík shook his head. "I couldn't find him. I thought surely he'd be asleep by now. I do hope nothing's happened to him."

"Wouldn't you know if something had? I mean, aren't shamans able to feel it when their loved ones …" He stopped short, unable to take his thought through to conclusion.

"Die? Yes. Ordinarily. But when dark sorcery is involved, the ordinary usually goes out the window." Malík shook his head sadly. When it was clear they could no longer track the lad with fairy powder, Malík had decided to wait till nightfall and try to find Ak'ten in the Dream Lands. Unfortunately, this night it seemed Ak'ten had better things to do than sleep. This had been Malík's third attempt in as many hours.

"Then I suggest we make camp for the night. Though I am loath to stop here," Kazkal said.

"Yes. Indeed," Malík muttered nervously.

"Ah, so you are concerned about camping in Meef territory as well," Kazkal guessed.

"Meef territory? I didn't even realize that we'd come so far as that."

"Yes. We have." Kazkal spat the name, "*Meefs*! They are a sick Tribe! Do you know the stories then?"

"Of course I do. I knew the Alpha Meef, as he now calls himself, when he was still a shaman."

"Yes," Kazkal said. "I suppose I should have figured that. It was only a hundred years ago, was it not?"

All the local gnome tribes both feared and abhorred the Meef Tribe. It was a tribe that was made of only one clan, Clan Meef. The Alpha Meef was the father of them all. He was both king and shaman. The Meefs were a very strange cult indeed. They had only one female, whom they shared, and all the males were named for jobs they showed proclivities for at birth. If two Meef gnomes showed the same abilities, they would be made to fight to the death. The Alpha Meef had gone from tribe to tribe, fathering sons, then stealing them away when they were infants. He had invented a language of inflection, a language that required only one word. It was a language that none could understand save for the Meefs themselves. It was clear that the old fiend had some agenda for his self-styled cult, but it remained unclear just what that agenda was. The shamans did not like it, but until the Meefs became an open threat, there was little they could justly do. For now, the Meefs were simply a blemish on the shaman collective and the gnome species as a whole.

Kazkal went on. "Well, if you weren't nervous about the Meefs, then what were you worried about? You seemed troubled. Was it just over Ak'ten?"

"No," Malík confessed. "Someone else I know lives near here. Someone I don't want to run into."

"Who could be worse than the Meefs, aside from gremlins, or—"

Before the great warrior could finish his thought, a huge net was thrown over him and the shaman, and they were quickly tackled to the ground. The night air was filled with various inflections of the word, "Meef!"

"Sick devils!" Kazkal struggled to free his axe from its straps, but could not get his arm free. The net had some magical properties it seemed. "If I could but reach my battleaxe, I would make short work of you!"

Malík remained calm. "Caution, son of Kinto. This is a very precarious situation. Tribe Meef is yet an enigma to us. We do not want to start a war inadvertently. We already have the gremlins to worry about, and if it came down to it, we'd rather have the Meefs on *our* side than theirs."

The Meefs began dragging the net along the ground.

"So what do you suggest?" Kazkal demanded grumpily. "For *this* is an unforgivable offense!"

"We must wait and see if we can reason with them. If not, then we fight. After all, I still have my staff, and you your axe."

"But they speak their deranged tongue only! How can they be reasoned with if we don't even know how to talk to them?"

"Alpha Meef was once a gnome shaman. He has surely not forgotten our tongue." Malík remained confident.

"I say we use your magic now and get out of this," Kazkal argued. "There is something you're not telling me!"

"Only that we must consider the possibility that this was Ak'ten's fate as well. Perhaps we will find him among the Meef tribe. For Fenrir is not the only fallen shaman in these parts. Ak'ten could yet be sleeping under any of their spells, and I would not be able to find him."

Kazkal's anger lessened. "I see. It is a wise point." He was silent for a moment, as they were dragged, listening to Meef chatter. Then, "But I will certainly let Ak'ten know how much I *appreciate* this adventure he's caused me when we find him!"

Malík would have nodded if the magical net had allowed. "I most heartily agree."

Once they were securely locked away in the Meef prison, weapons confiscated, it was clear that Ak'ten was not there.

"We should have done battle when yet we could! I should never have allowed even a shaman as great as you to convince me to hand over my weapon! This vexes me." Actually, Kazkal had dropped, more than handed over, the No'tall Battleaxe, and he'd laughed when the Meefs had failed to lift it.

Malík answered the warrior's protests. "Kazkal, I am sorry. But Ak'ten's absence means little at this point. We still must accept that there is some reason we are here."

"Yes," grumbled Kazkal. "We are here, because you said, 'Hand over your weapon, Kazkal.' That is the reason. The only reason."

Malík chuckled and shook his head. "We will see."

Just then, a messenger came with a small scroll and handed it to Malík through the bars. He then said, "Meef!" and went out the way he had come.

"Now we're getting somewhere," Malík said as he unrolled the message.

"How so? The only thing the message could say is, "Meef!' This is the most absurd situation I've ever been in! And I thought I'd have the *fairy powder* incident following me around to my dying day. That was nothing compared to this!"

"Ah," Malík smiled. "It's written in our own glyphs. We are to await a visit from the Alpha Meef himself." Then, as if suddenly realizing that he'd surrendered his staff, the shaman added, "We must be very cautious."

"A difficult thing without weapons," Kazkal grumbled. "At least we have a window." His tone changed abruptly. "Look!"

Malík went to the window and saw all the Meefs running out into the clearing between the trees that protected their underground village. A hooded figure was flying towards them, riding a bat. The bat landed, and the figure dismounted, cheered by the excited Meefs.

"A bat rider?" Malík asked.

"Yes," Kazkal spoke darkly. "Only Tribe Nebu-Ki is known to use bats. But what would they have to do with Tribe Meef?"

As if on cue, the figure threw back his hood, revealing the rider's identity. Kazkal growled, "Ben'du Soran! What business does that villain have here?"

"Villain?" Malík asked. "Ben'du Soran is hailed as the greatest warrior of the Nebu-Kis."

"Yes," Kazkal agreed, "but I have recently had dealings with him. He is not a moral gnome. He is a villain as I say. You must trust my warrior insights as I trust yours. Ben'du is a cat in mouse skins. There is no accord between us. There are warriors … and there are murderers."

Ben'du went to the back of his winged steed and opened a large satchel. He laid out his treasures and began selling them to the Meefs. Kazkal's face went pale, and he sank to a squatting position below the window.

"What is it?" Malík took a closer look at what Ben'du was selling. When he finally made it out, he gasped with horror. The warrior was selling the skins and teeth of gremlins. Some of the skins were even very small, as if from children. Malík turned from the window and sat beside Kazkal, who was trembling with rage. "He is more than a villain. I see your point."

"I didn't even know he was *this* bad," Kazkal said. "I knew he was a murderer. Not long ago, when I defeated the mud troll Grubello, Ben'du was there. We owed our lives to a gremlin innocent named Krat whom the mud troll held prisoner. When the ordeal was over, I considered the gremlin a friend. Such a friendship could have led to so many things. Perhaps a better understanding between our people. Perhaps an end to the Gremlin Wars. But Ben'du ran a sword through his back the first chance he got. It didn't matter to him that the gremlin had saved his life. It only mattered to him that the gremlin was a gremlin. The lesson I learned then was that there were worse things to be than that. One could be a murderer, or a back-stabbing coward of any race. I've tried to teach An'sep since not to hate the gremlins. Though we are at war, they are creatures much like ourselves, and peace would be a better end to the wars than annihilation. But I have hated Ben'du to this day. And now I loathe him all the more."

"Rightly so," Malík said angrily. After a moment, he added, "Still, one cannot help but see his arrival as advantageous."

"What do you mean," Kazkal asked in bafflement.

Malík stood. "You know him. You have fought at his side. I assume you have never greatly wronged him."

Kazkal stood. "I see where you are going with this, shaman, and I never have wronged him. Yet it is unlikely that he will help us."

"It's worth a try."

Kazkal nodded grimly. "Yes. I agree." He went to the window and called out, "Ben'du, Clan Soran, Tribe Nebu-Ki!"

Ben'du turned from his dealings and squinted at the far off window beneath the tree. "Is that the voice of Kazkal No'tall?"

"It is!"

"What are you doing in a Meef prison cell?"

"Long story."

Ben'du gestured to the crowd to hold on for a moment, and he made his way to the tree which held them, followed by several Meefs. He was soon facing them through the bars of their cell, and he handed his dark cloak over to one of his Meef admirers, communicating to the two gnomes that he had nothing to hide. He regarded them. "Well, well. How the mighty are fallen. Did you want something from me?"

Kazkal hated every word that came from his own mouth, as he said, "We were hoping you could get us out of this. Perhaps, since you seem to have some rapport with these creatures, you might be able to negotiate our release."

Ben'du laughed loudly, loving the sound of every word that issued forth from his self-righteous rival. He spoke hatefully. "I thought you were the great Kazkal No'tall! Surely you don't need *my* help." He turned his back to leave them, then added, "After all, they're only Meefs." He laughed some more as he retrieved and donned his cloak, pulled up his hood and went back to his business with the Meefs.

Kazkal watched in a rage as the warrior packed his wares and mounted his bat. "Ben'du, you fiend! I will not forget this!"

Ben'du shrugged with a laugh, as his bat lifted into the air. He shouted down to them, "Neither will I!" With that he flew back into the darkness from whence he had come.

"What now," Kazkal asked Malík.

The shaman shrugged. "Now we wait."

Kazkal rolled his eyes.

At that moment, the jailer Meef approached them and said in a haughty sort of way, "Meef."

"What did he say?" the warrior asked.

"Damned if I know," Malík huffed.

The jailer then handed Malík another thin scroll.

Malík opened it and read the glyphs to Kazkal. "You are hereby to be detained until morning, at which time the Alpha Meef will sentence you." He dropped the scroll angrily. "*Sentence* us? But what was our crime?"

"I told you we should have fought sooner." Kazkal folded his arms and leaned against the wall.

An outcry in the clearing, however, brought them both back to the little window. The Meefs were frantically gathering around a cloud of smoke that had just appeared in the center of the clearing. A mad cackle, too familiar to Malík, filled the night air, and as the smoke cleared away, his fears were realized. "Mighty Gods," he moaned. "What next?"

The shriveled crone of a gnome in the clearing cackled some more, then shouted, "Meef! Come on now, ya know why she's here!" She laughed and held out her hand, into which instantly appeared a large pot of tea. "Bring yer own cups now, loves! You Meefs never do bring 'em back for old Morrha! And mind you don't forget to pay!"

"What is *she* doing here?" Malík moaned.

Kazkal shrugged. "She's clearly here to sell tea. What do these Meefs use as currency that so many come to sell their wares here?"

The pair watched as a Meef dressed all in red came out to meet the crone most excitedly. He took her hand and shook it vigorously.

Kazkal turned to his wizened cell mate. "Who is this tea seller, that she warrants the attention of what I would assume to be the Alpha Meef?"

Malík put a hand to his forehead tiredly and sighed. "She is the very gnome I had hoped to avoid … Morrha the Moon Witch."

19
Beyond the Gnome Freeway

Zooming through the vast tunnels of the Gnome Freeway, Ak'ten finally decided he'd had enough of his disguise. He began squirming out of it as quickly as he could.

"Dude! What are you doing?" Pete spared a glance, as Ak'ten shoved his shirt and visor under his seat and began unzipping his pants.

"I'm getting out of these weird clothes. I don't need them for the time being anyway." He pulled down his baggy jeans.

"Yeah but …!" Pete saw from the corner of his eye that Ak'ten's own pants were on beneath the jeans. "Whew!" He laughed. "I was afraid you were goin' commando, dude!"

"Commando?"

Pete shook his head. "Never mind, dude."

Ak'ten held his arms out, feeling the wind on his chest. He smiled and sighed with satisfaction. "That feels *so* much better!" He put his hands behind his head and rested his feet on the dashboard, leaning back.

"We made it!" Pete shouted jubilantly, happy that he hadn't gotten them both killed. "This is our exit. It goes into the human sewer tunnels, but it's the only way to get to the surface right in front of the church. Well, the fastest way anyway." Pete swerved wildly to the right and took the ramp. Ak'ten was tossed from his relaxed pose and forced to hold on for dear life.

"Didn't I tell you to wear your seatbelt, Ak'ten?"

The other gnome smiled. "No, Pete, you didn't." It was an unexpected comfort to Ak'ten that Pete had used his real name for a change, instead of calling him dude. Ak'ten had deduced that *dude* was a fairly impersonal name, since Pete seemed to address just about everyone with the word. The use of his own name was a sign that Pete was beginning to regard Ak'ten as a real gnome, not just a novelty. For the same reason, it felt good to use Pete's name in response. Forbidden or not, a bond had begun to form between them.

The sewer tunnel was much darker than the artificially lit gnome freeway. Only the headlights of their own car now lit the way. Ak'ten noticed that the rattling of the car was getting slower. "Why's it slowing down?"

Pete looked perturbed. "We need to pull over and wind it up again's all." Pete drove the car a bit further, then brought it to a stop, turning the ignition key half-way back, so the lights at least would stay on.

Ak'ten opened the compartment for the key, returned to the rear of the car, and started winding again. He looked around at the darkness. "I don't like it here."

Pete, who was also looking around nervously, agreed. "Yeah, me neither, dude. But that old church isn't far off now. We're practically there!" He watched Ak'ten wind the car, all too aware of the complete silence that surrounded them. "Um, I think it's wound enough, man. This place is giving me the creeps big time."

"Me too." Ak'ten made one more twist. "There. All wound up." He grinned and jumped back into the car.

"Kick ass. Let's get out of here." Pete turned the ignition, and the car took off once more into the waiting darkness. As they drove on, Ak'ten, feeling the chill that came with travers-ing the depths of the unlit human sewer, reclaimed his own shirt and vest from the pocket of the discarded fat pants. Pete turned off the radio, feeling that the noise would have drawn attention from whatever lay lurking in the menacing darkness.

After a time driving in silence, it became clear that Pete had absolutely no idea where he was or where he was going. "Pete," Ak'ten finally asked, "how much farther do you suppose it is?"

"Um … not much. I mean, well … it's sort of dark. I think I missed our exit, but I can find it. I … Whoa!" Pete brought the car to a screeching halt, and Ak'ten was glad he'd been told to use the seatbelt. "Aaaaah! Bull frog!"

Ak'ten looked ahead at the massive, stone-like behemoth, as it puffed itself up and let fly a terrifying croak. Its eyes twitched as it studied them, then it turned slightly, as if setting a target. Ak'ten unbuckled his seatbelt, then Pete's, and shouted, "Get out! Jump!"

The two gnomes leapt out of the car, just as the great frog lashed out with its tongue and pulled the vehicle into its mouth, swallowing it whole. The darkness swallowed everything else.

Pete asked Ak'ten, "Do you think bull frogs can see in the dark?"

"I don't know, but I don't want to find out the hard way." He reached to his belt and found the small pouch full of fairy powder that he'd set out with in case of emergencies just such as this one. He hadn't taken the time to mix a proper charm dust, and fairy powder on its own was sometimes dangerously unpredictable. Still, it was something, and it would *probably* work. He hoped.

Pete was beside himself. "I'm so dead! It ate my parents' car! I am *so* dead!"

"Don't worry." Ak'ten pulled out a fistful of glowing powder. "I'll take care of it." He used the fairy powder to illuminate his surroundings until he found the giant frog. Before the frog had a chance to react, he blew the powder into its face, stunning it as he'd done to the snake days before. He

whipped out his flute and began to play the hypnotic tune once again. When the frog seemed relatively sedate, Ak'ten said, "The thing in your belly is bad for you. Spit it out, then hop far, far away from here. You need not eat for another day."

A sick look came over the frog then, and Ak'ten, still able to see enough from the glow of what powder still stuck to his hands, shouted, "Get out of the way!"

Just as he and Pete managed to get to either side of the great frog, it lurched and regurgitated a small ballet slipper, six marbles, three cockroaches, the remnants of another bull frog, a baseball, a bottle cap, and Pete's parents' car, headlights still blazing, now covered in mucus and simmering in places from the burn of frog stomach acid.

"Gross!" Pete shouted, trying not to gag. In the glow of the headlights, Pete then watched as the frog, looking content, turned and hopped away as quickly as its long legs would carry it.

"Whew!" Ak'ten sighed. "I'm glad I had that stuff with me."

"Hell, yeah, dude! Magic kicks ass! That was so cool! That … *peezwizz* frog did just what you said!" Pete was excited, even by his own standards.

"Well," Ak'ten said as he patted the smoking car. "Technology's pretty … *kick ass* too." He lifted his hand in disgust as frog ooze dripped from it. Then, shaking it off, added, "Do you realize how many days' walk we've covered in such a brief time? And it would be next to impossible to coax one of our squirrels into such a place as this."

Pete smiled, then crossed his arms and looked serious. "Too bad I have no idea where we are." He looked to Ak'ten imploringly. "I *do* know how to get there! We just must have missed it somewhere, and I'm too tired to think straight right now."

Ak'ten nodded understanding. "We should take a break then, calm our nerves."

"We can't take a break, dude! What if another bull frog shows up! Or one of those damn baby alligators people used to always flush!"

"We have to, Pete. We can't get back in the car till we clean it off a bit anyway. And rest is the best way to clear your head. I have a bit of magic to keep predators away." With that, Ak'ten went back to his pouch and sprinkled a circle around them and the car, and he cast a spell of protection.

Pete yawned. "Well, I guess after what I've seen so far, I have no reason to doubt your magic will do the trick. I guess we can take a short break." Pete turned the headlights off on the car, smiling at the pink glow of the circle that protected them. The two gnomes sat down by the car then, content to chat the night away. After a few minutes, they both lay down to continue talking, arms folded behind their heads. Within no time at all, they were sleeping sound as newborn babes.

20
Tea with the Moon Witch

The jailer Meef again approached Malík and Kazkal's cell. He announced with a hint of annoyance, "Meef."

"What did he say?" Kazkal asked.

"*Stop* asking me that!" Malík barked.

"He says you have a visitor!" came a shrieking, merry voice.

Malík actually jumped back at the sudden appearance of Morrha on the other side of the bars. "Morrha the Moon Witch! What have we to do with you?"

The moon witch cackled. "Plenty, Whiskers! Morrha can get those two gnomes out of hock, if they're willing to appease her, can't she now! Oh, yes, Morrha can do it!"

Malík rolled his eyes. Kazkal approached him and whispered, "This could be our—"

"Yes, he's right what he said! Your only chance! Alphy plans to have you skinned for blasphemy in his territory."

"*Alphy*?" Malík huffed incredulously.

Morrha pushed a crooked finger through the bars, pointing right at Malík's nose. "Now don't get jealous, Whiskers! You old fart! Morrha gave you your chance, she did! That ship has sailed, jus' like your little tug boat, pulling destiny behind him. Off into the night. Morrha knows what brings you out this far, and she knows where he's headed too! He told her." She smiled and folded her arms.

"Where?" Malík asked, suddenly filled with hope.

The moon witch shook a finger and cackled. "Uh-uh-uh! Not till you promise to have some tea with old Morrha now! If you do, Morrha will get you free. Otherwise, she'll just have to laugh when the Meefs make kites of you."

Kazkal nudged Malík. "Do it. This is what you were talking about before. The reason that we're here. She can put us back on the lad's trail."

Malík groaned tiredly. "Oh, all right." He looked the witch sternly in the eyes and raised a finger. "But no funny business, Morrha! We have a very important task."

"Yes, yes. Keeping the Dark Prince out of our hair does rank pretty highly where tasks are concerned." She extended her hand. "So, is it a deal then, my pretty Whiskers?"

Malík grumbled to himself, then extended his hand, grasping Morrha's. "It is a deal. Now get us out of here."

Morrha cackled some more and left them.

Kazkal was bothered. "Malík, how could she know of our quest? Of the threat we may face?"

"She was almost a shaman once," Malík explained. "She was incredibly gifted in the art of mind reading. Be careful what you think of, young warrior. She may use it against you. She is mad. She cannot be trusted entirely, though she's only ever told one lie. But we do need her, for otherwise we've lost the trail."

Kazkal nodded. "So what was the one lie?"

"It's of no importance," Malík said shortly.

Kazkal saw that there was no point in pressing. But he remained curious.

In little time, the jailer Meef approached their cell and unlocked the door, opening it. "Meef," he said with a genuine expression of friendliness.

"Well," Malík asked Kazkal grumpily, as the Meef opened the door. "Aren't you going to ask me what he's saying?"

Kazkal shrugged. "I believe he said we're free to go."

"How astute you are," Malík commented sarcastically.

After their weapons had been returned to them, Morrha met Malík and Kazkal at the exit of the prison tree. "That old Morrha got you out, she did! Offered them Meefs free tea! Meefs can't get enough of Morrha's tasty tea!" she cackled. "Now," she raised a knobby hand high above her head, "off we go!" A cloud of smoke rose out of the ground, and Malík and Kazkal broke into a fit of coughing. Morrha's laughter was the only other sound they heard.

When the smoke cleared, the pair was disoriented by the sudden change in scenery. They were no longer in the clearing of the Meef village. Instead, they were in a little gnome home, seated at a table, and Morrha was happily filling three cups with tea.

"By the gods!" Kazkal said.

"No!" the moon witch corrected him. "By Morrha! Hee hee hee!"

Kazkal looked around the little dwelling. It was a mess. There were pots of who-knew-what scattered about the main chamber, bones and toes of various creatures. A jar full of eyes on a shelf seemed to be staring right through him. "This is no wholesome abode," he said.

"Mind your manners, son of Kinto. This is the home of our rescuer." Malík passed Kazkal a cup. "Now, have some tea."

"Ah, Whiskers!" Morrha squawked. "Always so polite when he wants something, ain't he? Well," she asked, near a fit of hilarity, "what do you want, then?"

"You know very well. We are looking for—"

"Ak'ten, yes." She nodded her head with a smile. "Very nice lad. Morrha met him just yesterday, she did. Quite an idealistic little fish. Floated in on a stream and found himself in an ocean, didn't he, Malík?" She crowed with laughter.

Kazkal was impatient. "You met him? Was he alone? Where was he headed?"

Morrha looked at him crossly. "Have some tea, Commander, before Streptos takes it from you."

"Streptos!" Kazkal shouted. "What has *he* to do with it?"

"TEA!" Morrha shrieked.

Kazkal, sufficiently bothered by her outburst, sipped. "That's very good," he said, hoping it would appease her.

"Well of course it is! Ain't a gnome around don't like it! Not even them perverted ol' Meefs! Streptos, now. That one's up to strange things. Got some funny plans. Nothin' to do with your quest of course."

"Well, then," Malík interrupted. "Let's not waste any more time with it. Tell us about—"

"And what does *Whiskers* think of Morrha's tea, then?" the witch asked condescendingly.

"Oh," Malík said. "It's very nice, as always."

"Hee hee! You old schmoozer! Still in love with ol' Morrha, are you?"

"Now stop that! You know perfectly well that—"

"Ak'ten is headed to the human world," Morrha offered, ignoring the shaman's protest. "Gonna find the Darkgnomes in the city. He was alone when Morrha met him, but he met a friend soon after." She stuck her nose up mockingly in the air. "Old Malík," she shook her head, "would not approve." She grinned as wide as she possibly could. "Maybe Ak'ten will learn what a fart is for himself! Then he'll know what a fart his master is!" She cackled in a state of hysterics, holding her sides.

Malík and Kazkal just looked at each other. Kazkal was clearly ready to leave.

Malík took another sip of tea. "Is there anything else you can tell us regarding my apprentice, Morrha? Or should we be on our way?"

Morrha stopped laughing abruptly. She picked up a snail shell and put it to her ear. She appeared to be listening intently. When she put the shell down, she said, "Well, that don't sound a thing like the ocean, I imagine. Never seen the ocean actually." She scratched her head.

"Morrha …"

"Oh yes! Have some more tea." She refilled all the cups at the table, then sat back down and said, "Ak'ten ain't in too much trouble just yet. Still a ways to go, he got. Still on a quest to find the prince of devils. Morrha knows which way to point ya'. And she'll do so … in the morning."

"In the morning?" Kazkal rose to his feet.

"Will the warrior go back into the night, without shelter, to make camp? Or will he stay here, where gremlins, Meefs, and spiders can't get to him?" Morrha asked.

Malík stood and put a hand on Kazkal's shoulder. "I *hate* to say it, more than you could know, but Morrha is right. We would do better to camp here for the night than out there unprotected."

Grudgingly, Kazkal nodded his agreement.

"Ah! Morrha steers 'em right again! The guest beds are already prepared. So," she raised her seemingly bottomless pot, "have some more tea!"

21
The Missing Gnome Report

"Believe me, officers. We wouldn't have reported the car as stolen so soon, if we'd known that Pete was missing too!" Resna said in annoyance.

The same policegnome who'd been at her house a few nights before said, "Well, I'm not surprised, Mrs. Davidson. Those little troublemakers just don't get enough discipline at home is all. We'll make sure and correct that when we find them. Have you called Percival's mother?"

Resna was seething. "Yes, I called *Retro*'s mother. He's at home."

"Glad to see he's not following your son's example for once."

Scott Davidson spoke up then. "Don't talk to my wife like that, Jase. We're upset enough as it is without listening to your insults. If you had any kids of your own, we might almost value your opinion. But as it is, we don't. So let's focus on finding the boys and my car. This isn't my son's fault. He's had a new friend over for the past couple of nights that we don't know anything about really. His name's Ak'ten Underhill. Says his dad's name is Bill."

Jase and the tubby policegnome that had come with him exchanged a look. "Underhill?" Jase asked.

"Ak'ten?" The tubby cop asked. "That sounds foreign to me. Where was he from?"

"We don't know," Resna answered. "They met …" Suddenly it all made sense. "… outside."

Jase scratched his head. "I've never heard of Bill Underhill."

"It reminds me of that movie," the fat cop said. "You know? The one with Elijah Wood? Underhill was the alias he traveled under."

Just like Pete, Resna thought. *Taking his cues from a movie that reminded him of the present situation.* As far as she was concerned, that settled it. Ak'ten was an Old World gnome, and he had somehow talked Pete into helping him with something. *Could it have anything to do with Pete's "alien?"* she wondered. Her jaw tightened as she thought, *Absolutely it did.*

"Scott, officers, please excuse me." She opened the front door.

"Where are you going, dear?" Scott asked.

Resna smiled. "To see what I can find out from some of the other mothers."

Her husband shrugged. "Okay. What's wrong with the phone?"

"I just need some fresh air. Might as well take care of some things while I'm out." Resna waved sweetly, then closed the door behind her.

"See?" Scott said to the policegnomes. "Now you've upset her."

22
Dream Meeting

"Malík, we need to talk."

Malík turned around to find the voice. He didn't really want to talk to anyone. He was having such a nice time watering his garden, and there were fairies all around, singing silly songs. It made him so happy. "Who's there?" he asked.

"Io," said a very tiny owl.

"Io? Master, why are you a shrunken owl?"

"Because you're dreaming," said the owl. "I wanted to observe you for a while, before we spoke. Besides, I like owls."

Suddenly Malík remembered what was happening in the real world. "How may I be of service, Io?"

The tiny owl fluffed its feathers out. "You know well the legends of the Devil's Pearl." It was not a question. It was well known among the shamans that Malík had inherited the Tribe and the treasures of Sheto Qadash.

"Yes, of course." Malík answered warily.

"Therefore you know that whichever of our shamans Sheto entrusted with keys to finding it remain secret even to the chieftain of the Collective. So it came as an unsettling surprise when I learned that two of our shamans, who have recently been slain by unknown powers, were the keepers of these keys."

Malík's heart sank. "Master, which two shamans were these?"

The owl offered a sympathetic glance to his former apprentice. "Eldir-Mon and Diliac."

"I knew them well," Malík lamented. "Yet, never did I know they carried such burdens." A thought occurred to him then, and he regarded the owl. "How did you learn their secrets?"

"Our investigators found it written in their journals. We weren't sure the murders were connected until now, though we suspected it. Someone is trying to uncover the Devil's Pearl, and whoever it is now has Sheto's map and Shi-Nook's sword. I am warning you, because you are the only shaman I *know* may be a target, because you have Sheto's book. Even I do not know which of our shamans is the guardian of the Cloak of

Winds. The villain who seeks it may come for the book, hoping for a clue. Of course, we both know he won't find it."

"No, Master Io," Malík agreed. "No one knows who has the cloak. And I have more bad news. I do not think I am in danger as yet, for the one who seeks the Pearl believes me dead."

The owl puffed up. "You *know* who seeks the Pearl?"

"Yes. It is none other than Prince Fenrir himself. My apprentice encountered a deranged fairy. It seems the fallen prince is trying to make dark fairy powder by torturing them."

"How could you not tell me this at once, Malík!" The owl was not pleased. "I should have been informed. This is terrible. Fenrir had twenty-one years to study *The Book of Secrets* as your apprentice! If any of our enemies can find the Pearl, it is Prince Fenrir!"

"I know," Malík bowed his head. "Forgive me." He looked up again to meet the owl's angry gaze. "I am on an urgent quest."

"What could be so urgent that you forget to tell me—"

"My apprentice has gone looking for Fenrir."

"*What!?!?*"

"He intends to rescue the fairies from him. He doesn't realize what he's getting involved in. He's young and idealistic."

Io's bulging owl eyes narrowed. "He is to be brought before the Great Ghost in less than four years' time. He should have more self discipline by now. But you let him run amok! His appearance is unacceptable, his behavior is unpredictable. Now he goes to bring the eyes of Fenrir back upon your tribe."

"He is a special case. You know this," Malík said, standing his ground bravely.

The owl huffed. "Special case or not, the time of his apprenticeship grows short! If he is not *ready* by the time of his appointment, he will not be made a shaman."

"It is difficult, Io. Would it not be difficult for any shaman? There are times when I have very much wanted just to tell him the truth. Perhaps it would help him to know—"

"No!" Io boomed. "It would not do. It would only make things worse for him. He must *never* know. Besides, we only have your word on the matter as it is. The *truth* has yet to be tested."

"But you can see into my soul. You know the value of my *word*."

"Yes," The owl spoke calmly. "That is why we have indulged you these fifteen years. That is why, though I scold you, I will continue to turn a blind eye to the lad's unorthodox upbringing. For I value your judgment as well as your word. But I do not feel it hurts to remind you time and time again. You only have four years left to prepare him. At that point, all indulgences will cease. I know you can do this, Malík. We are all counting on it. Now go and find him."

23
When Gremlins Run

Malík awoke with a start and looked around. The sun had come up, and Kazkal sat polishing his gargantuan battle axe.

"Good morning, Malík."

"Good morning, Kazkal. Where's the moon witch?"

"Making breakfast."

"Oh, dear." Malík shook his head and stood, patting down his beard.

Morrha came out of her kitchen then with a tray of the-gods-knew-what. "Breakfast is served, gnomes! Come and get it!" She cackled and set the tray down on the table.

Malík and Kazkal took their seats. Kazkal studied the food with fading appetite. "What is it," he asked Malík, when Morrha had gone back into the kitchen, probably for tea.

"It's certainly … gray," Malík answered.

"Yes," Kazkal agreed. "And lumpy."

Morrha threw open the kitchen door then, with her all too familiar tea pot in tow. "And the best part of all—Morrha's tea!" She chuckled and filled their cups, then her own. In fact, she filled her own cup three times and chugged each serving before Kazkal had even taken a sip.

"What is it with you and tea?" the warrior asked.

"It gives Morrha her morning pep, it does! Nothin' like good tea, Morrha says. Now eat up, warrior, for you've a long day ahead."

"I hope you haven't had a vision, for yesterday was long enough to last me awhile," the warrior groaned.

Malík played with the gray, lumpy stuff on his plate, moving it about with his fork. "Morrha …"

"It's her own specialty! Steamed slug! With a dash of gravy," Morrha answered.

"You can steam slugs?" Kazkal asked.

"A *dash* of gravy?" said Malík.

"Yes, yes." Morrha nodded with a gnarly, full-toothed smile. "Eat up!"

Kazkal looked at Malík. "We warriors have a saying. Better to die from eating bad food, than to die from eating no food at all." He took a bite and swallowed. "If you swallow quickly, you don't have to taste it as much."

"Yes, I suppose it only needs get to our stomachs," Malík added.

Morrha looked at them both crossly and drank tea.

The shaman and the warrior wasted no more daylight than was necessary. After breakfast, Morrha pointed them in the direction they needed to go, as promised. They thanked Morrha and bid her farewell, traveling onward towards the forest's edge. At last, Kazkal asked, "So how do you suggest we proceed? If the human city is our destination, we will be in the land of monsters and heretics."

"Yes," Malík said. "We could go back for reinforcements, but that would waste precious hours. I suggest we simply press on. Proceed no matter what. Surely a shaman and a warrior can handle any obstacles that come our way."

Suddenly Kazkal went rigid, reaching for his battleaxe.

"What is it?" Malík asked in alarm.

Kazkal answered quietly, battleaxe now at the ready, "I hear gremlin feet, running towards us."

Malík readied his staff for battle. He tried to tell himself that they'd fared well against the gremlins the day before, but he couldn't help but remember that there had also been another two warriors in their company at the time.

Twenty gremlins leapt through the brush and ran right past them, paying them no mind at all. And once they'd passed, they kept on running, not looking back even once.

"How strange!" Malík said in surprise.

Kazkal shook his head urgently. "No, they were running in fear. We warriors have another saying on the battlefield. 'When gremlins run from anything other than us, we run too.' " The warrior made ready to run, but too late. The source of the gremlins' fear came monstrously into view. It was a mud troll, towering over them at just over a foot and a half in height. Malík made ready to smite her, but Kazkal stopped him just in time. "No, wait!"

"What?!? Are you blind?" Malík asked.

The mud troll looked down at them, a look of excitement overcoming her features. "No'tall! Jy'ty'tity *love* Kazkal No'tall!" The massive mud troll bent down then to scoop the warrior up and hug him like a rag doll. "You so good!"

"Rgh!" was all the warrior could manage in response, involuntarily dropping his great axe to the ground.

"Kazkal! I never knew you had such a way with the ladies," Malík said. "Are you sure you're all right?"

Kazkal managed to squirm into a breathable position in the creature's arms. "Yes. This is Jy'ty'tity. The mud troll Grubello was her husband."

"But," Malík was confused, "I thought you said you …" He thought better of saying it.

"Right," Kazkal said. "I slew her husband. But, as it turns out, she hated him. She pledged eternal gratitude."

"Yes!" the mud troll agreed enthusiastically. "Jy'ty'tity love Kazkal No'tall forever! Him give her freedom! Jy'ty'tity *hate* nasty Grubello mean head! She kick him head when it come off! She poopoo on Grubello's head!"

"I get the idea," Malík said with a bearded smirk.

"Who him?" Jy'ty'tity asked.

Kazkal answered, "This is Malík. He's the shaman of my tribe. We are trying to get to the edge of the forest. One of our friends has wandered into the human world, and we are on a quest to find him."

"Oh!" Jy'ty'tity dropped Kazkal in alarm. He managed to land well enough not to break anything. "Jy'ty'tity scared of humans!" She looked down at the two gnomes. "But Jy'ty'tity *love* good gnomes! She carry them to edge of forest. Go much faster than them small baby man legs."

With that, the massive mud troll scooped up the two gnomes and made her way with long strides to the edge of the forest.

Kazkal and Malík managed to grumble their uncertain thanks.

When the trio finally arrived at their destination, Jy'ty'tity seemed apprehensive. Sweat was beginning to fall from her brow like rain. She placed the gnomes down gently for once. "Ooh!" She wiped her forehead with a massive arm. "Here we am. Edge of forest. Human world." She gazed forward timidly at the gigantic buildings just beyond the trees.

"Thank you, Jy'ty'tity," Kazkal said. "We are in your debt for such speed and for protecting us from predators."

"No problem, Kaz … kal …" Suddenly, the great mud troll swooned.

"Jy'ty'tity!" Malík shouted. "Are you all right?"

"Look out!" Kazkal shouted, as the mud troll began to fall.

Jy'ty'tity hit the ground with an incredible splat-thud.

"What happened?" Kazkal asked. "She seemed just fine! I know she fears the humans, but would she really have fainted?"

"No," Malík answered with a shake of his head, studying the peeling skin around the mud troll's scalp. "She's molting. It happens annually and without warning to all mud trolls."

"*Molting*!?!? That's disgusting! How long will she be down?" the warrior asked.

"Two weeks."

"Two weeks!? We can't just leave her here! Not after she carried us like that. We can't just leave her at the edge of the forest for any human to find!"

"I agree," the shaman said. "But I can't just use my magic to float her back home, either. A floating mud troll would be anything but discrete, and while I floated her, we would be susceptible to attack. We must watch over her here until a solution presents itself."

"What? We can't do that!" Kazkal said. "Ak'ten could be in danger even as we speak! How long might it take for a solution to 'present itself'? And what if no solution comes to us at all?"

"Don't be so cynical, Kazkal. Haven't we made it this far?" Malík smiled through his long, white beard.

Grudgingly, Kazkal crossed his arms. "I suppose so." He sat down beside the fallen mud troll. "We will wait, for a little while. But if a solution does not present itself within a reasonable amount of time, we must rethink the mud troll issue.

Surely there is *something* we can do for her that won't get in the way of our quest."

"Yes," Malík answered. "So while we wait, we will put our minds to the task."

24
Resna's Discovery

Resna made her way through the dusty air shaft, flash light in tow, looking for the place where Pete had seen his 'alien.' She was determined to put this puzzle together. The more she thought about it, the more she was convinced that Ak'ten was the very Old World gnome she'd found Pete playing with five years before. "Okay," she said to herself as she at last approached the vent. "Think like Pete."

She turned off her flash light, finding the light coming through the vents from the human apartment to be adequate, and she saw in one of the thin grates of light something that made her heart stop. "Pete!" She scurried over to the little ball cap lying by the vent. She got down on her knees and held it to her heart. Tears fell silently from her big, blue eyes. "Now I know I'm thinking like you. You did come back here. You came to show Ak'ten where you saw the alien." Resna wiped the tears away and suddenly caught a faint, pink glow. "Aha!" she said, as she sprang back to her feet. "And there was evidence still here from your encounter. Something is not right about this." She shook her head. "So something up here gave you a direction. You needed to take the car." She caught a faint, sulfurous scent in the air. She went pale. "Darkgnomes were here. You saw them use their magic." She mulled over all the pieces, trying to see how it all connected. "The Darkgnomes were looking for the 'alien' as well." She closed her eyes and tapped her forehead with a clinched fist. "Think like Pete. Think like Pete." Her eyes flew open, and she gasped with the realization. "Ak'ten's trying to rescue the 'alien'! Pete's helping him!" A shadow of emotion covered her face. "They're trying to find the Darkgnomes."

Still clutching the little ball cap, Resna made her way back home.

25
Land of the Humans

Fully rested and back on the road, Pete managed to find his way to the proper exit without any further problems.

"It's amazing how well this car held up to being ingested by that bull frog," Ak'ten said.

"Told you, dude. Tonka. She can take all kinds of abuse." He took the car into a little hole in the wall and turned it off, daylight now peeking through the roof of the tunnel all around them. "This is the place. This is as close to that old church as I can take us in the car. This tunnel system doesn't really go beneath it anymore." He got out of the car, and Ak'ten followed suit. Pete looked up through the cracks above them. "Now we have to climb."

Ak'ten looked up, following Pete's gaze. "Shouldn't be too hard." He smiled and started climbing.

"Ak'ten, wait! It's crazy up there!" Pete started climbing after him. "You have to be prepared for the worst. Humans are *huge*! And they never notice us! So don't just step outside like it ain't no thing. You could get squashed by like a billion different things." For some reason, unknown even to him, the thought of being squashed by a billion different things suddenly made Pete laugh.

With even less understanding as to why, the thought of Pete laughing while a billion different things squashed him, suddenly made Ak'ten laugh. The two young gnomes tried to suppress their giggles, with little success, as they made their way towards the light of the outside world.

The roaring, screaming sounds of the gods-knew-what grew louder and louder the closer Ak'ten got to the surface. All at once, getting squashed didn't seem as funny. When he finally reached his destination, Ak'ten peeked his head out slowly. The great, iron beasts that Malík had often spoken of were everywhere. They were the fastest creatures Ak'ten had ever seen. Then it hit him. They weren't beasts at all. "Cars!" Ak'ten shouted over the noise. "The humans move about the world in *giant* cars!"

"Yeah, dude!" Pete shouted as he came up beside him. "Where do ya think we got the idea?"

The young gnomes looked at the sea of human cars that roared before them. "Where's the church?" Ak'ten asked.

"It's across the street. Right there." Pete pointed.

Ak'ten nodded his head, deciding to make a run for it. He poised for the run, but Pete caught his shoulder with one hand. "Ak'ten, wait! You're crazy! Wait for the stop light! All the cars will stop when the light turns red. *Then* we run!"

Ak'ten nodded uncertainly, feeling silly for not knowing about such things. He comforted himself with the fact that Pete would have been just as lost in his world.

The pair waited, and waited. Finally, the cars began to slow. When they had all stopped, Pete patted Ak'ten roughly on the shoulder and shouted, "Go now! Run!"

Ak'ten and Pete ran as fast as they could, trying, Ak'ten deduced, to make it across the street before the light changed again. It was a long, long way across the street. Ak'ten was determined to make it, but the sudden sound of engines roaring began to fill him with doubt and dread. Pete's hand on his shoulder again abruptly stopped him running.

"Damn, dude! We didn't make it!" As Pete spoke, they were between the front of one car and the back of another. Pete looked around. "We should be okay, as long as we stay *way* between the tires like this. Only a drunk would swerve enough to squash us then. Just be careful of anything dragging behind the car. That could really mess up your day."

Ak'ten nodded, full of adrenaline. As the cars began moving, passing over them, covering them with shadows, fumes, and noxious smoke, Ak'ten was more afraid than he'd been at any time in his life. A glance to his side told him that Pete felt the same way. After what seemed a very long time, the cars again came to a stop, one right on top of them, dripping a terribly odious fluid.

"Now!" Pete shouted.

The gnomes ran even faster this time, not wanting to repeat the experience. At just the right moment, they found themselves on the other side of the road, catching their breath against the curb as the cars rolled loudly onward. Pete patted Ak'ten on the back. "*That* was fun," he said.

"Now what?" Ak'ten asked.

"Now it gets worse," Pete answered, nodding towards the curb. "We have to climb up there, where there's human feet and bicycles."

"What's bicycles?" Ak'ten asked nervously.

"They're like cars, only really skinny and a whole lot quieter. You can't get between the wheels either. Bicycles can squash you good, dude."

"Are there more stop lights?" Ak'ten asked hopefully.

"No, dude. Those are only for cars. We have to run like you almost did the first time. Just dodge 'em."

Ak'ten nodded, fighting the physical demand to tremble. "Right then. Let's go."

Ak'ten climbed to the top of the curb, with a helpful push from Pete. Then he gave Pete his hands and helped the younger gnome up. Ak'ten turned around then to take in the horrific sight. No fewer than three bicycles headed their way, and he couldn't even count all the humans walking down the enormously wide walkway. "I thought you said this place was abandoned."

"It is, but there's a park nearby. So humans are still around *outside* of the church." As soon as there was a break in the traffic, Pete shouted, "Go for it!"

The two gnomes ran, almost getting stepped on more times than either of them dared to count. When they at last reached the other side of the sidewalk and were embraced by the calm of the path to the doors of the church, Ak'ten started laughing, unable to catch his breath. Pete followed suit, and they both fell over into the grass, gasping for air, choking on giggles.

When they at last pulled themselves together, it didn't take them long to get to the front of the building. Pete looked for a crack to squeeze through, considering the enormity of the two wooden doors. "There!" he shouted with excitement.

"Shouldn't we be more quiet?" Ak'ten asked.

Pete looked at him as if he were crazy.

"Darkgnomes?" Ak'ten reminded him.

"Oh yeah!" Pete shouted. Then he covered his mouth and, when he let go, whispered, "Oh yeah."

Before the two could slip into the crack, a mangled crow swooped down and stood before them. It only had one eye, and it turned its head sideways to get a better look at them. A groan came from the creature's belly.

Pete looked at Ak'ten. "Magic powder time, dude."

Ak'ten reached into his pouch. A look of surprise colored his face.

"What's wrong?" Pete asked.

Ak'ten simply looked down, to where his finger poked out through a hole in his now empty pouch. He shrugged. "Must have been the frog juice on the car."

Pete's eyes went wide, as he pulled Ak'ten to the side. The bird struck, just where Ak'ten had been standing. It turned its head sideways again, trying to find them. Pete shouted, "Run!" He kicked the bird in the leg, surprising it enough to send it back into the air. However, by the time the gnomes were squeezing into the crack, the bird had regained its composure and was fast returning for another try.

"Quick! Push!" Pete shouted, completely forgetting the Darkgnome threat that awaited them on the inside. Just as the bird landed and stuck its beak into the crack, the gnomes managed to push through, into the wall. It was much more spacious on the inside, and they soon found their way to an opening at the other end, inside the church. The room was faintly lit, making it clear that someone must have been inside. Ak'ten's jaw dropped as he looked around the massive room, marveling at the size of it all, the height of the walls, the seemingly eternal space between them. How titanic these humans must be to inhabit such a lair. The two gnomes tried to keep quiet as they yet again had to catch their breath. They noticed the sounds of muffled voices, laughter. Then the air was filled with a terrible scream. A tortured scream.

Ak'ten nodded darkly. "This must be the place," he said quietly.

"Yep," Pete swallowed. "Darkgnome central. And someone's being tortured."

"A fairy," Ak'ten said.

"We've gotta do something," Pete almost growled.

Somberly, Ak'ten answered, "That's why we're here."

26
Resna Sets Out

Resna, not wanting to alert Scott that she'd returned, made her way to the garage from the outside. She noted the garage door hovering above the ground. "Think like Pete," she repeated to herself. There probably wouldn't be anything inside to add any light to where he had gone. Pete was never one for making detailed plans. He was a very spontaneous gnome. He would have just said, "I know where we need to go," and then they would have gone there. No maps would have been drawn up, no strategies or battle plans written down. They would just head out into dangers unknown completely unprepared. It only comforted Resna slightly, as she squeezed the ball cap tighter at her chest, that Pete always seemed to manage just fine by the seat of his pants.

She turned around to look at the driveway, noting the skid marks. She followed the marks with her eyes all the way out into the alleyway. She walked down the slope of the driveway and peered down the alley, noting the identical marks that painted the cement as far as the eyes could see. "Good thing it's a Tonka," she mused. She shook her head, looking at the ball cap as if it were a friend, a helper in her quest. She nuzzled the cap gently to her face, looked back at the trail of skid marks. "This shouldn't be too hard," she said; and she made her way down the alley, following the trail of burnt rubber.

27
A Curious Pair

Ak'ten and Pete made their way through the shadows, following the screams of the tortured fairy. They went back into the walls, climbing upwards just enough. When they came to the chamber of torture, they found themselves looking down on it from a decorated hole in the wall, probably *meant* for observation. They were careful not to make a sound.

The sight before them was nightmarish indeed. A tall, muscular gnome, wearing a cape and fine slacks, but no shirt, was seated before a fairy in shackles. The fairy was trembling and sobbing. An orange glow filled the tiny chamber from a small fireplace. The gnome was poking at the fire with a long, iron rod. A sinister grin spread over his face, as he removed the glowing tip of it from the flames. "This doesn't have to go on forever, Ti-ta. All you have to do is give up."

The fairy wept some more, as she bowed her head. Then she sprang back up, glowing with giggles and nonsensical rhymes. The gnome jabbed her side violently with the hot iron. He then stood over her, grabbed one of her wings, and ripped it almost in half. The fairy screeched and wailed in agony.

Tears were streaming down Pete's face, as he turned to Ak'ten and whispered as quietly as he could, "We have to do something *now*."

Ak'ten was dazed by the sight before him, so stunned that the tears he would have expected didn't come. "We will," he whispered back.

The pair turned to leave, and were met by another Darkgnome, staring back at them. "I don't think so," said the Darkgnome stranger. Before Ak'ten and Pete could finish a gasp, the Darkgnome threw out his palm, hitting them with an energy blast that instantly robbed them of consciousness. The two gnomes slumped to the floor, while the Darkgnome quietly delighted.

"What's going on up there," came the voice of the other Darkgnome.

"I just captured two young spies, Lord Fenrir! A very curious pair at that," Mephistopheles answered.

A black shadow appeared beside him then, and Fenrir stepped through it. He looked at the fallen youths. "Ah, yes.

Very curious. It is more than strange to see an Old World gnome and a Techgnome spying *together*. Even if they have come seeking to join us, it is strange that they would come as a pair. We will question them, when they awake." He crossed his arms, studying them. Then he smiled at his most talented disciple. "Put them where they can see the fairy in her cell. Let them think by the sight of her that we mean to treat them as we've treated her. Fear is the quickest way to uncover the truth."

Mephisto bowed theatrically. "Consider it done, my lord."

28
Ri-ni

"This is too frustrating!" Kazkal raged. "We have waited long enough! We simply must move forward."

Malík answered calmly. "And what would you have us do with Jy'ty'tity, son of Kinto? Would you leave her here for predators to feed upon? Or would you have us take her along, floating magically above the ground, calling attention to us wherever we go?"

"Forgive me, Malík. I am restless. I am a gnome of action, and I want to get to Ak'ten as soon as possible."

"I understand, Kazkal. But we must remain patient, or we may miss the answers that we seek."

At that moment, a weak looking fairy flew towards them from beneath the nearest human building. Malík paid close attention to her bittersweet songs as she approached. "Oh, my!" he said.

"What?" Kazkal asked.

Malík ignored the warrior for the moment, calling the fairy to him. The fairy flitted over, barely keeping herself in the air. She seemed pleased at having someone to share her silly rhymes with. Malík asked her questions and, to Kazkal's bewilderment, behaved as if she were actually answering them with her nonsense and gibberish. The fairy engaged in innumerable pointless statements that were clear to the warrior only in their lack of clarity. Then, after the fairy made several gestures which were no less than dramatically acrobatic, Malík turned to Kazkal with a solemn look on his face.

"What in the name of the gods was that all about?" Kazkal asked.

"It seems," Malík answered, "that Ak'ten and a young Techgnome have been captured by Fenrir."

"Is he all right? Wait!" Kazkal suddenly realized that he was taking the word of a fairy. "How do we know this? Nothing she said made sense."

The fairy giggled, then coughed. A light sprinkle of fairy powder twinkled to the ground, and she moaned.

"I thought only fat fairies could release powder," Kazkal said in confusion.

"It is true," Malík answered. "But this fairy has been wounded. She is leaking."

"Leaking?"

"Her name," Malík went on, "is Ri-ni. She and her sister were captured by Darkgnomes days ago. She says that two others had been captured before them. Ri-ni managed to escape, but the Darkgnomes hurt her, and she was lost in a human home for days. But most important to us, fairies have no sense of what they're supposed to be looking at, really. So they often see things through each other's eyes. She can see Ak'ten and the other gnome through her sister's eyes. She says they are in a cage, and that they are sleeping." Malík smiled.

"Why do you smile, Malík?" Kazkal asked. "So Ak'ten finally sleeps, and you can find the way from him to the Darkgnome stronghold! I understand that, but still none of our conundrums have been solved! We still may have a long way to travel on foot, we still have to find some way of protecting Jy'ty'tity! By the time we can actually get to Ak'ten, it will be too late!"

Malík continued to smile. "On the contrary, my good warrior, we now have the solution to all our troubles. I only ask for a little more patience, and that you would be kind to Ri-ni while I am in trance." Malík then muttered something to the fairy, who giggled, flew in a loop, and went to sit on top of Jy'ty'tity, where she winked and winked at no one.

Kazkal shook his head, unsure what to make of it all.

Malík nodded appreciation at Kazkal, then went and sat cross-legged on the ground, closing his eyes.

Kazkal tiredly put a hand to his forehead and reminded himself, "It is not for warriors to understand shamans, only to trust them."

Malík traveled the Dream Lands, looking for his lost apprentice. He found him soon enough, surrounded by screaming fairies. The lad was kneeling on the ground, weeping. Malík studied the fairies. They were all leaking and had torn wings. Some were horribly burnt. He rushed to bring Ak'ten to his senses. He grabbed the lad by the shoulders. "Ak'ten, you're dreaming."

Suddenly the youth noticed Malík. "Malík? What ...?" He suddenly remembered what was happening in the real world. "You should have come along, Malík!" He was angry now, still aware of the mangled dream fairies that surrounded him. "These dream images are a reflection of the things I've seen!"

"I am coming, Ak'ten. Kazkal is with me." He led Ak'ten away from the nightmare, and they made their way to Malík's own dream. They sat down in the garden. "Let's talk here. It's a bit more serene, don't you think?"

Ak'ten turned around. He couldn't even see his own dream anymore. All that surrounded them were trees, flowers, and birds, and the sun shone brightly above them. Ak'ten smiled. "Yes. You're dream's pretty kick-ass compared to mine."

"Kick-ass? What do you ...?" Malík shook his head. Perhaps the lad was still slightly lost in dream awareness. "Ak'ten, I need you to tell me exactly where you are."

"That won't be easy, Malík. We mostly traveled through tunnels. Hey, this is the first time you've ever visited my dream."

Malík tried to remain patient. "This is the first time I've had to. Now stay focused. If something wakes you up, we will lose contact. Can you show me an image of the place? Something I could find?" Malík gestured to their surroundings. "Show me here. Use the Dream Lands as your canvas."

Ak'ten concentrated, and Malík's peaceful garden was replaced by a busy human street. "By the gods!" Malík shouted in alarm.

"It was a perilous journey, Malík," Ak'ten confessed. "But we made our way to the building across the way. Pete says it's a human church that now serves as the Darkgnome stronghold. That's where we are."

Malík studied the building very carefully, memorizing every detail.

"Very well. We will be with you shortly."

"But, Malík, it takes days on foot! We used Techgnome magic to get there!"

"Techgnome *magic*?" Malík was distressed. "I can see we will have much to discuss when we get back home. Now trust me, lad. We're on our way."

"But, Malík! You can't come by any of our ways! It's far too dangerous! The human world is—"

Malík put a hand on Ak'ten's head. "Wake up, Ak'ten." As the image of Ak'ten vanished from the Dream Lands, Malík said, "You need to keep your guard up." Malík looked one more time in the direction of the building, but saw only his tranquil garden. Malík opened his eyes and regarded Kazkal with a smile. "I have seen the Darkgnome stronghold."

"Excellent, then let's get going!" Kazkal said with relief.

Just then the fairy went berserk.

"Well, what is she saying?" Kazkal asked.

The shaman looked serious. "She says that Ak'ten will find his way back here, and we must be ready to rescue him *then*. We have to wait."

"Why didn't she say that before? How can we take her word?" Kazkal was beyond frustrated.

"Fairies never lie. And they can't tell the past and future from the present. They see all things, but don't know what they see. They are a strange people," Malík said.

"You've got that right," Kazkal grumbled. "Look, only a moment ago you were ready to go! You said all our problems had been solved, which, I imagine includes Jy'ty'tity *and* our lack of swift transportation. So, I am going to take your word over the fairy's. I am going into the city to rescue Ak'ten, with or without you." Kazkal began walking away.

Exasperated, Malík said, "Hold, Kazkal No'tall. I cannot let you go alone. You would never reach the stronghold in time, and I will need you here when Ak'ten returns. As I know how bullheaded you can be when you've made up your mind, and as I'd rather not have one more lost hero to rescue from the perils of the human city, I will come with you. But give me only a fraction of a second more."

Kazkal turned angrily and saw, to his continued dismay, a company of fifteen fairies, flying towards them.

"Here comes a part of the solution," Malík said.

The fairies met their wounded sister atop Jy'ty'tity and flew around her, singing happy tunes. Ri-ni was elated, as they bandaged her wound with flower petals. She then did a non-sensical song and dance for them, and they all giggled and squeaked. Ri-ni and the other fifteen fairies then flew about gathering flowers and tying them together around the molting mud troll. Within a matter of seconds, Jy'ty'tity was perfectly hidden from the world in a lovely cocoon.

Malík explained to Kazkal, "The fairies will now watch over her until she wakes up. She will be quite safe."

"That solves one problem, but there is still the matter of speed."

"Yes," Malík agreed. "That problem was solved much earlier, when Ri-ni got here."

"How so?" Kazkal asked, more curious now than skeptical.

Malík went over to the place where Ri-ni had leaked. He knelt down and scooped up the powder she'd lost. He put it in his pouch then and removed a flute from inside of his robe. Not long after the shaman began to play, a plump-looking blue jay sat down beside him and began to sing along. Malík slowly put away his flute and reached into his pouch. He reached up to pet the creature on its head, thus covering its blue crest in fairy powder. "We need a ride through the air, my friend," Malík explained to the blue jay. Malík then held up his hand before the bird and sent him the image that Ak'ten had shown him. "We would be grateful if you could take us there."

The blue jay twittered excitedly, lowering its wings for the gnomes to climb on.

"Does that mean he knows the place?" Kazkal asked.

"I'm not sure," Malík confessed. "But it certainly sounds like it." With that, Malík climbed upon the blue jay's back. He looked at Kazkal, who hadn't moved a centimeter. "What's this? I thought you were eager to press on."

Kazkal gritted his teeth and made his way towards the bird. "It is nothing, Malík. Only that this warrior is more comfortable with both feet on the ground." He climbed on the bird's back behind the much older gnome. "But while the brave do know fear, only cowards can be stopped by it."

The bird took to the air then, and Kazkal held on for dear life, vexed by Malík's never ending supply of confidence.

29
Prisoners of the Dark Prince

Pete awoke to find Ak'ten sitting alert beside him, arms folded, brooding. "What happened?" he asked groggily.

Ak'ten, pleased to see Pete awake at last, whispered, "We got caught … dude."

"No joke!" Pete cracked. He sat up, noticing the bars that surrounded them. "We're in a cage!"

"No joke," Ak'ten parroted. He nodded forward. "Look."

Pete followed Ak'ten's gaze to a human-made jar. "The fairy!" Pete studied the tiny, pink creature trapped in the glass prison. She looked very sad, but she was awake. "She isn't …?"

"No," Ak'ten answered. "They haven't been able to turn her yet."

"Whew! Well that's good, at least."

A ferocious roar from another room caught their attention. They both turned instinctively to face the wall, though they knew they couldn't see through it.

At that moment, the gnome they'd seen torturing the fairy strode quietly into the room. He cleared his throat, and they turned, both angrily, to face him. "Welcome to Darkgnome Headquarters. May I ask, before I kill you, what brings you by?"

Pete and Ak'ten only glared at him.

Fenrir continued. "I see. No answer. It is very curious that an Old World gnome and a Techgnome would be found spying on me as a pair. How did this come about?"

Still, they only glared at him.

"Very well. We'll just have to get on with things. Are you here seeking to join the Darkgnome Legion? Or are you spies? And if you are spies, *who* exactly are you spying for?"

"We are not spies," Ak'ten answered. "So to speak."

"And we sure as *hell* aren't here to become Darkgnomes!" Pete shouted. "We're just here for the ali— *fairy*."

Ak'ten looked at Pete, as if to shush him.

Fenrir laughed. "I see. Little heroes, here to rescue the poor fairy." He looked over at the jar, at the sorrowful creature pressing hands against the glass. "Quite a bang up job you did, too." He grinned menacingly. "Now you're in the same boat yourselves. And who will come and rescue you?"

Ak'ten whispered to his friend, "Clear your thoughts. This could be Fenrir."

Fenrir started. "How do you know me, lad?" He eyed Pete. "How do *either* of you know me?"

Silence. Ak'ten concentrated on blocking his thoughts.

Fenrir focused, which was the most important part of shaman mind reading. He came up on a blank with Ak'ten. A wall. This in itself gave him a partial answer. "So you're a shaman's apprentice." He chuckled, as Ak'ten's concentration was very briefly interrupted. He then looked to Pete. "Your friend won't know that trick, then. Unless *you* taught it to him. Which would make you quite the little heretic." He eyed Ak'ten. "You're clever, rebellious, certainly both very bold. I could use gnomes like you." He focused on Pete. Pete was thinking determinedly about baseball. That was his own mind-clearing trick he'd learned to use because of teachers asking him to stand up at awkward moments.

"Fine!" Fenrir raged. "I'll come back later." He strode towards the exit, then turned his head slightly. "Just so you don't suffer from false hope … you won't be leaving this place alive." He left them then.

Ak'ten and Pete both breathed a sigh of relief, realizing only then that they'd scarcely been breathing at all.

The fairy tapped the glass weakly, then slumped to the base of the jar. There was fairy powder all around her. Ak'ten decided that he had been right about the other fairy. It *had* been wounded, and had been bleeding—just as this fairy was now bleeding profusely. If they were going to save her at all, they would have to act fast. And if they were going to act fast, they were going to have to get out of their cage.

Fenrir returned to his chamber, calling Mephisto and Necros to follow him.

"What did they say?" Mephisto asked excitedly. "Who sent them?"

"They divulged nothing!" Fenrir growled.

"Well why didn't you just—?" Mephisto stopped abruptly, reading the deadly look on his master's face.

"The Old World lad is a shaman's apprentice. He was able to thwart my efforts. As for the other one … he has all the mental tricks of a fourteen-year-old male at his command. They test me." He jabbed a finger in Mephisto's direction. "Fly on the wall!"

With that, the cocky gnome was changed instantly into a fly. Necros gasped in horror as Mephisto buzzed around. "Don't worry, Necros," Fenrir offered. "He's still in full command of his faculties. I've been dying to use this thing." Fenrir walked into the command center and returned with a very tiny camera. "Come here, Mephisto. I need you to be my fly on the wall in there."

The fly landed and allowed Fenrir to strap the contraption to its head. The Dark Prince turned it on, satisfied by the nearly microscopic green light that was now flashing off and on. His lips curled into a sinister grin. "Now go," he said.

"Find a discrete place to hide. I'll be seeing what you see. And I can send further commands through the headset."

Necros opened the door for him, and Mephisto buzzed away.

"Come on," Fenrir commanded Necros. He led the way into the control room, where he brought up an image on one of the computer screens and laughed. "Now we'll be able to hear whatever they have to say to each other about where they came from and what they plan to do."

Necros watched the image zooming through the church, until it finally came to rest high above the prisoners. Fenrir hit a button, and the camera zoomed in.

30
A Spell of Deception

The blue jay landed on the doorstep of the old church after little time at all. Kazkal dismounted with all speed and sighed, relieved to be on terra firma once more. Malík was much slower to dismount, not having found the journey harrowing in the least. When his feet were on the ground, he patted the bird on the head with a chuckle. "Thank you, my friend. You have saved us much more than you can know. Wait here for us."

Kazkal rubbed his head. "Quite a useful trick, Malík. Now if only this rescue mission will go as smoothly."

"Of that, I have every doubt," Malík replied.

"How comforting." Kazkal eyed the crack in the wall. "Well, let's get going then."

"Wait, Kazkal!" Malík implored the warrior.

Kazkal rolled his eyes. "Oh, what now?"

"We can't go in there like this. It would put our tribe in danger. He was my own student, and you, though a child when he last saw you, have grown to resemble your father far too much. If Fenrir saw us, he would know that Tribe Qadash still lived. We would put our people in mortal danger."

"So what do you suggest, shaman?" Kazkal asked, conceding the point.

The jewel in Malík's staff lit up. "Disguises of course." He zapped Kazkal quickly.

The warrior stood back, surprised by the darkness of his skin. He pulled a strand of hair before his eyes, seeing that it had gone from fair blonde to pitch black. He felt his face. The broadness of his chin was gone, replaced by a much narrower one. "I wook wike …" he began to say in a very squeaky voice. "Ahh!" he squealed. "What's wong wif me? What have you done to my voice! I sound wike a wittwe peezwizz!"

Malík laughed more than he knew was appropriate, but quickly regained his composure. "Er … sorry, son of Kinto. This sort of magic isn't my strong point. I've never been fond of deception spells." He saw by the glare on Kazkal's narrow, dark face, that the warrior was less than willing to be understanding. "Oh, all right. Let me try and fix it."

Kazkal raised a finger. "Just be suwe not to make it any wowse, you damn owe shaman!" he squeaked.

"Oh, pish posh! You do fret too much." Malík zapped him again. "There, see if that's better. Oh, wait!" He zapped Kazkal's face, widening his nose and mouth. He studied him some more. "Now stop grinning like that. It's creepy."

"I can't" Kazkal boomed in an incredibly deep voice. His eyes glinted, adding genuineness to his mad looking grin, as he heard the new voice. It was still strange, but at least he didn't sound like a peezwizz anymore. "Now that ith bettew." He stopped at the sound of the words. "What! I thound even wowth! You exthpanded my tongue! And I'm thtiw talking wike a peethwith! Damn youw gnawwed thtaff, thaman! Thith bettew be tempowawy!"

"Oh … just don't talk to anyone!" Malík turned uncomfortably away from the strange countenance of Kazkal then. "Now for me," he said, zapping himself with the staff. He turned back around and asked, "How do I look?"

Kazkal studied the shaman's bright red hair and corpse-like, gray, flaking skin, the dust and cob webs covering his cloak, big, pointy hat—and he chuckled through the wide grin he couldn't conceal, as drool started to drip from his unclosable mouth. "Vewy nithe. I'd dawe thay pewfect."

"Really? You're not just saying that?" Malík asked, uncertain.

"No. Weawy. You wook fabuwouthe. I'd nevew know it wath you. That'th fow thuwe."

"Really, Kazkal. Don't talk. It's freaky. Now let's get going." Malík led the way into the crack in the wall. "I hope this leads us somewhere. It's unlikely our lad opened the front doors."

"I espethiawy wike the hat. It'th vewy pointy," Kazkal added, following the shaman in.

"I mean it, Kazkal. Stop talking," the shaman pleaded.

"You didn't even change you'we voithe," Kazkal muttered into the darkness.

"Well then, I just won't talk either."

"That'th good. Make a nithe change."

"Be *quiet!*"

"Thowy."

The pair moved into the darkness, following the fragile thread of hope.

31
The Escape

"Dude! I'm not gonna die here!" Pete stood up and crossed his arms defiantly in the cage.

Ak'ten looked up, his concentration broken. "Neither am I, Pete. I was just trying to think of how to do something."

"How to do what? Bend the bars and step through to freedom?"

"Yes," Ak'ten answered with a small grin.

Pete leaned down. "Dude! Can you do that?"

Ak'ten shrugged. "I don't know. But there is a way. Shaman's powers come from the spirit realm. We channel energy. The key to all magic is focus. Singleness of mind. The staff of a shaman is only a tool. A focal point. There are ways to do magic without a staff. Without even charms like fairy powder. But only the greatest shamans have mastered it. I'm not supposed to be able to learn that sort of thing until I'm declared a shaman four years from now, but when Malík's not around, I sometimes get into his books." He regarded Pete thoughtfully, wondering if Techgnomes even had things like that. "A book is like a bunch of scrolls all bound together … with … pages … um …" How could he explain?

"Dude! I know what a book is! I just hate them is all."

"You hate books?"

"Well," Pete reconsidered. "Not so much. Just reading them."

"Oh." Ak'ten was amazed.

In his control room, Fenrir's eyes had gone wide with feelings too powerful to tame. *Malík*. The boy had said *Malík*.

No longer able to take it, Necros asked, "Master … are you all right? Should we do something to prevent their escape?" He noticed the wobble of the camera. "Mephisto seems antsy. Should he reveal himself?"

Fenrir spoke quietly. "Did that lad just say *Malík*?"

Necros started, as he let the words play back in his mind. "Yes, I believe he did. I can't believe I missed it. I was just too caught up in the idea that they plan to escape."

Fenrir waved it off. "They can't get out the way that they plan. This apprentice isn't far enough along. Surely he hasn't even fashioned a staff yet. So how could he do anything so advanced as bend the bars without one? We don't need to worry." He hit a button and spoke into the microphone on his headset. "Hold your position, Mephisto. They aren't going anywhere."

He turned, staring right through Necros as though he weren't there at all, a wild look in his glassy, brown eyes. "If Malík still lives, then so does Tribe Qadash!"

Necros put a hand on his master's shoulder, trying to bring him out of it. "Master, I beg you not to jump to conclusions. The lad may have referred to a different Malík. It's not as if your master were the only gnome ever to bear that name."

Fenrir seemed to finally notice Necros. "Yes, but a *shaman* named Malík? A shaman in *this* area! What are the chances?"

"Slim, I admit. But again, what are the chances of surviving a shamans' duel that one has lost?" Necros said pointedly.

"A good point. Unless, of course, one throws the contest in order to shake his adversary off of his trail. He might have faked it. His defeat, his destruction. *Everything.* If so, how arrogant I was to think I'd defeated my own great master so easily."

"They're talking again," Necros cut in.

"Turn it up," Fenrir commanded.

"... But just because you read a book doesn't mean you can do everything it says, dude!" Pete argued. "We can't just sit here, while you concentrate like you have to let out a huge turd, and wait for Fenrir to come back and kill us!"

Ak'ten opened his eyes. "Do you have a better idea?"

Pete looked at the fairy in her jar. "No," he said somberly. "I guess not. I just want there to be another way."

"There is something," Ak'ten offered. "My master and Kazkal No'tall, the greatest warrior of our tribe, are looking for me. Malík told me in a dream."

"A *dream*? Dude, you do know dreams aren't real …"

Ak'ten looked at Pete as though he were the most ignorant gnome he'd ever engaged in conversation. "Shamans can travel the Dream Lands."

"For real? Kick ass! Can you come and find me in my dreams?"

Ak'ten considered, then said rather uncertainly, as he shrugged, "I think so. I've never really tried it before."

"Cool, dude. That is *sweet*!"

"Kazkal *No'tall*," Fenrir was crazed with excitement. "That settles it!"

"How do you mean?"

"No'tall was the clan name of our greatest warriors in Tribe Qadash. I defeated Meso No'tall and slew his son Kinto on the battlefield a decade and a half ago! And Kinto had a son!" He sobered then, abruptly. "Malík *will* find us, Necros. He's already found us. The lad has to have shown him in the Dream Realm."

"If this shaman is as powerful as you say, perhaps we should go into hiding, kill the apprentice so he can make no further contact …"

"No," Fenrir said wildly. "We will stay and see him for ourselves. If Malík lives still, I will turn it to my advantage. Tribe Qadash *must* die! Don't you understand? They have the book! That book could create terrible adversity where our mission to find the Devil's Pearl is concerned. If someone else gets to it first … No. We will stay, and if need be, I will engage him once again."

"Master …"

"No. It is my will."

Necros bowed solemnly. "Your will be done, Lord Fenrir."

Ak'ten focused. He tried to see the smallest fibers of the bars with his mind. Tried to feel them. To change them. He drifted. He found his center, the magic within him. Life magic. He tried to aim it at the bars with his will alone. Eyes still closed, he held out his arm, sweat glistening on his face. Pete watched in absolute silence.

"My Lord!" Necros called. "His hand!"

Fenrir glared at the screen. "How interesting. Perhaps there's more to this apprentice than we thought."

***

Ak'ten opened his eyes and began to breathe heavily, wiping the sweat from his brow. He looked over to Pete, noticing the other gnome's stunned appearance. "What? Did it work?"

"I don't know, dude, but you're hand glowed. I've never seen any gnome do *that* before."

Ak'ten stood, shakily. "That took a lot out of me. I should recover quickly though. I just have to find my center again." He walked over to the bars. They didn't look any different. He reached out, touched one. He wrapped a fist around it and pulled. It gave, bending like rubber in his hand. Ak'ten smiled at Pete, then he bent the bar some more and stepped through to the other side. "Come on, Pete! What are you waiting for?"

Pete bent two bars aside. "Whoa! Once again, magic kicks serious ass!" He stepped through with a bounce and a giggle. He noticed the fairy smiling in her jar, coughing or laughing, he couldn't quite tell.

The image on the screen was bouncing crazily. "Hold, Mephisto! I can't see what's happening," Fenrir commanded into the headset. The fly steadied himself then, and Fenrir saw to his astonishment that his young prisoners had indeed escaped. "Very good!" he said. "Malík has quite a powerful apprentice. Not even I could have done that at his age." He considered. "Of course, I never actually tried."

"Shall I ready the Darkgnomes?" Necros asked.

Fenrir patiently stroked his chin. "Not just yet."

"But, my lord, they're trying to rescue the fairy," Necros said, perplexed.

"Ah, so they are." Fenrir studied the screen. He noticed how agitated Necros had become, and he smiled sedately. "But this is most promising, Necros. Don't you see?"

Necros shook his head, not seeing at all. "After that display of unexpected power, surely they will succeed."

"It doesn't matter. We don't really need another one at this point. It was just a precaution. Let them take her. But don't underestimate them. They may take note if we don't give chase. Have the Darkgnomes appear to try and stop them. But feign defeat, fall back, and follow them to the secret caverns of Tribe Qadash from the shadows. Have them return here to debrief, once that's accomplished. Then we'll determine how best to slaughter them … again. This time, however, I will see *every* body!"

A very agitated buzzing filled his earpiece. "Calm down, Mephisto. We're going to let them go. Trust me. They are digging themselves a very deep grave."

The fairy managed to fly briefly within her prison, but fell. Even hope could not keep her aloft for long. Fairy powder was all over the base of the jar. "It's too big," Pete said, as he helped Ak'ten try once again to push it over.

"You're right," Ak'ten agreed. "We have to find another way. And fast."

Pete's eyes lit up. "I know. Squat down in front of it, facing it."

Ak'ten did.

"Now," Pete said, as he began to climb up on the other boy's shoulders, "I'll stand on your shoulders, and you stand up."

"But it still won't be high enough," Ak'ten said as he stood.

"I know, trust me," Pete said. When Ak'ten had stood to his full height, Pete could just barely reach to top of the lid with the tips of his fingers. "Now here's where it gets tough. I hope you're as strong as you look. Can't help noticing all your muscles since you Old Worlds are always naked."

"I'm not naked!" Ak'ten protested.

"Well … scantily clad then. But you get my meaning. So here's the plan. Push my feet with your hands, stretch your arms up as far as you can."

Ak'ten frowned. "I don't have *that* much muscle, Pete."

"Well, you've got more muscle than I do. Do you have a better idea?"

Ak'ten looked at the dying fairy on the other side of the glass. She reached out to him, putting her palm up against the side of the jar. "No," he said wearily. "I don't." He wriggled his fingers under Pete's feet. His nose wrinkled. "Did you step in something, Pete?"

"Huh? No. I just have nasty feet."

"Oh," Ak'ten said. "Well that's something for motivation at least." He pushed with all his might, stretching his arms and lifting Pete as high as he could. "Hurry," He grunted through gnashed teeth, feeling his arms quake. "I can't hold it …"

Pete grabbed hold of the top of the lid and pulled himself up. "Yes!" He stood atop the jar triumphant.

Ak'ten scratched his head. "Now what?"

"What?" Pete asked, not following.

"Now that you've gotten yourself up there, what do you plan to do?" Ak'ten asked slowly.

"Oh, yeah! Um …" Pete looked around. "I'm gonna topple it." He pointed behind him. "Hold the base of the jar, so it doesn't roll."

Ak'ten stretched out his arms. "I hope I can. You sort of pushed my arms to the limit. I'm not used to lifting gnomes our age." Ak'ten made his way to the base of the jar, behind Pete. There was nowhere really to grab hold. He just put his hands against the glass. The fairy winked at him and smiled, then started coughing again, bleeding powder. "Don't worry, little fairy. We're going to get you out of there."

"Here goes, Ak'ten! Ready?"

Ak'ten couldn't say more than, "Y—" before Pete grabbed hold of the top of the jar, jumping backwards and pulling the whole thing over on its side with a clunk. To Ak'ten's chagrin, it did roll a bit, but somehow the place he'd put his hands turned out to be just the right spot. He let go as soon as he felt the jar was steady and looked out around it. "Pete! Are you …?"

Pete looked around the side, dusting himself off. "Dusty up there." He grinned. "I'm fine, dude. Went just as I planned it. Now hold it steady while I unscrew the lid."

Ak'ten nodded and went back to his position. He heard the scrape of tin against glass, as Pete turned the enormous lid. He heard a fairy squeal with delight, so he ran to the other side, just as Pete was going in to get the fairy.

Pete was in awe. "Are you all right?" he asked.

The fairy blew a raspberry at him happily, then began to cry. She smiled and waved. "Pete!" she said.

Pete turned to Ak'ten, who looked nervous. "She knows me!"

Ak'ten shrugged, looking over his shoulder, then back again. "She's a fairy. They know lots of things. Now pick her up, and let's get out of here."

Pete studied the fragile creature. "I don't know how. The wings …"

"I'll show you," Ak'ten said, understanding. He passed Pete in the toppled jar and knelt down beside the wounded fairy, scooping her up gently, careful not to crush her little wings with his arms. "Now let's go," he said.

"Right," agreed Pete, and the three of them made their escape.

Fenrir spoke into his headpiece. "Mephisto, follow them." He spoke then to himself. "Whatever happens now, their efforts have been in vain." He laughed softly, as a distant roar came to his ears from another room in the building.

32
Shamans' Duel

Ak'ten and Pete ran as quickly as they could, though Ak'ten was slowed down by the exhaustion he'd been fighting since his feat with the bars and by the added weight, though slight, of the fairy in his arms. Pete did his best to stay with his friend, stopping and running nervously in place, which really looked more like bouncing, whenever he got ahead of him. "Come on, dude! We're almost there," he whispered as loudly as he could.

Ak'ten glanced suspiciously at the fly that seemed to have been trailing them. "Something isn't right. There aren't *any* Darkgnomes in our way."

"You're complaining about *that*?"

"No, I just don't trust it." Ak'ten stopped when he was right beside Pete. "Look there."

Pete turned his head. "Uh-oh." He studied the figures moving towards them in the darkness. "What do we do?"

Ak'ten looked around him, trying not to let it show that his arms were beginning to tremble from fatigue. He looked straight ahead at the approaching figures. "We go forward," he said with resolve. Glancing at the now unconscious fairy, he added grimly, "We have no choice."

Pete nodded at the figures. "We can take them. Let's move."

As the two pairs neared each other, they began to make out each other's features. The strange pair heading towards Ak'ten and Pete quickened their pace. Pete gasped as he got a good look at the shorter one's face. Was this a gnome, or something else? The thing was grinning horribly, drooling. "Ak'ten!" it boomed.

Now it was Ak'ten's turn to gasp. He and Pete froze where they were. Both of the others were visible now. The creature that had spoken was unfamiliar to him, though it had spoken his name. How had it learned his name? Had Fenrir managed to probe his mind after all? And the taller one with the pointed hat looked equally terrible—robe covered in cobwebs, skin flaking off.

Ak'ten spoke. "Who goes there?" His arms were trembling too much to hide.

The deranged-looking creature with the grin seemed to notice his weakness. "Give me the faiwy, Ak'ten," it said.

"No," Ak'ten shook his head, backing up. "Come no closer. We *will* fight you, if we must."

"Not in the thape you theem to be in, wad. I don't think tho." The menacing form moved closer.

"Don't!" Pete shouted. "You'll regret it. He bent the bars of our cage with magic from his hands! Imagine what he could do to *you*!" He smiled.

"Is this true?" the taller one asked quietly.

Ak'ten squinted his eyes. The voice was familiar. "Yes," he said. "It is true."

The figure with the pointed hat moved closer, stepping into the light a bit more. He revealed his staff. "You speak the truth. I can see that. How incredible."

"Malík?" Ak'ten asked uncertainly. "Is that …?" He looked over to the grinning demon. "How could it …?"

"Dithguitheth," the creature said. "And appawentwy, mine ith much bettew than hith."

"Yes, Ak'ten, it is us. We had to disguise ourselves. You should have known there would be consequences if ever Fenrir learned that we still exist."

"But he doesn't know. And we've got his fairy," Ak'ten argued.

"We?" Malík studied the young Techgnome at Ak'ten's side. "Yes. We will deal with this once we've escaped." He turned to Kazkal. "You see? I told you we didn't need to come and rescue them." He straightened proudly. "The fairy was right."

"Bah!" Kazkal said. "It ith cointhidenth."

"Dude," Ak'ten said to Kazkal. "You're really freaky looking."

"Dude?" Kazkal asked.

"Yeah," Pete said. "And you talk like total peezwizz."

Kazkal growled.

"Oh, right," Malík said. He zapped Kazkal once again with his staff, toning down the demonic grin. "No more need for that."

"What?" Kazkal asked. "See here, Malík!" He stopped. "You fixed it! My speech is back to normal." He paused. "Wait a minute! What do you mean, 'No more need?' What was the need for *that*?"

Malík looked at the warrior, as if he should not have to ask such things. "It was *funny*," he said. "I *needed* a laugh."

"Damn you, shaman!" Kazkal crossed his arms, certain that he would *never* understand the inner workings of Malík's crazy mind.

Back in the control room, Fenrir was frantic. "Damn it! Why doesn't he stop buzzing his wings like that! He can't even *hear* me!" Fenrir was going mad, trying to prove to himself that his suspicions were true, but he couldn't hear *anything* over the speakers aside from the furious buzzing of Mephisto's wings. He tore the headset from his ears and threw it to the ground. "I must know, Necros. Change in plan. Send a small group out to confront them. At least *one* of the intruders must remain alive to lead us back to the tribe. So feel free to kill the Techgnome. But I must have time to gauge the power of this shaman. I can feel it. I just need to know if it's Malík."

"Can't you tell by looking at him?" Necros asked.

"No. That doesn't look at all like Malík. But it could be a disguise. Though Malík was never much for deception spells."

"What about his staff," Necros suggested, as he nodded towards the screen.

Fenrir looked. "No. It isn't the staff I remember. But that could be because I broke his staff in two when last we did battle. It is the finishing gesture of such a duel. I must go down there and see him for myself!"

"But, Master!" Necros all but shouted. "If this *is* your own teacher, and you were unable to defeat him before, he could destroy you now. You jeopardize the entire operation!"

Fenrir turned on Necros with a snarl. "It is my will!" He summoned his staff to him and waved it before them, opening a shadow portal and walking through, closing it behind him.

Necros shook his head with resignation. "Your will be done."

Malík led the way to the front of the church, and Ak'ten stopped, arms shaking violently. "I can't …"

Pete ran over, gently lifting the fairy out of Ak'ten's arms the way he'd been shown. "I got her, dude. Let's go."

Ak'ten nodded his appreciation. "Thank you."

Kazkal turned. "No. This heretic cannot be allowed to—"

"You're wrong about him, Kazkal!" Ak'ten snapped bitterly.

The warrior was stunned. Never before had Ak'ten seemed angry with him. There was something frightening about the set of the lad's jaw and the menacing gleam in his eyes.

Malík stopped as well, turning around. "We will discuss all of this later. For now, we simply move." His face paled, as he heard something with his shaman's ears. He looked at the door, determining whether they still had enough time. "Oh, no," he said. "Not again."

"What is it?" Kazkal asked. He looked to the shaman's apprentice, a fear dawning on him. "Damn. That's what I was afraid of."

Ak'ten had gone just as pale as his master, as the eerie, silent voices filled his magical ears. *Good blood. Good blood. Tainted* … "Arachnis!"

Kazkal reached for the axe on his back, but was stopped by a gentle strike from Malík's staff. "No, Kazkal. You must not reveal the No'tall Battleaxe. It would be recognized by our enemy."

Kazkal nodded, then reached for the sword at his belt. "I was trained with the sword anyway." He unsheathed the beautifully decorated silver and gold sword and saw Pete admiring it. In spite of the fact that it was a Techgnome admiring the blade, Kazkal couldn't help but smile appreciatively. His uncle Jenjo, named for a cousin who had fallen in battle just before his birth, had not taken the path of the warrior, but was no less valuable to the defense of the tribe, having become a master swordsmith. When Kazkal made the choice to follow the path of the warrior, his uncle had fashioned him the most beautiful sword he could imagine, for Kazkal had grown to replace Jenjo's much beloved brother Kinto. Kazkal couldn't help thinking how fitting it would be to slay Fenrir, the murderer of Kinto, with this sword fashioned in his memory. The honor of the kill would be with both Kazkal and his uncle.

"We mustn't think on vengeance this day, son of Kinto," Malík said, having picked up on the warrior's thoughts. "We must get out as discretely as possible and live to fight another day."

Kazkal gritted his teeth. "All warriors must answer the call of Nubus."

"Yes. And today is not your day, my friend," Malík said affectionately.

Kazkal shook his head. "Exactly. For Fenrir was a warrior too. A warrior who has yet to answer the call of Nubus."

"What's the call of Nubus?" Pete whispered to Ak'ten.

"Death," Ak'ten answered simply. "It is a warrior's death, when the Red God Nubus calls him home in battle."

"Oh," Pete said, just as something very large pounced on him and knocked him to the ground. The fairy was launched out of his arms. "No!" he shouted, as the thing held him to the ground.

Malík called out, as he blasted the great spider atop the Techgnome youth with his staff. "Ka— The fairy!"

Kazkal ran with all speed and caught the fairy just before she hit the ground, dropping his sword to make it possible.

Ak'ten ran to help Pete up and, as he knelt down, found himself looking directly into the eyes of a great spider.

Good Blood … Tainted blood … Good blood …

Why were these monsters having such conflicting thoughts? He felt sure that none of his friends had tainted blood. Then he saw the Darkgnome rider mounted on the great arachnid, and he felt he understood. The Darkgnomes all had tainted blood, and the spiders picked up on that, differentiating between riders and victims.

The rider grinned at Ak'ten hatefully, and the spider leapt. Ak'ten closed his eyes and braced himself, only to hear the creature land behind him. He opened his eyes and turned to see it had leapt over him and gone for Kazkal, landing just in front of the warrior. He saw Kazkal's sword on the ground. "Oh, no!"

Pete sat bolt upright. "His sword! The fairy!"

Ak'ten nodded. "I know!" He called to his master. "Ma—" He realized the folly in using names at this point. "Master! The warrior!" He pointed, and Malík followed, seeing Kazkal's predicament, as the spider crept slowly closer, twitching its horrific black fangs in anticipation.

Good Blood.

Malík nodded and pointed his staff, just before another great spider leapt upon him from behind.

"No!" Ak'ten shouted. With dread, he saw the other spider leap onto Kazkal, knocking him down. The fairy skidded across the floor, and another spider and rider came creeping from the shadows after her. *What have I done*? Ak'ten thought frantically. *This can't be the way it goes! They can't all die because of me!*

Suddenly, Pete was on his feet. The younger gnome ran out into the middle of things, snatched up Kazkal's sword, swooning slightly, due to its unexpected weight. He then made his way to the fairy.

Ak'ten made to follow him, unsure what to do. He had no weapon, and he was so tired from all he'd done before. He ran to Pete's side. The spider clicked its fangs hungrily. The rider on its back grinned with malice. "Give me the sword," Ak'ten said. "Go and get the fairy."

Pete nodded slowly, feeling a fear much colder than he'd previously thought possible, and handed the sword to Ak'ten. The pair of them backed up slowly. Ak'ten stayed right in front of Pete, covering him, listening to the spider's thoughts. *Tainted blood … good blood … sweet blood.* "Come no closer," Ak'ten warned. "I will slay you *and* your pet."

The rider put his heal in the spider's side, and it went into a springing position. "We'll see about that, lad." The spider leapt suddenly, landing on the other side of Ak'ten. The rider looked confused, since he'd expected his beast to go right for the shaman's apprentice. He snarled at the spider. "You're not afraid of him just 'cause he's got a sword, are you?" He gritted his teeth, eyeing Pete and the wounded fairy now securely in his arms. He kicked the spider with both heels.

The fairy woke up then and wiggled her fingers tiredly. "Good blood, sweet blood. Bread crumbs. Cummerbunds." She giggled and hiccupped, then winked and fell asleep.

The spider suddenly bucked and threw his rider across the floor. It began twitching as flowers sprouted from its body, killing it instantly.

Malík, meanwhile, had managed to zap the spider that was attacking him. It had caught fire and was writhing in agony as it shriveled and died. The rider was rolling along the ground, trying to put out the flames on his clothes.

Kazkal had not fared so well. He was growling in fear and disgust, holding onto the spider's very fangs with his fists. The rider kicked the spider harder and harder.

Ak'ten ran to the scene, slashing the spider across its backside. The spider jumped and turned on Ak'ten, stunned by the sudden pain. Kazkal took advantage of the moment to run to Ak'ten's side and grab the sword from him. He then sank the blade without preamble into the spider's head. He pulled it out with a victorious yell, and strode right up to the rider, who removed a large dagger from his belt and blocked Kazkal's blow. Kazkal moved the Darkgnome back, keeping him on the defensive. Finally, he found an opening and slashed the villain across the chest. He then lifted up his leg and kicked him to the ground, holding his sword at the ready, warning him not to make any sudden moves.

"Enough," came a very loud voice from the giant banister half way across the room. Suddenly, Kazkal found himself in a bubble, floating up off the ground, hovering slightly. He stabbed at the bubble with his sword, managing only to stretch it out. He knew the No'tall Battleaxe would make short work of the magical trap, but would also reveal them, for he recognized the villain looking down at them all.

Ak'ten was also trapped in a hovering bubble, pushing against it to no avail. He looked over at Pete and the fairy, in their bubble. Pete gestured towards Malík. Ak'ten looked and saw that the shaman had not been imprisoned.

Malík stared at the figure atop the banister, a sea of emotions flooding him all at once. Standing there, smugly surveying them all, was the enemy. A gnome he'd raised from infancy and taught everything he could. The gnome who'd tried to kill him and all of Tribe Qadash so many years ago. And yet he dared not say the name aloud. *Fenrir.*

The Dark Prince chuckled. "Greetings, shaman. I see you've come to collect your apprentice. His skills are quite impressive. You must be proud."

Malík only nodded.

Fenrir went on. "Tell me, shaman, what tribe do you serve?" Fenrir knew how Malík was loath to tell a lie.

The shaman did his best to disguise his own voice, knowing that silence would give too much away. He must not reveal how much he had to hide. "I am not a fool, sir. The Darkgnomes are powerful, and my apprentice is reckless and brave; a deadly combination." He glared at Ak'ten, as the young gnome winced inside his bubble at the remark. "I have no desire to make an enemy of your kind for myself, for my apprentice, or for my tribe. So they shall remain nameless, in case you would do them harm on our account."

Fenrir nodded, smiled. He would reveal Malík somehow. He knew the old gnome well; knew where the line would be drawn. "Very well then, master shaman. I understand." He stroked the head of his cobra staff as though it were a cherished pet. "I too was once trained in the ways of the shamans. I found them wanting, but I know how much you must value your tribe and your apprentice. I will let you go, unharmed. I will take you at your word, provided you do one simple thing for me." He offered Malík his most sinister grin. "Leave the fairy behind. She's our prisoner by right."

Malík hesitated, knowing he could do no such thing. His hopes for a peaceful resolution were undone. He glanced at his companions in their bubbles. He couldn't save them if he were destroyed. There was a reason he'd been left alone, while they'd been captured. Fenrir was suspicious. He turned to the prince, shaking his head. "I will not do this. I will fight you, if I must." He questioned his opponent. "Have you ever fought a shaman before? Do you know the potential destruction I could unleash? Surely you must. And I doubt you've kept in practice yourself, having found us wanting. I suggest you let us go. It would be to your own advantage as much as to ours."

Fenrir shook his head. "I think not. I would like to see you try. I challenge you to a shamans' duel."

Ak'ten gasped in his bubble. He had never actually seen such a duel, but he'd heard stories. He knew Malík had been in duels before; had even dueled Fenrir and faked his own demise. What would be the outcome now? There was little room for Malík to create a deception without leaving the rest of them behind. He would have to fight Fenrir for real. Ak'ten wondered fearfully if his old master were still up to the challenge. The realization froze his soul. Malík may still die, because of him.

"I accept," Malík said. "What are the terms? To first blood, or to unconsciousness?"

"To death," Fenrir answered smugly. "I am no coward. I destroyed my own master long ago." He played the part. "You remind me of him, in a way, actually."

Malík surprised Ak'ten then by not hesitating at all. "To the death then." He tapped his staff on the ground, forming a magical energy disk beneath his feet. The disk lifted him off the ground and carried him towards Fenrir. He landed on the banister, then let the disk disappear.

Pete rolled his bubble, hamster-style, over to Ak'ten's bubble. "Ak'ten!" he shouted, but it was clear the sound was contained. He pushed his bubble right up against Ak'ten's and heard a strange, sucking sound, as the bubbles merged. "Freaky!"

"Pete!" Ak'ten was amazed. "How did you know that would happen?"

Pete shrugged. "I didn't, dude. So what's going on? I could hear them, but I guess sound only travels through these things one way. What's a shamans' duel?"

"It's not good. It's the sort of fight where each shaman uses his full power to try and destroy the other. Malík has already surprised me. I've never seen that disk trick."

"Do you think he'll win?" Pete asked hopefully.

Ak'ten considered. "I don't know, Pete. I can only hope the gods are still with him. But I can't help thinking of the prophesy."

"What prophesy?"

"There was a gnome who was to be born that would grow to be the only gnome who could defeat Fenrir."

"So, was he born?"

Ak'ten shook his head sadly. "No. Fenrir learned of the prophesy and destroyed the poor hero before he ever had the chance. Tore him from his mother's womb."

"Holy crap! Then that means …"

"Malík will lose," Ak'ten finished. "He is not the one."

Suddenly, the loud, sucking sound came again, as Kazkal, having seen Pete's discovery, merged his bubble with theirs. "This does not bode well," he said. "Fear not. I will use the axe, if I must. If Malík is defeated."

Ak'ten appreciated Kazkal's words of hope, but he knew the warrior had reached the same conclusion he had. The truth was, he was willing to use his axe *when* Malík was defeated. All this battle could do was buy them time to strategize. Tears welled up in Ak'ten's eyes. He had caused the death of Malík—his master, his friend, his only real family.

Atop the banister, the two sorcerers prepared for combat. They bowed to each other, then crossed staffs. They backed away from each other then, circling like boxers, each waiting for the other to make the first move.

Fenrir struck first, lighting Malík's robes on fire with a blast from his cobra staff.

Malík knew that Fenrir was holding back. It was a setup, designed to bring his guard down. Fenrir was anticipating that Malík would take the time to douse the flames before he struck back. Fenrir was wrong. Malík leveled his staff, blasting Fenrir backwards onto the banister. Wood from the structure began

to splinter, reaching up, growing over the fallen prince, pulling him into the banister itself.

Fenrir yelped, surprised by the move, as Malík at last doused the flames on his robes. Fenrir squeezed his staff, covering himself in a red glow that rent the wood, forcing it to release him. He then caused the wood to quickly form into arrows, and he launched them magically at Malík.

Malík blocked the arrows, creating a shield of light.

Fenrir wasted no time then, changing the wood beneath his old master's feet into tar.

Malík sank to his knees, before the tar gave out and he fell to the ground beneath the banister.

Fenrir leapt after him, zapping the ground beside the mass of tar that now held Malík tightly.

A hungry Venus flytrap sprouted in the spot, just as Malík managed to turn the tar into feathers and send them flying towards Fenrir, blocking him from view. The carnivorous plant snapped at Malík's staff.

Malík smacked it in the head with the business end of his staff, turning it to ash. He blew the ashes, and they dissipated.

Fenrir, meanwhile, waved his staff within the feathers, converting the loose swarm into a single, feathered serpent.

The serpent charged at Malík, who removed the ground from beneath it, sending it deep beneath the church.

Fenrir tapped his staff on the ground, changing Malík's clothes into ants.

Malík tapped his staff three times, restoring his own clothes and turning Fenrir's clothes to ice. He then sent a power blast right towards Fenrir's staff hand, knocking the weapon from his grasp. This was the main objective in a shamans' duel: to disarm one's opponent.

Fenrir smiled, as Malík came towards him in victory.

The old shaman caught the gleam in his former apprentice's eye only a moment too late. He turned to see the snake, now sporting a pair of feathered wings, just before it struck, swallowing him whole.

The cobra staff flew back into Fenrir's hand, and he restored his clothes. He watched the snake, anticipating. "Come on, you old fool. I know you're still in the game."

Ak'ten's heart sank in his chest. A heartbeat later, he was raging, pushing against the bubble with all his strength. He turned in exasperation to Kazkal. "Use the axe! Use it now!"

"No, wait!" Kazkal pointed.

The winged snake reared up, changing into a miniature tornado, Malík riding atop it.

Fenrir clung to his staff, as the winds pulled him in violently. "All right! No more parlor tricks!" His staff glowed, killing the winds. He then blasted Malík with pure power from his staff.

Malík parried the blow with his own staff, as he fell to the ground, and sent an equal burst of energy at Fenrir, who did likewise.

The pair traded blows several more times, before Fenrir raged, "This is getting us nowhere!" He then blasted Malík with a ray made not of magical light, but of thorns.

Malík quickly held up his staff, changing the course and makeup of the blow, sending a pillar of roaring fire right at Fenrir, who screamed horribly, as the pillar approached him.

Suddenly, the fire went out, leaving naught but smoke. Fenrir was nowhere to be seen.

Malík studied the ground. "No. You can't be defeated that easily."

A shout from behind distracted him. "We're free! You did it!"

The shaman turned to see his apprentice and the others having hit the ground. A sign that a sorcerer had been destroyed was that all his spells began to fail. Malík turned back to the spot where he had apparently destroyed Fenrir. "Not possible," he mumbled.

He strode quickly to the others. "Come on. We must leave quickly, while we still can."

Pete was staring at Malík in awe. "You kick ass!"

"What do you mean, Malík?" Ak'ten asked. "You won! Fenrir's …" A look from his master silenced him.

"No, Ak'ten. This is a trap. But we may turn it to our advantage." He kept up his pace, leading them right to the crack in the wall through which they had all entered.

Mephisto buzzed into the control room, after the group had escaped.

Fenrir was waiting for him. He waved a hand, and Mephisto returned to his original form.

"Did you get that last bit," Mephisto asked happily.

"I certainly did," Fenrir answered. "There is no doubt."

Necros entered the room. "Master, I have given your orders, but the gnomes I chose are afraid of the shaman. They don't see the point of engaging one so powerful."

"They aren't to engage him at all. Just to follow him. He will no doubt be returning to the caverns of Tribe Qadash. I just want to know the place. Then they come back here, and we return later to annihilate them." Fenrir laughed. "Now, leave me. I want to bask in the moment."

The two gnomes bowed and left the control room. Fenrir rewound the footage just a bit, and he watched it again.

"What do you mean, Malík? You won! Fenrir's …" And then Mephisto had made his way back, as he'd been ordered to do just before the lad had uttered that magical name.

"Malík," Fenrir snarled the name, as he turned off the screen. "Crafty, old fool. I am learning from you still. You will not fool me again."

33
Journey's End

Outside of the building, Malík gave a whistle, and the blue jay flew down to meet him. Malík patted the bird on the head, then turned to regard its intended passengers. He looked at the fairy sadly. He stepped over to Pete, who was holding her, and he lifted her arm, glancing at the wound. He winced. "Get on the bird, lads."

"We're gonna ride on a bird? Kick ass!" Pete beamed.

Malík knew it was not a socially acceptable thing to let a Techgnome ride along. He looked over at Kazkal, as the young ones climbed onto the blue jay's back.

Kazkal nodded. "It is the right thing. He is brave."

Malík smiled, and the pair of them climbed onto the bird. "Try and cover her from the wind, my young friend," Malík said to Pete. "Fairies are fragile creatures and not used to traveling at such speeds."

Kazkal whispered to Malík, as their ride took to the sky. "Will the fairy survive?"

Malík caught Ak'ten trying to listen casually. He took the lad's feelings into account, when he answered, "There is always hope." However, the sorrow in Malík's eyes told Kazkal what the shaman really thought.

Back at Fenrir's fortress, Necros entered the Dark Prince's chamber. "Forgive the interruption, master."

Fenrir regarded him coldly. "That all depends. Surely they don't have the location already?"

"No, my lord. But I think it's time," Necros said with a smile.

"Time?" Suddenly Fenrir understood. "Time! Excellent." He made his way quickly from the room and traveled the corridors until he arrived at the prisoner's cell. He peered through the small, barred window. There she was, fat beyond all reason. Her skin was stretched out, deep dark purple. Her hair was black and stringy, eyes glazed and creamy, canines sharp like the teeth of a gremlin. She roared monstrously at the sight of him. "Yes," he said. "That's my girl. Are you ready to pop?"

The dark fairy roared again. No laughter. No gleam in her dead-looking eyes. She began to quiver violently, growling like an animal. Then it happened. The fairy burst.

Fenrir was laughing joyously when Necros came up behind him. He grabbed the other gnome's shoulder and smiled. "Victory!"

Necros looked in through the window and let himself smile along with his master. The little, dark fairy had recovered. She was slight, eyes black, a severe look on her harsh purple face. She was terrifying. And she flew around a great mound of distinctly purple fairy powder. Dark fairy powder.

Malík landed the blue jay at the edge of the forest, where he'd found Ak'ten with Pete, he now knew, all those years before. "Why are we landing?" Ak'ten asked.

"Because," Malík answered, climbing from the bird, "this is where we must part ways."

The others climbed off of the bird behind him. Malík tapped his staff on the ground, removing his and Kazkal's disguises. "Whoa!" Pete said. "Y'all look way better this way. But, I was getting used to you the other way." He wanted to scratch his head, but remembered the fairy in his arms. He looked at her. "We have to get her home."

"*We* will," Malík said pointedly. "You, on the other hand, must return to your own world."

"But …" Pete started.

"You are a brave gnome," Kazkal offered. "But this is the way of things."

Ak'ten went over to Pete, put a hand on his shoulder, looking him in the eyes affectionately. He glanced down at the fairy. Her whole body suddenly blinked, fading out, then back again. He looked to his teacher. "Malík! What's wrong with her?"

Malík looked very sad. He knew he had to tell them the truth. "She is dying, Ak'ten. I'm afraid we were too late to save her."

"No!" Ak'ten shouted. "She'll be all right."

"We just have to get her home!" Pete said, and he immediately ran for the forest, followed by Ak'ten.

Malík rolled his eyes. "Oh, gods."

Kazkal shook his head. "They are brave, but still have wisdom to gain. Shall we go after them?"

"We must," Malík said. "We've been followed."

"Followed?" Kazkal asked. "How?" He looked into the distance and saw the crow land. Several gnomes climbed from it. He counted four. "Right." He wasted no more time, as he followed the young gnomes into the wood, Malík right behind him.

Pete had stopped when they found him. "Where do we take her?" She flickered again in his arms.

"What's wrong?" Ak'ten asked, noticing the serious look on Kazkal's face.

"Darkgnomes," Kazkal answered grimly. His warrior senses kicked in, ears alert to every sound around them. "Get down," he shouted to Malík as he spun around, hurling his giant axe ahead of him.

A loud thud and a cry of pain followed, and a Darkgnome wandered out of the brush, the No'tall Battleaxe buried in his chest. He fell very quickly to his death.

Three more Darkgnomes sprang forth then. One of them spoke hatefully. "We were only supposed to follow you! But this changes everything, Kazkal, Clan No'tall!"

Kazkal squinted, finally recognizing the Darkgnome as a warrior from another tribe who'd vanished years before. Only now he was adorned in the standard black attire of the Darkgnomes, and his skin was as ghostly pale as a living gnome could manage. "Riven Torn! It is an evil day indeed when a warrior joins the heretics' way! Aside from your leader, I thought the Darkgnomes were only for Techs!"

Riven laughed. "You know nothing, barbarian. And today, you will meet Nubus face to face!"

"The gods alone know my fate," Kazkal said, drawing his sword.

Riven also drew a sword, while the other two Darkgnomes drew ferocious daggers. Riven's sword met Kazkal's, and the two of them began to duel.

One of the Darkgnomes glared at Malík and cocked his arm to throw the dagger in his hand, but Malík blasted him with an intense, laser-like beam of power from his staff, right through the heart. The Darkgnome looked surprised. He met the eyes of his companion, then fell to the ground dead, smoke still issuing from his tiny but deadly wound.

The remaining Darkgnome snarled at Malík, dropping his blade to the ground and preparing to do some magical thing, but was suddenly snatched up by a passing bird, crushed in its beak, and swallowed whole. The bird circled above, apparently surveying the scene.

Kazkal, meanwhile, had gained the upper hand. "You're out of practice, Riven. The Techgnome ways have softened you. You are weak."

Riven snarled and growled, pulling his sword up and trying to get at Kazkal's side.

Kazkal, however, was not at all out of practice. He swung around quickly, sinking his blade into Riven's abdomen, then pulling it out roughly. "It is you who will be meeting Nubus this day, Darkgnome. Perhaps if you beg him for mercy, he will forgive you for abandoning him."

Riven fell, holding his wound, looking furiously at Kazkal.

"I'm sorry that we cannot risk your escape." Kazkal kicked the Darkgnome down on his back and prepared to quickly slit his throat.

"Wait!" Riven grunted.

Kazkal hesitated with a sneer. "What?" He practically spat the question.

"I was a hero once, you know this. I didn't want things to go this way, but now I cannot go home to Tribe Nebu-Ki, or seek shelter with my mother's people in Tribe Riven."

"You seemed rather zealous only a moment before, when you strove to kill me. Why should I hear your plea?" Kazkal asked skeptically.

"Because," Riven gripped his wound tightly. "In all the years that I've been allied with the Darkgnomes, I never betrayed my warrior's oath to protect your tribe from Fenrir. He never learned from my lips that Tribe Qadash still lived. I may have gone to the Darkgnomes, son of Kinto, but I took my honor with me. Now, if I return, my great master will destroy me, for I have failed him irredeemably. I beg you for my life, noble Kazkal, that I may one day make myself useful again … to someone. And I ask you to keep my secret, as I've kept yours. A warriors' pact." He winced, as he removed a blood drenched hand from his abdomen, offering it to his victor.

Kazkal was torn. What was the right thing to do? If he made this pact, Riven may yet betray him. However, if he killed the Darkgnome, he may be destroying a gnome of honor, who may, as he'd suggested, become useful in the future. Kazkal thought hard, staring at the trembling hand before him, watching the crimson blood run down Riven's arm. A pact had long existed between the three tribes in the Gremlin Territories. None would speak of the existence of Tribe Qadash in their midst to outsiders. Not only was this a matter of honor, but of prudence. For, if the Dark Prince had come for Tribe Qadash, then Tribe Nebu-Ki and Tribe Riven were sworn to come to their aid, and would be wiped out right beside them. Ending this protection for Qadash would have brought Riven Torn great rewards with his dark prince, yet he had remained silent for years. Now, it seemed clear, he could no longer return to the Darkgnomes anyway. Kazkal weighed safety against honor in his mind, wishing he had his magical axe in hand to show him whether or not this was an innocent gnome.

At last, he decided.

"Thank you, Kazkal," Riven breathed quietly, as the other warrior's hand gripped his. "Our pact is sealed in my own blood. I will remember you, whatever becomes of me after this day. Even if only Nubus awaits my testimony."

Kazkal released his grip and readied his sword. "Now help me, Riven. Cry out, as my sword passes by you, and lie as dead until we are gone."

Riven nodded, and Kazkal swung the sword, making it seem as though he'd slit his enemy's throat.

"Kick ass!" Pete shouted, as he watched from a distance.

"Yeah!" Ak'ten chimed in.

"There's that awesome bird!" Pete pointed, as the bird came in for a landing. His jaw hit the ground when he saw his mother climbing from its back. "Mom!?!? What the hell?"

Suddenly the fairy began flickering much more rapidly.

"The fairy!" Pete ran a bit farther into the forest. "Where do you live?" He saw a large group of fairies, flying around the large mass of flowers that, unbeknownst to him, kept safe a molting mud troll. "Help!" he shouted.

Ak'ten came running behind him. "Pete! Lay her down! Maybe they can help her."

The fairies flew over, as Ak'ten and Pete kneeled down beside the fairy. "Ti-ta," they chanted, as they wept quietly and laughed aloud, holding their faces.

The fairy looked at Pete and smiled. "And then …" said the fairy. She began to simply fade.

Tears were streaming down Ak'ten's face, as he put a hand on Pete's shoulder.

"No! You can't die! We *saved* you!" Pete began clapping his hands violently. "I do believe in fairies! I do! I do!" It had worked in *Peter Pan.* Surely, if fairies were real, it would work for him as well.

The fairy giggled and reached for him. "Pete." It was barely a whisper. Then she vanished before his eyes and did not flicker back again.

Pete lost control of his tears then. "No! Clap, Ak'ten! Clap! That's how you bring back fairies from the dead!"

Another hand touched his shoulder then, and both young gnomes turned around.

Resna smiled down at her son. "No, Pete. That's the end of it. I'm afraid life doesn't work the same as fairy tales." A tear rolled down her own cheek.

"But we … we *saved* her, Mom." Pete was desperate. He looked down at the ground where she'd lain. "We saved her."

"I know, Pete. You saved her from dying away from her home. You saved her, whether she lived or not." Pete hugged her, still weeping. She held him to her and looked at Ak'ten with a little grin of not-at-all-surprised, as she studied his Old World attire.

Ak'ten backed up, ashamed of his deception, wiping the tears from his eyes. He turned and saw Malík standing right behind him. "We failed her, Malík. We failed."

Malík put a hand on Ak'ten's head, mussing his long, black hair. "No, lad. It's like the Techgnome says. You saved her just as surely as you brought her home. But there's a lesson to be gained."

"Must there always be, Malík?" Ak'ten sniffed.

"Yes, Ak'ten. There must. There is no such thing as failure, so long as we find the lesson. And this one is, despite our best intentions, even victory does not always take the form we'd like it to."

Ak'ten looked down, saying nothing at all, feeling there had been a slight reprimand in his master's voice.

Malík looked to Pete's mother. The female was a puzzle. A Techgnome who could ride a bird. He studied her face. "There's something familiar about you," he said at last. "Have we—?"

"No," Resna cut him off sharply, as she placed Pete's cap on his head. "That's not possible. I do not consort with pagans."

Pete backed away, looking at his mother with hurt in his eyes. There had been a slight reprimand for him in her voice, even though she was speaking to Malík.

Malík looked at Ak'ten, as he answered her. "And we do *not* consort with heretics." He looked at Resna then. "A tragedy has just barely been avoided this day, because of the impulsiveness of these two lads. A tragedy which would never have been a threat, had they not taken off on their own."

"But, Malík," Ak'ten pleaded. "We were just trying to save her."

Kazkal broke in, as he cleaned the blood from his axe with a leaf. "Yes, and save her you did. You are *very* brave, Ak'ten. But bravery must be tempered with wisdom, or it is of no use to anyone."

"Pete," Resna said. "Say goodbye to your friend."

Pete looked to his mother, then over at Ak'ten, and he smiled. The smile was contagious.

Ak'ten met Pete half way.

Pete held out his hand, and Ak'ten took it. "Goodbye, Ak'ten."

"Goodbye, Pete."

Both young gnomes had a gleam in their eyes that said this was not goodbye at all. Just a show for the adults. They'd been through too much together ever to forget the friendship they had forged. They had bonded strongly and knew their mischievous natures would bring them both back to the edge of the forest, where adventure would be waiting.

Pete walked back to his mother, and Ak'ten to Malík. They waved at each other one last time, as they were each ushered off towards their different homes.

As they walked home through the crisp, mowed grass of the human world, Pete asked his mother, "Are you gonna tell Dad?"

"Yes," Resna answered. "I'm afraid I must. He's going to want a very good explanation as to why his car is sitting in the sewer, and to where his only son has *been* for all this time."

Pete perked up excitedly. "Are you gonna tell him about the fairy? Are you gonna tell him about how you swooped down on that kick-ass bird and killed that Darkgnome?"

"What?" she said. "Pete, you have the most insane imagination. Such an exaggerator."

Pete was unfazed. "How in the hell did you learn to ride birds anyway? Didn't that fairy freak you out? Or did you think it was an alien? Come on! How did you do it?"

Resna rolled her eyes, unable to fight the smile that was forming in response to her son's admiration. "I read a lot of books, Pete."

"Well how the hell come you don't ever read *those* books to me?"

"Maybe you should read them yourself, Pete," Resna suggested with a grin.

"Um … no. What's for dinner?" Pete said, as he grabbed her by the shoulder and quickly led her home.

34
Defeated and Victorious

That night, at the Darkgnome headquarters, Fenrir was pacing in his study, fondling the pouch in his hand, savoring the victory of acquiring yet another key, but still considering the failure of his Darkgnomes to track the Qadash gnomes home. His one-eyed crow had returned without passengers. That was all the evidence he needed. They'd been put to death.

His shadow stopped moving in sync with his body, and he spoke to it. "Hello, Belial."

Your Darkgnomes have failed you, Fenrir.

Fenrir tensed. How could Belial have known about that?

I met them in … passing. They'd been slain by warriors from the Qadash tribe.

"Yes," Fenrir admitted. "It seems Malík somehow managed to fool us. He survived. They've had fifteen years to recover. That's not much time, if you think about it. I will find them again. I will see every body with my own eyes. You can watch me as I break Malík's staff and impale him with it."

You are arrogant, Fenrir. Why should I trust you still?

"Because of my latest victory, of course."

Ah … the pouch …

"Yes. I figured you knew that already. I suppose you were just testing me to see if I'd let you know. Did I pass?"

The shadow cackled. *Of course, my poppet, as always. Keep up the good work.* Then, just as quickly as he had come, Belial was gone once more, leaving Fenrir his shadow.

Necros knocked on the door. "Master, may I enter?"

"Come, Necros. I believe I already know what news you will bring," Fenrir said.

Necros entered the room, somewhat stooped and afraid. "Master, Riven and his men have failed, it appears. Your crow returned without them."

"Yes, I know. But let's not dwell on our failures, Necros." Fenrir offered his trusted number one a genuine smile. "Let us focus," he held up the pouch of dark fairy powder, "on our victories."

Necros straightened up, as he smiled and followed Fenrir to the control room.

Fenrir opened the secret compartment that held the other keys he'd acquired, and he placed the dark fairy powder beside them. "We're so close, Necros." He continued to gaze at his magical treasures. "Once I have the Devil's Pearl, no one will ever escape me again."

35
Family Secrets

Pete was in bed, but still wide awake. So he wasn't startled when the door to his room creaked open. "Hi, Mom."

Resna came in. Everything had calmed down. Scott had been very angry about the whole thing, but quietly amazed at his son's courage. She hadn't told him everything, of course, and had sent Pete to his room more to keep him from correcting her version of things than for actual punishment. They'd decided to ground him severely of course, but to Pete's relief, had opted not to kill him. The car was now home, and there was nothing wrong with it that couldn't be fixed. Even if it had been lost, however, the Davidsons would have been happy just to have Pete back in one piece.

"So did you tell Dad?" he asked.

"Yes. You know I did. I already told you."

"I know, but I mean, did you tell him the *rest*?"

"The rest? Pete, I think you're the one who needs to hear the rest."

Pete sat up. "What do you mean?"

"No one's ever told you about your uncle Zak, have they?" Resna asked.

"Yeah. He died a long time ago, before I was born. He was Dad's brother."

"Did they tell you how he died?"

"No. I just figured he was old."

Resna laughed. "Pete, he was very nearly the same age as your father. He was very young. But he went astray, got involved with the wrong sorts of gnomes, long before I met your father."

"Was he a Darkgnome?" Pete asked, not knowing what had brought the notion to his mind.

"Yes," Resna answered, actually managing to shock him.

"Are you *serious*?" Pete shouted.

"Shh!" Resna tried to quiet him. "Keep it down, Pete. I'm telling you this, so that you know why to drop the matter where your father's concerned. You ran off and got yourself captured by Darkgnomes, Pete. I don't think you left out any details, when you told me everything that happened. What you didn't know was that your uncle ran away and *joined* the

Darkgnomes. He realized all too late the mistake he had made. He was really a very good person. He betrayed them, tried to leave them. They killed him." Resna's eyes were beginning to water.

"Did you know him?" Pete asked, wondering at his mother's tears.

"Yes. I knew him. I knew him when he was trying to turn his life around. It's how I met your father. So, Pete, you must keep all the details under your hat. Your father was very upset about the Darkgnomes today. It was very hard on him losing his brother. And now, *you've* made enemies of the people who killed him as well. It's not something he wants to think about. He would die if anything ever happened to you, and this has opened up a very old wound."

"Okay, Mom," Pete said. "I promise. I won't say anything to Dad about it."

"Good." She kissed him on the forehead. "And, Pete, promise me one more thing."

"Yeah?"

"Promise me you'll never see that Ak'ten again. He's a danger to you. Old World gnomes are pagans. They believe in strange things."

"Like flying around on birds? And fairies?" Pete asked incredulously.

"Pete, promise me."

"And magic! Mom, it's for real! And it kicks some *serious* a—"

"Pete! Promise me!"

Pete smiled. "All right. I promise."

"Thanks, Pete." Resna kissed him again as she stood to leave. "I love you."

"I love you too, Mom."

Resna closed the door, and Pete uncrossed his fingers. "I promise, Mom. I promise that I won't let stupid prejudices take away my friend." He giggled, proud of his never ending cleverness. He rolled over and closed his eyes, thinking about the next time he would meet Ak'ten, as he fell asleep. Then he was dreaming of the adventures they would have.

36
A Time for Dreams

Ak'ten finished telling Malík all that had happened in the dim glow of the candlelight. He noticed the stoic expression on his master's face. "What troubles you, Malík?"

"What *troubles* me? You never cease to amaze me, lad. I am troubled by a great many things. I believe that Fenrir figured us out, or else he wouldn't have had us followed. He allowed us to escape, Ak'ten. He feigned his defeat, just as surely as I once feigned mine with him. After all, the prophesy was quite specific. And the child of the prophesy was lost."

"So no one can defeat Fenrir? Ever?" Ak'ten asked.

Malík rocked back in his chair and studied the boy. "Well, I'd say there's always hope, Ak'ten. We must never give up on that." He snapped out of his thoughtfulness. "And now to the matter of your heresy with the Techgnome. You know how dangerous heretics are, Ak'ten. You know how dangerous Darkgnomes are! I have told you all of these things. Yet you still ran off to find out for yourself."

"But Pete isn't dangerous."

"That's what you think. He's a Techgnome. He has nothing to do with the gods, or their plans. You must stay away from him from this point forward. And on the matter of you getting into my books and practicing *advanced* magic …" Malík smiled. "Good job." Then, sternly, he added, "But don't do it again. We will go over all of those lessons in time. You have my word. You are a very fine apprentice. But you still have a long way to go on your journey. We have four years to get you ready for your time before the Great Ghost. I have been warned that you are to shape up. The Collective will suffer no disobedience from you, when the day comes for you to join them in their ranks. Perhaps we should cut your hair."

Ak'ten gasped. "No!"

Malík considered the lad, smiling at the sight of him. "Oh, I suppose I can indulge you for a while longer. I have grown rather accustomed to it by now. But we must go before King Nesu in the morning. We must tell him everything. We stopped the Darkgnomes from following us this time, but I am sure, now that they are on to us, they will continue to search us out. The tribe is in danger. You must stay close from now on.

No more wandering to the edge of the forest and meeting strange friends, like Pete, or Morrha the Moon Witch. I've warned you, and I expect you to listen."

"But no one else would listen to me! Pete was the only gnome in the world who was willing to help!"

"We will speak more tomorrow. As for me, I'm going to bed. I am very worn and looking forward to the comfort of my own pillow beneath my head. You will do the same." Malík stood up, putting out the light, and Ak'ten followed suit. They both went to their rooms and closed the doors.

Ak'ten lay down in his bed and thought about all he had been through in the past few days. He couldn't promise never to see Pete again. Actually, he felt that he simply *must* see Pete again. He would have to keep him updated after all. Especially since no one else would ever likely lift a finger in defense against the evil of the Darkgnomes. Pete was the only one brave enough, aside from himself. It was true what Malík had said. There was still a long way to go on his journey. In fact, as far as Ak'ten was concerned, the journey had just begun.

Ak'ten leaned over and blew out the candle by his bed. He fell asleep just as soon as his head hit the pillow. It had been a very long day. As he slept, he dreamt of frightening things: Darkgnomes and tortured fairies, but these dreams were lined with good things, such as Pete, their adventure, and a future when no one would scoff at the idea that two gnomes, from two very different worlds, could be friends.

The adventures of the
METROGNOMES
will continue with Book II
ARADIA'S WAND

www.ingramcontent.com/pod-product-compliance
Lightning Source LLC
Chambersburg PA
CBHW030820310726
48980CB00006B/574/J
9781618150707